Has she truly lost him or simply found herself? Every sunrise moves her closer to the answer.

GOOD MORNING,
BEAUTIFUL

DLR Publications, LLC.

Paperback: 978-1-7340526-3-3

Ebook: 978-1-7340526-2-6

Good Morning Beautiful

Cover Illustration and Design by: Marcela King

Edited by: Jessica Covington

Good Morning, Beautiful

Daines L. Reed

Dedicated to my husband, Abram Reed, who makes me feel extraordinarily beautiful in real life.

ACKNOWLEDGMENTS

The completion of this novel would have been wholly impossible without God's incredible grace and mercy. For that, I am utterly grateful.

To my husband Abram Reed, who unknowingly became my creative partner in this writing process. Your willingness to listen to my ideas, discussing my characters as though they are real people, and offering your own plot twists and juicy details truly brought this story to life. Your contributions to this story were so vital, and your perspective on relationships were so insightful, you practically deserve a writing credit—for you, I am overwhelmingly grateful.

To my parents, Joseph and Carolyn, my children, Ti-Ras, Chelsey, and Holly: You have provided me with the space and freedom to write during special occasions and even the holidays. Family always comes before work, but you must have known this novel was not a matter of work—it's the creative outlet I've always needed. I can never repay you for your patience and understanding. More importantly, I know you believe in me—it's a phenomenal blessing.

To my dearest friends: Erica Maye, Frankie Singleton, Lorina Noble, and Adriane Beals—your support, encouragement, and enthusiasm have pushed me through to the finish line. I'm grateful for this kind of irreplaceable love.

Leonora Thompson, your support and response to my first novel moved me to tears. After all these years, you didn't have to reach out with so much love, but you did, and it's meant the world to me.

Sala J: You are the epitome of Girl Power and Self-Love! You are a literal shining light and your positive vibes have given me a new level of confidence. Thanks for spreading the love and supporting my work! I can't wait to write your story someday…

To the pearl girls: Jenny Gandhi, Suzie Dubrinski, Vickey Bingham, Jen Mason, Kristin and Babs and Marcie and Loren and Shannon and Pattigene… the list is long--- you ladies have been so genuinely happy for me. You'll never know how humble and loved you've made me feel. THANK YOU!

Ms. Marcela King: You were a Godsend. I'm so thankful that our paths have crossed. Your artwork gave my story life. Thank you for listening to my needs and blessing my book cover with your design. You are a true artist—but you're also a Believer—and that's more important to me than you'll ever know.

To my readers, to YOU: This novel is more than just another book. It is the tangible result of what happens when God tells you to put your butt in the chair and write. I wrote! And I'm honored to share my work with you. Thank you for your purchase. I hope you will enjoy it.

****

She was optimistic about love, not because she believed in fairytales, but in spite of them. ~D. Reed

****

****

Unfortunately, I have seen you. I have seen the truth about who you really are, and no matter how hard I try, I cannot unsee the truth. ~Also, D. Reed

****

CHAPTER ONE

Four minutes. According to SavvyCrush.com, a woman should wait a minimum of four minutes before responding to a text from a man. That is, if she doesn't want to look too desperate.

This bit of info crosses my mind when I hear my iPhone text notification, which sounds like a perfect, single droplet of water. It causes me to stop wiping down the kitchen counter and glance at the clock on the stove. 8:19 P.M. From where I stand, I can see my phone screen become illuminated for a moment and then go dim, but I don't touch it.

To be clear, my waiting has nothing to do with desperation or the lack thereof. I'm trying to train him— assuming it *is* him—to understand I'm not just sitting by the phone waiting for a text, and that's why I hold off for exactly seven minutes before checking the text message waiting, unopened on my phone.

I scrub at a nonexistent spot on the counter and move closer to the phone but stick to my self-imposed waiting period. I won't pick it up or check to see who the text is from until 8:26.

Technically, I could check it now and still wait to reply. It's not like anyone would know. But I figure, if I can resist the urge to look at the message for a few more minutes, then somehow I won't look so desperate to myself.

8:21P.M. Sitting at the counter with the iPad I gave mama for her birthday, I try to remember the last time I saw her use the device. My intention was to give her a way to download books online and maybe even subscribe to a few magazines or newspapers. The online reviews showed this model to be popular for older adults because the backlit screen and adjustable font sizes are easier on the eyes. I had even set it up so she could try a few audiobooks.

Shame on me for trying to enlighten her with modern technology.

According to her, there is no substitute for the feeling of a real book in your hands, and how do we know the government isn't using the internet to keep track of what we're reading? So, the iPad-as-a-gift was a fail and, rather than let it collect dust on her nightstand, I've been using it for my own entertainment.

While I wait to check my message, I do an internet search for: '*what does it mean to dream of a snake and a lizard?*'

I had two separate dreams last night, one about an apparently harmless snake, the other about a harmless lizard. I say *apparently harmless* because I touched both in the dream, when in real life, I'm deathly afraid of them. Not afraid as in I-prefer-not-to-be-around-them. I mean afraid as in jump-over-a-table, run-through-a-wall, run-my-car-off-the-road afraid.

In both dreams, the reptiles had gotten into the house, first the snake and later the lizard, and I chased them in and out of the rooms, behind dressers and beds, along baseboards, until I caught them. Meanwhile, everyone (not sure who everyone was) lounged around, unfazed by the chase.

I know there is symbolism in dreams. Mama said a dream about fish means someone is pregnant and I've heard all sorts of other explanations for the meanings behind our dreams. I've been obsessed with Googling my dreams lately, hoping I'll have one that means I'm getting married and having children soon.

According to the internet, if you dream about snakes it "may represent something that you are afraid of facing, accepting or dealing with in waking life: snakes may symbolize someone or something that you view as threatening to your physical or emotional well-being."

If you dream about lizards, it "may represent your basic instincts and reactions; it may symbolize one or more fears that you are not dealing with; it may represent someone that you see as cold-blooded or thick-skinned; however, since it sheds its skin, it may also represent rebirth or renewal."

If you dream about snakes and lizards together it said "as two of the oldest and most durable creatures on earth, these may portray the power of your survival instincts, both good and bad."

Mulling over this information briefly, I bookmark the website and plan to revisit it later. I close the browser and click on Cookie Crush and then jump over to Pinterest, but nothing catches my eye. Next, I open Words with Friends and start a new game.

Three (okay, maybe five) of mama's Lorna Doones disappear before I can come up with a good word using the letters E,L,D,A,R, and O. While *Abster125* ponders his or her next move, I go back to Pinterest and search for new hairstyles, before finally allowing myself to check the time again: 8:32.

When I look at the message it is him, and it simply says,

Him: *whats up?*

That's it. Without any context clues, the message is annoyingly vague. I mean, he hasn't texted me since last Sunday after church, when he normally texts me every day. Today is Thursday.

Having waited another five minutes before responding, I text back,

Me: *Nothing. Just cleaning the kitchen.*

And then—crickets. Nothing else from him. And, after an hour, I want to text him back and ask why he even texted me at all? But I don't. Self-control.

Instead, I get to work, prepping my lunch for tomorrow—I've been trying to follow Weight Watcher's guidelines for portion control and meal-prepping to prevent mindless eating—then I stash my lunch in the refrigerator, grab my phone and the iPad and head for my bathroom. It's the retreat I look forward to at the end of the day. I light a new, almond-scented candle, begin filling the bathtub, shed my clothes and pause to study myself in front of the bathroom mirror.

I'm heavy. At a few ounces over 278 pounds, I've gained about forty pounds over the last two years. There are stretch marks on my boobs and my butt cheeks. How? Why? I don't have any children. I grab a chunk of my thigh meat and squeeze it. The cellulite disappears. When I release my grip, it returns. I place one hand under each butt cheek and lift, turning sideways to see what it would look like if I were to start doing squats again. I let them drop.

Next, I lean closer to the mirror and study my face from all angles. It's pretty, and I don't mean that in a conceited way. I've always been told that I'm pretty. No one thinks twice before telling me I'm pretty with a caveat—I have a pretty face for a heavy-set girl.

As I'm using the backside of my hand to push the chubby area under my chin up to my jaw, I pause and listen. For a moment, I wonder if I've heard a noise coming from the hallway, but there is only silence.

I reach over to shut off the bathwater, an action which causes the turkey wing part of my arm and my boobs to swing in unison. I stand again. I lift one arm and try to make a muscle. Then, I wave at myself in the mirror. The turkey wing is jangling and so is the corresponding boob. I slide one hand under each boob, lift, and then push them together. I let them drop. I like my breasts, but they're heavy. Maybe I should check to see if my insurance covers breast lift surgery.

When I lift them up again and turn sideways to see how they'd look if they sat up higher, I definitely hear something from the hallway: "Cent! Cynthia!"

I drop my heavy boobs, grab my robe from the hook behind the door and hurry to her room. I know she doesn't want anything important, but she'll act like somebody's torturing her if I don't come running when she calls.

"What, Ma? I was trying to take a bath!"

Her room is dark except for the bright light of the judge show she's watching on TV. She fumbles around with the remote control, presses a button and the channel changes. Sitting up and reaching for the bedside lamp, she peers at the remote and mumbles to herself.

"Mama! What do you need? I was about to get in the tub."

She presses another button and Judge Mathis reappears on the screen. Another button is pressed, and the volume is silenced. She places the remote on her lap, satisfied, and lies back on her pillows, looking at me.

"Oh. I thought you were in the kitchen and I just wanted you to bring me some of that Arma Parma."

I'm at a loss as to what she wants. "Some *what*?"

Now, she's frustrated. "Arma. Parma. ArmaParma! Armall Parmall—I don't know how to say it! I've been in here all day, waiting for you to bring me something to drink and you didn't even come to check on me!"

I can't contain my annoyance. "Mama! Yes I did! I came in here when you were watching Divorce Court and I put those two bottles of water on your nightstand. Now, don't act like you don't remember that! And I don't even know what ArmaParma is!"

She glares at me. I know I'm hollering, but she just pushes my buttons. It seems like I can just walk into a room-- no, sometimes it's just the sound of her voice-- and I'm instantly irritated. And then I feel guilty. She's my mother. I love her and I would do anything for her. The Bible says to honor and obey your parents. But, Lord, have mercy!

I take a deep breath and relax my shoulders. "What is Arma Parma, Mama?"

She dismisses me. "Don't worry about it. I'll drink the water. Go 'head and get your bath."

Guilt won't let me walk away. "No, Ma, it's fine. Just tell me what you need."

She picks at her nightgown and mumbles, "I just wanted some of that thing that tastes like lemonade and sweet tea you had the other day. The one you brought me from Chick-fil-A and you said you could make it at home.

I stand still for a moment, confused, and then I laugh. I bust out laughing and I get so weak that I have to lean on the door frame for support.

"Mama! An Arnold Palmer? It's called an Ar-Nold Palm-Er! What in the world is Arma Parma?" I can barely breathe from the laughing, but I can't stop.

"Come one, Mama! Arma Parma? Now you know that's funny!"

She's too stubborn to smile. Instead, she picks at the edge of her blanket for a second, then picks up the remote control and presses a button, ignoring me.

When I bring the glass of half-sweet tea, half-lemonade back into the room and hand it to her, I hold on for a few extra seconds until she looks at me.

"Here's your Arma Parma, ma'am."

She laughs then, finally, and swats at my backside. "Get on outta here, girl!"

Though I may be a little thicker than I was in my youth, I'm still swift enough to avoid her playful whooping. I scoot just out of her reach, wink at her as I slip out of her room, and pull the door closed behind me.

After my bath, I brush and floss, scrub my face, and apply my monthly glycolic facial peel. While I wait for the peel to begin working, I slather shea butter on my feet, pull on my spa socks, and then rub more shea butter over my stretch marks. Next, I slip into panties and an oversized tee shirt, lay across my bed, and tap my phone screen to check for new messages. There are none.

I scroll through Facebook, Instagram, Pinterest, but nothing seems to pique my interest. I return to my text messages and shoot him a one-word message:

Me: *wow.*

I watch as tiny bubbles appear under my message and I can tell that he's typing a response, but after a moment, the bubbles disappear, and I'm pissed at myself for waiting for his reply. Then, after I rinse and moisturize my face, just before I power my phone off, he responds:

Him: *Don't be like that.*

Me: *like what?*

Him: *you're mad bc I didn't text you right back.*

Me: *I'm not mad*

Him: *yeah right*

Him: *you can't fault me for stuff like that. That being said, im serious when I say I want to take it slow. I did just get out of a relationship and I don't wanna rush in bc that's not fair to you. But I like being with you and we always have great experiences together.*

Me: *I understand*

Him: *I hope that's okay. I just want to be honest.*

Me: *I know you've been through a lot. I've told you before, I respect your need for more time.*

Him: *I mean I'm not saying I can't see us evolving into something more, I just don't want to rush into it!*

Me: *well I'm not going to rush you! I'll let you go at your own pace.*

After I press send, I wait. He doesn't reply but I wait a little longer—so he won't say I'm pressuring him. I lay on my bed, thinking about his fear of getting into a new relationship. I recognize it as fear because, why else, after two years of hanging out with me, does he continue to remind me that he's *just gotten out of a relationship*? How much time does he need?

When I wake up, at 4:15 A.M., having fallen asleep holding the phone, I see he hasn't responded, place it on the charger and go back to sleep.

Chapter Two

When morning comes and I turn on my phone, I'm greeted by a message from the Sprinkle of Jesus app:

Stop accepting things that are unacceptable.

It's the simplest message, but it causes tears to burn behind my eyelids. It's been two years since my friend Ruth died suddenly, but I feel as though I can hear her voice saying the words out loud. *Stop accepting things that are unacceptable.* And she's right. She *was* right.

I can still remember the day she told me to download the app on my phone. She had told me she used daily affirmations to keep her mind focused on the Lord. She'd said I needed to do the same thing: Focus my mind on the Lord and stop worrying about finding a man and having a baby. She'd said those desires would manifest in my life only in God's time and not mine.

I had said, '*Yeah, but does God realize that I'm almost forty? I'm running out of time to have kids.*'

And I remember the way she looked when she whispered, *If the Lord saw fit to give Sarah and Abraham a baby at the age of ninety then there ain't nothing He can't do. Genesis 18 and 14 says, Is anything too hard for the Lord?*'

I had laughed at first—I knew the story of how Sarah couldn't conceive and had given up all hope. How she had allowed her husband to make a baby with her servant as a last resort, only to finally conceive a child at the age of ninety—but the laughter had gotten hung up in my throat when I caught a glimpse of Ruth's expression. She was so serious.

That's when I knew her faith was so much stronger than mine. That's when I knew I needed to do better. I followed her advice, knowing she'd never steered me in the wrong direction, and downloaded the app.

I'm so thankful for her advice. When the daily messages pop up on my phone, I feel as though she's still here with me. I mean, how could I have known she *wouldn't* be here anymore?

I haven't told anyone about the brokenness I have endured since she left me.

Since she left us.

Since she passed away or the Lord called her home.

Whatever you want to call it—she's gone. And I am broken.

The loss of a friend, I now understand, is an ailment no one can help you with. *No one but the Lord*, is what she would say about it. *It's me and you, Lord,* she'd probably say too. And it's true. The death of a dear friend is something people can't understand unless they have experienced it firsthand.

I have learned, the death of a friend puts you into an unfortunate category which is almost completely unrecognized by society. There's no space to grieve properly and your job won't give you any time off for bereavement. After all, it's not like you lost your mother or father. It's not the death of a child or a spouse.

People will give you their condolences, say they are sorry to hear such-and-such has passed, ask how it happened, and send prayers up, but afterwards, they will go on with their lives.

And I'm trying to go on with mine, too. But I can't just *go on*. At least, not in the same way. My life has been interrupted. I've been knocked off-course, and I'm getting back on track, so to speak, but I'm not the same as I was before.

Life without Ruth is like this: One time, I broke my pinky toe. Fractured it, actually. And it hurt like the devil, but the doctor couldn't do anything about it. It looked fine on the outside, even though the x-ray showed a hairline fracture.

The doctor said it didn't need a cast, splint, or boot. He said it just needed time to heal, maybe six weeks or so. I was able to walk on it, and I'm sure I looked alright from the outside, but when I stepped a certain way or when I wore certain shoes, the pain shot through my foot something terrible. Sometimes, it felt like it would never stop hurting, and I contemplated seeing another doctor for a second opinion.

But it did get better in six weeks, as the doctor had said, even though it still gives me problems every now and then. For instance, when the lady pulls my toes too far apart during a pedicure. Oh! It hurts like a mother, and nobody can see it or understand it except me. So, yeah, I can run again and I can wear heels, but my pinky toe isn't like it was before. It's alright, but it's not okay.

And that's how I've been living since Ruth left. I'm alright, but I'm not okay. She was just gone one day, and a little piece of me is broken because of it. That sounds selfish. I hope that I added some value to her life, too. That I didn't just take and take from her without giving something in return.

So, I still cry for her at the most unexpected moments. I still lose my breath when some little thing reminds me of her during the day. And then I'm embarrassed in front of myself because, if she is looking down on me from heaven, she would tell me to get myself together and keep it moving. She was stronger than me.

I have found a few small ways to hold on to her. I still have her name and number saved in my phone. I still text her sometimes. And I still have her bible and her hammer—the only protection she ever needed.

Sitting on the edge of the bed, I'm aware of the moisture that has become trapped beneath my chin and my chest. Every time I cry, the tears run down my cheeks and slide up under my chin before joining together, one from each side, and drop down onto my chest. But my chin—my chins—shouldn't be able to touch my chest anyway, and that's why I need to get up and get moving.

I give myself a quick pep talk—*Sit up. Hold your head up. Get to the gym.*

I'm already late. My personal trainer, Vito, will be livid, and ain't nobody trying to hear his mouth this morning.

Another text comes through:

Him: *Good morning, beautiful.*

So, he left me hanging last night. It's so typical of him, though, to not reply to my message on one day and remember to send me a good morning text on the next. I don't have time for his games today. Instead of replying, I make sure Mama is situated for the day, lay out her meds and make sure she has food. Then I spend ten minutes looking for my keys, and another ten minutes trying to get my blender to produce a decently blended smoothie before I grab my lunch bag and hit the door.

Before backing out of the driveway, I pull out my cell phone and send him the coldest, blandest response I can think of to convey my disinterest:

Me: *gm*

I don't dignify my response with any punctuation, emojis, or memes. Instead, rather than allowing myself to wait for his reply, I toss the phone into my purse, turn the radio up and drive to the gym.

When I arrive at the gym, Vito, my personal trainer, has a massive attitude. He doesn't even look at me. He just points to the treadmills and barks, "Get warmed up!"

Granted, I am twenty minutes late—technically seventeen minutes late—for my thirty minute session, but I couldn't find my keys this morning, I couldn't find the right mixing blade for my smoothie blender, I had to stop and get gas, and I…Hell, I just didn't want to come.

I hate working out. I hate the way the sweat-marks on my t-shirt are always right underneath my boobs. I hate the way Vito tries to tell me I can do more sets and more reps. I know my body! I know when I can go a little further and when I can't.

Still, I can't let Vito think he can just talk to me any kind of way, so I take my time strolling to the treadmill, and I toss a casual comment over my shoulder as I pass him: "Why do I pay you to tell me to run on the treadmill? I can run on the treadmill by myself, not have to hear your mouth anymore, and save the $80 a week I pay you."

He rewards my taunting with silence. Since he doesn't take the bait, I push my earbuds into my ears and start running. Within three minutes, I can feel my hair start to curl around the edges as heat and sweat escape from my scalp. No matter how much I blow it straight, no matter how much money I spend on hair products that promise to keep my straightened hair from fluffing up into a lion's mane, no matter how tight I wrap it and tie it down before I work out, I always end up leaving the gym with a baby afro.

After the workout as I'm on my way to work, another text message comes through:

Him: *I can't start my day until I see your face. Send me a pic.*

The message makes me smile despite my annoyance with him. Whatever has been bothering him the last few days seems to be a non-factor now.

At the stoplight, I take a few selfies from different angles, making use of the copper glow the morning sunlight provides. The problem is my sweated-out hair is still a hot mess and no angle is good enough to camouflage it. It probably wouldn't be a bad idea to move my workout to the afternoon. Or I could just cut my hair off and eliminate the whole what-do-I-do-with-this-hair dilemma.

What I do know is I cannot send him a selfie right now, so I dial his number instead. In one and a half rings, his voicemail picks up and the traffic light turns green. Hearing his real voice would've been nice—it's really the only reason I called, and since I don't have any other message to leave, I hang up and head to work.

CHAPTER THREE

At work, I put three drops of peppermint essential oil into the reservoir of my aromatherapy diffuser, turn on the soft white string lights draped across the bookshelf behind my desk, and turn my computer on. I'm greeted by an obscene number of unread email messages, a handful of encrypted direct messages from various employees, and an unfinished hand of solitaire still running on the toolbar.

My role as a hospital administrator has evolved over the years, but I've been able to streamline my department, delegating tasks and training new hires so our team runs efficiently, and I don't have people up in my face all day. I'm not the Big Boss, and that's okay. The way I've been able to set things up, I can come in here, do my thing, and go home with no worries.

I change my intra-office work status to *In Meeting* so I won't be disturbed and log on to CelebrityBloggerDaily. com for my morning fix of celebrity gossip. It's my guilty pleasure. So-and-so had a baby, Mister and Missus Whatever are getting divorced, DJ YadaYada was spotted leaving a bar with the latest Flavor of the Week Model.

On the lower half of the page, I see a short article announcing one of the ladies from the Real Housewives of Something has launched a new line of gender-neutral baby products. I click the link and browse the cute onesies, booties, diaper covers, and diaper bags. If I were having a baby—correction: WHEN I have a baby—I'll buy this, and this, and one of these—no, two of these… In minutes, my virtual shopping cart is loaded with my selections.

I hear two brief knocks on the door and then someone is barging right into my office without waiting to be invited. I panic a little, clicking all over the computer screen to minimize the evidence of my online shopping. Upper management is cracking down on us, trying to prohibit employees from using the internet for personal business. As the screen vanishes, I use a phony smile to hide the guilt on my face, but let it drop once I see who's coming through my door.

"Cynthia?" The new girl who was hired to work on insurance verifications just bursts into my office uninvited and stops dead in her tracks as she looks around. "Oh my God! It's so nice in here! Wow!"

She seems to have forgotten why she came into my office. I can tell by the way her eyes take in every detail of my decor and I'm immediately annoyed. "I haven't been in here before…"

I stop fumbling with my mouse, sit back in my chair, and exhale. "What's up, Tiffany?"

Before the question leaves my lips, she's already leaning over my desk, waving a verification sheet in my face and talking a mile-a-minute. "I called to get a breakdown for this patient, and I'm following the checklist like you said, but the insurance representatives act like they don't want to give me any information! I asked the lady about the frequency for a prior approval, right? She tells me once a year. Okay. But is that once in a calendar year or once every twelve months? That's all I asked her! And she popped an attitude with me! She just kept repeating, 'Once a year, once a year!'"

I dig deep down in my Spirit for some patience. She's new and I'm still training her. "Okay, first, calm down. Now, what was her name and representative ID number?"

Tiffany is a deer in headlights. She's blinking and stunned as if I've just spoken to her in Hebrew.

I smile at her like she's a kindergartener. "You always get the representative's name and ID number from the start, right? That way, if the call escalates, you have something to reference when you ask to speak to her supervisor. And what insurance is it?"

We both look at the top of the sheet and see that the carrier is AmbuAssure.

"Okay, AmbuAssure is typically on the calendar year—January 1st through December 31st. The rep should have explained this, but sometimes they can be impatient and you can't let that get to you. At the end of the day, you aren't calling them to make new friends. You're trying to get this information and reduce the chances of a claim being rejected because of incorrect information. After you've worked with these insurances for a while, you'll start to learn how they work."

Tiffany rubs her temples and manages a slow smile. "I know you're right, Cynthia. It's not hard. I just… I'm tired, I guess. My patience is on zero lately."

She reaches out to push my office door closed and lowers her voice a bit. "I'm pregnant. I just found out. I'm only a few weeks and I haven't told anybody, not even my boyfriend. I am so exhausted! It's like I can't think clearly, right now! But I'm so excited. This will be my first, you know?"

She sits down in front of my desk and continues chattering as though we're on a coffee break.

"You have kids, right Cynthia? How old are they?"

I stiffen immediately, instinctively. "I don't have any children. Not yet, anyway."

She looks embarrassed, and I let her marinate in her own discomfort for a moment, until she starts stuttering for a response.

"I'm sorry! I thought somebody told me that you…I guess I just figured you did because you're so…"

"Old?" I offer the word that would complete her sentence.

Tiffany's energy changes as soon as the word leaps out of my mouth and I instantly feel self-conscious and petty. I pray every day for the Lord to help me to control my tongue and my attitude. I've already failed today.

"Nurturing. I was going to say you're so nurturing. I figured you were probably a great mom." Tiffany's words are dry as she rises from the chair, the elation of her pregnancy reveal drained from her expression and she moves towards the door.

"Congratulations on your pregnancy! Let me know when the baby shower is!" I try to undo the damage my insecurity has caused. I've stolen her joy this morning. *Way to go, Cynthia.*

"You want me to leave the door open or closed?" She is already across the threshold, back towards me, hand on the doorknob.

Before I can answer, she swings it shut.

I sit for a moment when she leaves, tapping my nails on the mouse and then click to reopen my shopping cart. The cocktail of impulsiveness and guilt sends me to the checkout screen where I click on the box that says: Is this purchase a gift? —and I type in Tiffany's name.

Later, when my stomach begins a long, slow grumble, I grab my car keys. I did meal prep for today, but by the time lunch rolls around, I realize the boiled egg, hummus, celery sticks, four cubes of grilled chicken, and cheese stick won't satisfy me. Plus, I need to get out of the office for some fresh air, so I jump in the car to go for a snack.

While I wait for someone to bring out my fresh French fries, I dial Julene's number. After Ruth's unexpected death, Julene has become more of a sister than a friend to me. She answers on the first ring. "Hey what's up?"

"Nothing. Trying to get some lunch and they gone give me these cold fries!"

She laughs as though cold fries aren't a true emergency. "Where are you? And how many points are fries?"

I confess, "At the burger drive-in next to the hospital! I'm hungry! And what do they give me? Cold fries! They shouldn't even have cold fries at lunch time! They should be hot off the fryer! They know fries come with every meal, so why wouldn't they keep cooking them?"

I blatantly ignore the question about counting points. Sometimes I regret asking her to be my weight loss accountability partner.

I notice movement out of the corner of my eye and roll the window down as a boy walks up to my car with a tray of milkshakes. "Hold on Ju. Hang on a sec."

The boy attempts to shove the tray of milkshakes through my open window, and I stop him. "Those aren't mine. I'm waiting on some hot fries." He looks confused, but says, "Yes ma'am, one moment, please."

"And look!" I'm shouting behind him as he turns to leave. I hand him my drink. "You might as well make me a fresh strawberry limeade since I had to wait. And I don't want that strawberry syrup. Just some fresh strawberries and the limeade."

"Yes ma'am."

"And make sure my fries are hot!"

"Oh, they will be, ma'am. Sorry about the wait."

I smile at him, "It's okay."

I pick up the phone again, knowing Julene has heard the entire exchange. "I know people be thinking I'm just a bitch." I have to laugh at myself. "I don't give a damn. When I'm spending my hard-earned money, I want my stuff to be right! And today is Friday! Fryday! Fry day, Friday! Confucius say, '*May nary a point be counted on Fryday!*'"

Julene laughs at my joke. "Now I'm wanting some fries! You got me hungry. But hold up—I thought you were meal-prepping. And saving money. Didn't you bring your lunch?"

"I know, right? I ate it earlier. I just wanted some fries and a strawberry limeade for a quick snack. But no! I gotta wait an extra ten minutes for some fresh hot damn fries. I don't even know how many points it's going to cost me. But hey! Weight Watchers doesn't need to know, right? Anyway… so, Victor texted me last night. Totally out of the blue."

Julene laughs, knowing the history of my on and off 'friendship' with him. "So what did the serial texter want from you last night? Wait. What time was it when he texted you?"

"Well, first of all, it wasn't a booty call. It was only like, eight-something in the evening."

She stops me before I can explain. "Of course it wasn't a booty call! It wasn't a *call* at all! I'm telling you, I've never seen a man have so much time to text, but can't actually pick up the phone and call. Or, better yet, take you out on a date."

"I know, I know. We've been through this already! But I don't text him as much anymore. Most days, he hits me up first. In the morning, it's '*Good morning, Beautiful.*' When he's on lunch, it's some corny meme on Facebook. When he's travelling for work, it's '*Why didn't you text me back last night? Who's taking up all of your time?*'" I laugh as I give Julene the rundown of my daily schedule with Victor. "And I text him back, like, '*Nobody's getting my time except my Mama.*' Most of the time, I don't even text him back at all."

On the other end of the line, Julene is silent. I know she doesn't believe me.

"It's the truth! I told you, I'm minding my own business, trying to get my life together, and he wants to be my top priority, but it seems like whenever we get close, whenever we seem to be vibing, he pulls away from me. At this point, I'm saying forget it. I'm not getting my hopes up over him again. It's whatever."

"Well, I think he's just lame for taking up your time without actually dating you. It's like people don't date anymore. Unless texting is the new dating. That's it! Y'all are Text-Dating! I'm so out of the loop with this stuff!"

Her discovery makes me laugh. "Ain't nobody got time for no Text-Dating! I need me a real man and a real date! I'm sick of being everybody's homegirl."

Another kid appears at my window with a crumpled bag and a limeade. Rolling the window down, I grab my lunch, thank the kid, and tell Julene I'll call her later.

"Wait, you're not coming back to work today? You know I'm there from 2-11 today." She sounds disappointed.

"I'll be back for a little while, but I'm off-site later this afternoon. They have me leading the training and procedural updates at the skilled care and rehab facilities. I don't love it, but it keeps me moving around during the day instead of sitting at my desk eating snacks all afternoon!"

"Ugh. I thought we were working together today! But that's cool. Go on over there and teach your little lessons or whatnot. Holler at me later, though."

When Julene hangs up, I head back to my office to finish up a few tasks before I leave for the off-site training. I make a point to smile warmly when I pass Tiffany's desk in the call-center space outside my office door, but she ignores me. It stings a little and I recommit myself to a more positive attitude when I interact with my team. Knowing I can't do anything more about her hurt feelings today, I make sure my computer is locked, shut off the lights and diffuser, and let my team know I'll be at the rehab facility for the rest of the day if they need me.

By the time I finish bringing the back-office team up to speed at the rehab facility located on north end of our hospital's campus, I have three missed calls from mama and three text messages from Victor. I'm not in the mood to hear from either one of them. If mama had been having a true emergency, the home security monitoring service would have contacted me by now.

I open Victor's messages. One is a meme of Madea with the caption: *Halleluyer! Praise the Lordt! It's Friday.*

Victor: *Can you help me out with something?*

Victor: *Call me when you get a chance. If u can make time 4 me.*

I roll my eyes at the phone. What does he mean, make time for him, when he's the one who never has time for me?

I dial his number, though. After one and a half rings, I hear his voicemail message: *It's a great day to praise the Lord. You've reached the phone of Victor Randall III. I'm sorry that I'm unable to...*

Hanging up, I shoot him a text:

Me: *Just got off work. How are you?*

Victor: *I'm good. I had needed your help with something, but you weren't available. Don't worry about it.*

Me: *Awww...* 😊 *... You needed me? I feel so special...* 😇 *You have my full attention now. What did you need?*

Victor: *In meeting. Talk later.*

Next, I call Mama. She answers on the first ring. "Where have you been? I've been calling you all day! What if it was an emergency?"

"Mama, you know I was at work. I was literally in the middle of a training session when you called, but you have my full attention now. What did you need?"

She dives right into her list of daily complaints. "Well, for one thing, I haven't had a bowel movement since last night. Something is wrong with my stomach. Doctor Sherman said he can see me Monday morning at 11:30. I was watching The Doctors on TV this morning and they said constipation could be a warning sign of stomach cancer. They said you shouldn't ignore the symptoms, so I went ahead and made me an appointment."

"Ma, you don't need no doctor! And nothing is wrong with your stomach. Drink some prune juice and some warm water. Or some tea! There's tea up in the pantry. You can make it yourself."

She's grumbling in the phone.

"Ma, is that why you were blowing my phone up? Because you haven't pooped in eighteen hours?"

"No. I called to ask you if you're still saving your money, because I saw on the news that old sorry excuse for a president is talking about cutting all kinds of public assistance and community programs and changing healthcare policies. If you don't get your ducks in a row, you won't be able to afford to live in this country by the time you're my age. Mark my words."

She kills me with this stuff.

"Yeah, Ma. You know I'm saving. You know we set up the trust fund right after Ruth died and I'm contributing regularly. And stop letting the news get you all riled up. You know he can't do half the things he claims he'll do. He just likes to keep everybody stirred up."

"Well, I don't know about that. Either he's going to have us all living like refugees, or he's going to lead our country into another war. I just pray that man will just die in his sleep before he can do anymore damage."

"Mama! You can't pray for someone's death! Lord Jesus!" I consider her choice of words for a moment. "But I have to say, that's about the kindest way I've ever heard someone say they wished someone would die. Most people would say, 'I wish he would choke on his dinner or I wish he would get hit by a car.' I've never heard 'die in his sleep' before."

She laughs. "Well, let me clarify: I can't stand him and I do wish he was dead. God already knows my heart, so I done already made peace with that. I used to pray that someone would just shoot his ass but seem like they can't dammit do that. So, lately I've just been praying that he'll go to sleep and not wake up."

"Mama! I can't do this with you! Stop watching the news! And you could have waited to tell me this when I got home! I have a few stops to make and then I'll be there."

"Okay, then, Imma let you go. But I had one more thing to ask you."

"I'm listening."

"They say there's a tornado coming tomorrow. What time you plan on getting home tomorrow because the weather is supposed to be bad?"

"I'm hanging up, now. Bye Ma."

That evening, as I'm preparing the lesson for my youth trustee's meeting, InVest, I feel pretty good about the state of our group's affairs. It's hard to believe only a few years have passed since we established our trust fund. I mean, who would have thought the working-class black ladies of Landis Vereen Memorial Hospital would have been able to come together—stick together—and come up with a way to establish a plan for generational financial independence? Of course, it didn't take long for us to find out this thing takes a lot more work than we had initially thought.

Since a large part of our mission is to train our children—well, not my children, but the children in our families—to eventually manage the trust themselves, I volunteered to host their monthly 'Little Trustees' meeting. We decided to call it InVest and it quickly became my pet project. As I'm thumbing through my notes on, I'm interrupted by a text message:

Victor: *I have my daughter tomorrow. Do you want to go to the movies with us?*

Me: *Movies? What are we seeing?*

Me: *And can we sneak in our own snacks like we did last time?*

He hates that I smuggle snacks in my purse, but his daughter loves it and I can't justify spending extravagant amounts of money at the theater concession stand.

He sends a meme of Madea pulling a box of fried chicken out of her bosom.

Victor: *Your Bougie-Ghetto ass would probably do this. LOLOL. But okay.*

I send a picture of Beyoncé pulling a bottle of hot sauce out of her purse.

Me: *I just like to be prepared. Don't play. You love to see what I pull out of my bag!*

Victor: *The matinee starts at 11:10 in the morning. You meeting us there? Afterwards, lunch at Fun Fair Park?*

Pause.

Me: *I have InVest in the morning.*

Victor: *What?*

Me: *InVest. My Little Trustees meeting? I do this every month.*

Victor: *Can't someone else cover for you?*

Me: *It's my project. I have to do it.*

Victor: *Can't you do it earlier?*

Me: *Hair appointment is earlier.*

Victor: *Just say you don't want to go with us. Stop making excuses.*

Me: *Not saying I don't want to go. Just have to take care of my responsibilities first.*

Victor: *Excuses.*

Me: *Can we push the movie back to 2:30?*

Victor: *The matinee is all shows before 12. And I'm taking her to lunch after. Don't worry about it.*

Me: *I'll meet you at Fun Fair Park for lunch after my meeting.*

And…crickets from him. Figures.

Chapter Four

Saturday morning, after my hair appointment, I head to the activities room at church to set up for InVest, my Little Trustees meeting.

The tiny, windowless box of a room is drab and uninspiring. If I'd had time, I would have hung some pictures and string lights, lit a few candles, or at least brought in my diffuser. Maybe a colorful rug in the center of the floor would soften it up a bit. I'll get this room decorated eventually, but even in this utilitarian setting, spending time with the kids is one of my favorite pastimes.

Just as I begin thumbing through my notes for today's lesson, my young trustees begin to file in.

"Hey Miss Cynthia." The older kids— Ms. Emma Lee's granddaughters Amethyst and Mecca— slide past me with earbuds dangling from their ears and take seats in the farthest corner of the room.

"Hi Miss Cynthia!" The younger children crowd around me.

"Hi babies! Where are my hugs?" Suddenly, there are little arms winding around my waist, wrapping around my thighs, pulling on my arms. The younger children haven't yet learned to feel self-conscious about showing affection and I'm thankful.

A tiny hand is walloping my butt and giggling, "It moves! It moves! Watch!" Before the next punch lands on my rear, I reach behind my back and swat the young offender away. I love the little ones. "Okay, okay, let's take our seats!"

Right away, my little angels are tussling and fussing, fighting for this seat and that seat, falling onto the floor, whining for me. I catch Amethyst and Mecca rolling their eyes at each other.

I clap-clap-clapclapclap and wait for my little students to respond. A few clap with me, catching on to the rhythm, until I have everyone's attention. Once all eyes are on me and everyone is clapping on beat, I call the class to order.

"I'm so glad to see all of you! Who would like to help us begin by leading our mission statement?"

Joseph, Ms. Irene's youngest grandson, jumps up and runs to stand next to me. Facing the American flag, hand over heart, he begins, "Our Father, who art..."

The rest of the children are giggling and Joseph's stair-step older sister Mackenzie interrupts. "Nooo...! You done mixed up the Pledge of Allegiance and the Lord's Prayer! She wants our *mission thingy*."

Joseph looks near tears. "We 'posed to pray first. Nana says always start by praying."

He turns pleading eyes towards me, and I nod. "Please lead us in prayer, Joseph."

He grabs my hand, and I resist the urge to pull away from the warm stickiness of his palm. I make a mental note to give him a squirt of hand sanitizer before we began our activity.

His small voice is stronger when he begins again, "Our Father, who art…"

When his prayer concludes and we all say 'Amen,' I walk the children through our mission statement:

I desire to be successfully, financially independent.

I have faith in God and in myself.

I can see my bright future.

I will learn to be fiscally responsible.

I will work hard to earn the life that I love.

I will honor and protect the blessings that God bestows upon me.

I will be decisive and persistent.

I am the positive energy that I wish to attract.

I can achieve what I believe I can achieve.

I will trust my gut.

"Alright, you guys! That was perfect!" I clap my hands together and look around the room at my little angels. There are only seven children here this morning. Two are Ms. Emma Lee's grandchildren and three are Julene's kids. The last two are Irene's grandchildren.

Early on—when we first formed the children's group—there were nearly twenty children, ranging in age from four years old to sixteen. The number of children in attendance dwindled significantly after the first few months of the InVest program's launch.

When we first began, everyone was just so excited to be part of something so visionary. In our rural Georgia community, there are few wealthy black families.

The idea of establishing a multi-family trust fund and breaking the chains of our struggles had gotten everyone's hopes up. Everybody started walking around talking about how '*We bout to be rich, we got our own money,*' but few seemed to grasp the truth about how long it would take to see the fruits of our efforts become tangible. It was an exciting mission, but its appeal definitely began to dull the moment I tried to establish some order and rules to our meetings.

The meetings for the elders— the founding members— ran without any disruption. Aside from the shock of Ruth's death, we continued to follow the advice from our attorney. We met regularly and prayed continually. We read widely and deeply, taking chances on books that would teach us new things, broaden our perspectives, and challenge our financial attitudes. And we kept on contributing, increasing our investments each year as we learned more about budgeting and holding each other accountable.

But the little trustees… I couldn't get a handle on those meetings after the first few months. I had—I *have*— such high hopes for these children. I get excited about activities and projects and lesson plans that will teach them how to be good stewards of the trust when they are of age. My future children will join this venture and I want to make it something we can all be proud of.

So, yeah, I set rules:

1. Be on time
2. Use good manners
3. Pay attention
4. Attend all meetings

I just thought it was important to bring some order to the meetings and let the parents know that this isn't some kind of free day care where you can drop your kid off while you go and run errands. The kids need to be here, be prepared, and participate. I get it, some of them are too little to understand a whole lot, but still… And they need to be picked up ON TIME. You would have thought I was asking the kids to pay a cover charge by the way some of the parents got offended and stopped bringing their kids.

I couldn't even get my own cousin to bring her children to the meetings! She stopped bringing them when I wouldn't commit to giving them a ride home afterwards.

I would have helped her out by dropping them off once or twice, but she expected me to do it every time. Just because I don't have kids of my own doesn't mean she should assume I'll always be available to chauffer hers around.

The small class size doesn't dampen my enthusiasm for the cause, though, and I jump right in to the day's session.

"Okay, guys. We're going to continue our lesson from last week about how to save money."

Mackenzie's little hand shoots up. "I have some monies at home that my Nana gave me. I already have about seven dollars from my birthday."

I raise my eyebrows. "Did you put some of your birthday money in the bank like we talked about?"

She pulls her hand in slowly and looks me directly in the eye. "My daddy said my birthday money is for me and my Nana got more money in the bank for me."

Her statement makes my eye twitch. There is no way Irene's son should have known anything about the money in the bank. I make a mental note to bring this up at the next Founder's meeting. The adult children are not to have knowledge or access to the status of the trust. Period.

Rather than let the kids see my frustration, I try to take advantage of this teachable moment. "What did we learn at our last meeting? We must always put aside a little bit of money for ourselves, by ourselves, right?" I scan the room for nodding heads, for understanding.

"Pay yourself first." Mecca recites the lesson in a monotone voice without even lifting her head from the screen of her cellphone. "Are we ever going to do anything in here besides talk about saving money? When are we gonna do something fun?"

I study her for a moment. She's a beautiful girl with skin so smooth and dark you'd assume she's wearing makeup although her grandmother would never allow it. Her thick, naturally curly hair is pulled up into a puff ball on the crown of her head, and the fine baby hair along her edges are swirled as though she'd used the flourish of a paint brush. She appears so much older than I know she is, but her face hasn't yet lost its baby-softness. I sigh.

"That's right, Mecca!" I exaggerate the excitement in my voice, partly to show her that her negative attitude has no place here, and partly so as not to steal the joy from the younger children. "No matter if the money comes from a birthday gift or a job, we must always remember to first put a bit aside for ourselves. A part of all that you earn is yours to keep. Remember?" The babies nod. The big kids mumble.

"Right. And what are we keeping it for?"

"A new phone, I hope. My screen been cracked for almost a year!"

I walk towards her corner of the room and entertain her comment. "Alright, a new phone. So, how much does a new phone cost?"

She glances up at me, slightly interested. "Probably like $600."

"What if I paid you $100 a week to keep my hair looking as pretty as yours? How long would it take you to get that new phone?"

"Six weeks, I guess. If I just save what you give me."

"And at the end of the six weeks, when you buy that phone, what would you have?"

Amethyst joins the conversation. "Uh, easy. A new phone!"

I pause for a moment, giving her time to think about her answer. "You sure about that? Would you feel comfortable with zero dollars and a new phone that will eventually be worthless?"

"Nope. That's why I would just save the money that you give me for like, the next ten weeks after that, and then I'll have a new phone and a thousand dollars."

Joseph pipes up, intrigued by the idea of one thousand dollars. "When you get the thousand dollars will you buy me a phone too? I've been wanting one and my Nana said I'm not old enough but my other cousin gots one and she's younger than me!"

Mecca rolls her eyes in Joseph's direction. "Boy, no! Didn't you just hear Miss Cynthia say we need to save money?"

I side-eye her and smile at Joseph. "She didn't save her money, did she, Joseph?"

Joseph tattles on Mecca as if this scenario has actually happened. "Nope! Nope! She bought a phone! And won't even buy me one! And she gots a whole thousand dollars!"

I hold my hand up. "No she doesn't have a thousand dollars. Maybe I don't need her to do my hair anymore after she buys the phone. Maybe she just spent all of her money on a phone and now she's broke."

I turn towards Mecca. "You can't save the money for six weeks and then spend it all. Maybe you can spend $540 on something if you think it's a smart purchase, but you have to save the other $60 or ten percent for yourself. That's what I'm trying to teach you. Put it up somewhere, preferably in the bank, and keep it, but don't spend it. What if something happens? What if your grandmother has an emergency and needs your help? She needs $60 for her prescription and you can't help her? Don't let your grandma die because you wanted a new phone."

Her sweet, warm, baby face goes cold. Her mouth opens slightly and her lips move softly, in search of words which refuse to form. She glances at her sister and then at the floor.

I've gone too far. I know it as soon as the words leave my lips. Again. Set a guard, O Lord, over my mouth.

But these, kids! They're so self-centered and entitled. It's as if they were born saying, '*Me, me, me, me, me. I want, I want.*' Meanwhile, a grandmother has dedicated her life to raising children who aren't her own! She's put herself in last place when she knows she's in the last season of her life! Where's the gratitude? Where's the appreciation? I don't say any of this out loud, though. I've already hurt her feelings. We've wasted a big chunk of our meeting time and I don't know if what I've said makes sense or not.

I rub my neck and sit down on the low stool beside the worn pulpit stand. "Who wants to give Miss Cynthia a neck massage?"

Irene's grandchildren, Mackenzie and Joseph, race to my side, squeezing and pounding my shoulders with their small fists.

Mackenzie pauses, mid-squeeze, "Are you going to pay us for this good massage, Miss Cynthia?"

I pretend to think it over. "Hmm… I'll give you ten dimes."

I fish a handful of change from my purse. "Now how many dimes are you supposed to save just for you?"

She looks at her brother, performs some quick math on her fingers, and looks at me again. "You said to save one dime out of every ten dimes. So, I have to keep one, just in case somebody kill my Nana and I can buy candy with nine."

I gave her a high-five. "That's my girl. Nobody's going to kill your Nana, though, okay? And you don't have to spend the whole nine on candy, but that was excellent math!"

I wink at Mecca and Amethyst, who are eyeballing me from their corner. "Why are y'all still over there? Come on over here and let me buy you a massage."

The youngest looks at the oldest and waits for her to make a move. Then they both race across the room and pull up chairs next to me.

I pull another handful of coins from my purse and give each girl some change. "I'll give you the money and let you treat yourself. Your massage will cost a dollar each."

Amethyst studies her money and looks over at me. "This ain't enough!"

"What?" I lean over and count her money. "I gave you ten dimes. One dollar. That's exact change!"

"Nope. You said we have to save a dime from it, so now we only got nine dimes for the massage. That ain't enough!"

I can't help but laugh. "My, my, my. Thank you for paying attention!"

I hand her a few more coins and tilt my neck so that Mackenzie can get the upper part of my shoulder a little better.

"Amethyst, what do you want to do when you grow up?" She stops giggling from her massage and peeks at me, then at her sister.

"Well I like doing makeup and stuff. I used to want to be a makeup artist, like style people for photo shoots and stuff. But my grandma said I need to be a nurse or teacher or something."

She sounds as though she has resigned herself to her grandmother's wishes.

I probe a little deeper into the topic. "A nurse and a makeup artist are completely different. Why do you think she wants you to do that?"

"She said I need to go to college and get a degree so I can make a lot of money. She said makeup isn't a career."

My stomach clenches faintly as I remember my own dreams as a young girl. This wasn't the life I had imagined. No husband, no kids, and working in the basement of an old hospital.

I had envisioned a beautiful life where I worked as an event coordinator, putting on lavish weddings and high-end parties. I'd imagined I would only take a few of the most exclusive events each year so I could be at home caring for my family. I would drive a big-bodied Mercedes Benz and take trips to Atlanta, New York, and Los Angeles to shop. I would volunteer with youth groups, ladies' ministries at church, and probably donate my event services to a few of the lucky couples who win free weddings on some of the national morning shows Mama always watches.

Without moving beyond Mackenzie's reach, I stretch my hands out and grab Amethyst on one side and Mecca on the other.

"Girls, my mama gave me the same advice. *Go to college, get a good job.* But I found out a job isn't really a good job if you don't love it. You have to find the thing you love, master it, and figure out how to earn enough to support yourself. Nurses earn a lot of money. But they work very hard and they see a lot of things that aren't very nice. The best nurses are the ones who love what they do, even when it isn't very pretty."

I peek at their faces on either side of me. I can't tell if they are understanding me or not.

"Basically, I'm saying it doesn't matter how much money you make if you aren't happy while you're doing it. Even though you're young, you can make some choices about the kind of life that you want to live and set some goals to make it happen. But first," I squeeze their hands, "you gotta be smart about your money. Ain't nobody gonna pay your way in this world. You want it? You gotta make it happen. And you gotta pay for it yourself."

Just then, I hear Ms. Emma Lee coughing near the doorway. I stand up.

"Okay you guys! Our time is up! Let's put the chairs back in the corner and grab yourselves a juice from the mini fridge!"

Mackenzie eyes my with hesitation. "How much we gotta pay?"

That makes me laugh, but I notice that Ms. Emma Lee hasn't cracked a smile.

I cut my laughter short. "It's free, pumpkin, go ahead and get what you want."

"Girls, go on ahead and get in the car. I'll be out in a minute." Ms. Emma Lee directs her grandchildren with a voice so calm and so steely, Mecca and Amethyst don't even stop for juice on their way to the door.

Julene walks in, just as the girls are leaving, to collect her own children. Her expression tells me she can sense she's walked in on something serious, and she shuffles her children out of the room without making a sound.

The room immediately becomes still and cold but I do my best to remain pleasant as I hug and kiss the last of the children goodbye.

Ms. Emma Lees eyes pierce the side of my face so lethally, I forget for a moment I am a fully-grown woman. Why do I feel as though she's about to send me to the yard to get a switch?

As the last child leaves the room, she clears her throat. "Look here. I'm an old woman and I don't have a bunch of time to beat around the bush when I got a problem. Imma tell you, I like what you're doing with the kids, but you don't have no right undermining me and telling them how they need to be living their lives."

My mouth swings open, but I close it while I rack my brain for a response. What is she even talking about? "Ms. Emma Lee, I'm confused. You were there at the Founders meeting when we agreed to start working with the children. We all agreed to teach them early about the financial…"

She holds up a hand and my mouth swings shut again. Heat burns my armpits until they tingle.

"Cynthia, I like you. You know I do. I love you like a daughter. But you don't never try to get in between me and my grands. They mean everything to me and I am everything to them. I took responsibility for them-- to raise them up and get them to where they can take care of themselves when I'm not here. So, when I tell them to go to school and get a real degree—one they can depend on when that mortgage and that light bill come due— you don't have no right to tell them anything different."

"That's not what I was saying! Of course they need college educations, but I was just challenging them to look at the big picture, think for themselves…"

"Baby, them are my babies—my grands—not yours, so that's for me to teach them, not you. I was standing in the doorway for a long time. A long time, listening to you tell them how your mama gave you the same advice as I'm giving. Making it sound like we too old to make good sense."

I shake my head slowly, wanting to undo the misunderstanding. "I wasn't telling them to disobey you. I was just sharing my experience—what I wish I had done differently. I only told them what I would tell my own…"

She doesn't let me finish. "Bingo! When you have your own kids, you can tell them whatever you want. But these is mines. And when it comes to mines, you don't dabble in that. So, I thank you for everything you been doing, I believe your heart is in the right place, but if you can't respect my wishes then maybe Mecca and Amethyst don't need to be coming to these meetings."

When she shuffles out of the room, I sit down on the stool and close my eyes. I replay the morning's events in my mind, searching for my mistakes. Ms. Emma Lee had scorched me with her comments. I'm insulted. Threatened.

It's not like I'm making this stuff up out of the blue. She was there when we, the founders, had studied and discussed the ideas of setting your mind and heart on goals that you wish to achieve with a burning desire. About deciding what you want and formulating a concrete plan to get it. Of fearless, independent thinking. Of creating the life you want and then living it.

At the time, she was on board with it. Now that we're talking about her family, she's changing her tune. And getting mad at me? And eavesdropping on my class?

Ms. Emma Lee's words shoot around in my mind like darts and I can't stop thinking about how the morning had turned out, can't figure out how I turned out to be the bad guy when I'd only tried to uphold the values we had established when we formed the trust in the first place.

My purse buzzes, low and dull, as though it is bigger and deeper than it really is. Reaching over, I sink my hand inside without looking, using my fingers like an ant uses antennas, to feel for my phone. The buzzing has stopped by the time I find it, trapped beneath the inner lining of my purse and the fake leather exterior. It must have slipped through the hole in the bottom corner. I'd planned to fix the hole, but today I'm thinking I probably need to just get a new purse.

I click the phone on and a string of notifications appear. Multiple text messages from Victor, missed calls from Mama, and Julene had reacted to my recent Facebook post.

I open Victor's texts.

First there's a selfie of him and his daughter, Empress, sitting in the movie theater. She's holding up a box of Mike and Ikes, and he's holding a huge blue slushee, tilted towards the camera as if to say cheers.

Victor: *wish you were here!!*

Next there's a selfie of him, standing outside of the women's restroom, next to the sign of the stick figure in a skirt, holding up his daughter's My Little Pony purse, his face bewildered.

Victor: *I am now her official purse holder! Lol! Anything for daddy's angel! SMH*

Victor: *we're here. We parked in Lot J. R U OTW?*

Victor: *we're going inside. just meet us at the food court when you get here.*

I look at my watch. It's 1:43 now. He must have been texting me the whole time I was getting chewed out by Ms. Emma Lee.

Me: *sorry meeting ran over. I'm otw. Starving too. Order me a grilled chicken wrap please? And a fruit cup. Please and thank you.*

Tossing the phone back into my purse, I hurry to get the activities room cleaned before I leave. I move the snacks and treats into the compact refrigerator and stash the bottled water, bowls, and serving dishes inside of the cabinet. Then I switch off the room light, pull the door shut, and hustle to my car.

CHAPTER FIVE

P ulling out of the church parking lot, I look at the time again. It's 1:48. I call Victor's phone.

It rings a few times before switching over to his voicemail. I hang up and dial him again. Clearly, he has his phone with him because he's been texting me all morning. One and a half rings and then I hear his voicemail again. Okay, so he's mad. I get it, I'm running a little late.

By the time I find a parking spot in Lot K—because of course, Lot J was full—it's just a few minutes after 2. He still isn't answering his phone, but I find him and the little princess in the food court, finishing off a basket of French fries.

"Hey y'all!" I hug Victor and run around the table to hug and tickle Empress. When she smiles at me, I see that her front tooth, the one that fell out last year, is just beginning to grow in. The edge of the tooth peeks through her gums at a slight angle, taking up more than half of the available space. She is adorable—a tiny, feminine version on Victor.

"Are you two having fun?" Sitting on the small picnic bench that connects to the table, I grab a stray fry and swirl it around the edge of the ketchup mound. "Where's mine?"

He doesn't look up at me. It's as though I'm not there. I ignore his petty attitude and my hunger and move on.

"How was the movie?" I'm looking at Victor, who is scrolling through his phone, looking at something too important to acknowledge my question.

Empress answers, "It was so funny, Miss Cin-D-Uh!" Without her front tooth, she struggles with pronunciation, but it's adorable.

She's babbling on, fumbling over the jokes and describing the funny scenes, but my eyes are fixed on Victor, who never looks at me. Not once. Until I go for another fry.

"Are you supposed to be eating that?" He asks the dagger of a question without even looking at me.

Empress looks at him, realizes he's speaking to me, and shifts her eyes my way.

"What?" I hear him clearly. But I need to know if he meant to say it so rudely.

"Are those fries on your diet?" His voice has the most unfriendly edge. I can feel Empress's eyes on me, but my embarrassment won't let me look at her right now.

Popping the fry in my mouth, I speak directly to the portion of his face that I can see. "Not exactly, but I haven't eaten all day and I asked you to order me something that would have been healthier…" I cast my eyes around the table, emphasizing the absence of my lunch. "Why didn't you order me something?"

Finally. Finally, he glances up from his phone, and says, "You didn't ask me to get you food."

I am incredulous. "I texted. I told you the class ran over. I asked you to order my lunch."

His eyes go back to the phone. "You texted me? When?"

"Miss Cindy Uh?" Empress is tugging at my arm, "Did you get it? It was a joke! The fox said 'What do you think I am, a typewriter?'"

She is overcome with giggles and I see her eyes darting around the table, fully expecting everyone present to find it funny too. She's oblivious to the adult drama unfolding right in front of her. He is fixated on his phone, but I give Empress the laughter she seeks.

And then, as though nothing is wrong, he puts his phone down, balls up a tiny piece of tissue and shoots it through his straw, hitting her squarely in the forehead. She dissolves into giggles, searching around and above, wondering where the shot came from.

A grin sweeps across his face, the first smile he's flashed since I got here, and I take note of how handsome he is. Deep, thick eyebrows that lay down and shine as though he styles them himself. Bright, clean white eyes. A perfectly trimmed mustache-- one that outlines his big lips. Soft brown lips that have never touched a cigar or cigarette, occasionally sipping on cognac or prosecco. There's a dimple in his right cheek—a scar, really—from when he threw a rock through a window as a child and karma repaid him with a shard of glass to the face.

She reaches for her own straw and struggles to force a piece of tissue into the end of it. Blowing with all her little girl might, she can't manage to send the tissue ball more than a few inches beyond the tip of her straw. She's laughing hysterically and so is he, and my heart is moved by the power of this daddy-daughter relationship.

He loves his daughter, I can see it in this moment, and I'm glad that he thinks enough of me to invite me on their outings. I imagine for a moment that we are a family. I grab a tiny bit of tissue, roll it between my fingers, place it in the palm of my hand and flick it at him, landing the shot in the center of his chest.

He pauses only for a second, determines the shot was from me, and redirects his attention towards Empress. He grabs a rogue French fry from the table and pretends to look up at the sky while flicking it under the table, targeting Empress again. When she peeks under the table to search for the fry missile, he reaches over and hides her juice box behind the napkin holder.

Now I'm a bystander-- an onlooker. The awkwardness has crept into my consciousness, making me aware of the stupid frozen smile on my face. Attempting to look unbothered, I pull out my phone and scroll through Facebook.

Julene has posted new pictures of her kids.

An old girlfriend from high school has gotten engaged and shared some pictures from her engagement photo shoot. She's used the hashtag #SaveTheDate on all of her pictures.

An old high school boyfriend, one whom I still consider a good friend, has posted a new progress picture for his fitness journal. I can't tell if he's doing it on his own or if he's joined a fitness group, but he posts pictures almost every week of his meals, his physique, his sweaty face after a run.

I consider commenting on one of his pictures but change my mind. The last thing I need right now is for Victor to think I'm checking out some other guy while I'm sitting here with him.

That's when I notice the table has suddenly become quiet and I lift my eyes to see Victor and Empress have taken a seat at a nearby face-painting artist's booth. They've walked away without a word to me.

I grab my bag, slide my phone in it, and walk back to my car. I can take a hint.

In the morning, I don't want to go to church. I haven't heard from Victor since I left him at Fun Fair Park yesterday and that lets me know just how simple and petty he can be. Honestly, how can he be mad at me for running a little late when he knew I had an obligation to the kids? And then he has the audacity to give me the silent treatment in front of his daughter?

I consider skipping church just to avoid running in to him, but he'd see I wasn't there and think that he'd gotten the best of me.

After lying in bed for another ten minutes, I finally decide to get up and get dressed.

Pulling into the church parking lot, I scan the parked cars to see if he's there. When I don't see his car in the usual spot, I breathe a sigh of relief. The main lot is full, and the men of the security ministry wave me towards the gravel overflow lot. I hesitate to drive over there, hoping to find a better spot in the main lot so I won't have to walk through the gravel in heels.

It could be my imagination, but I can swear my balance has been off-kilter since I've gained this weight back. Even in wedges, I feel a little unsteady.

No parking spot opens for me and I follow Brother Campbell's gesture into the overflow parking lot. As soon as I turn in I see Victor standing there, laughing with the other men of the ministry, waving a flag and guiding cars into open spaces.

He sees my car. I know he sees it, but he turns his back, continuing to direct the vehicles on his row.

It's fine. I don't even know why this 'argument' is dragging on, but whatever. Ain't nobody got time for his games.

After I park, I realize the distance from the gravel lot to the church is going to be a challenge. As soon as I step out of the car, my ankle starts wobbling. When I can't find steady footing on the rocks, I sit down in the front seat and try to remember if I have any flats stashed in the car somewhere.

I don't.

I stand again, straighten my skirt, and get my head on right. That's what Vito always yells at me when I start slowing down or tell him that I can't do some new exercise. *Get your head on right, Thomas!* That means, decide you're going to do something and then do it.

I pull myself together and head towards the church, ankles wobbling. I'm getting closer to the ministry men who are no longer waving cars through, but just standing around telling jokes, goofing off instead of going in the church.

Why don't they just go inside?

Lord have mercy, I would rather do anything—anything!—other than walk past him right now. But I've ventured too far away from my car to turn back now and a few of the men have already acknowledged me, tipping their hats and smiling. As I approach, everyone except Victor is greeting me.

I feel more like I'm in high school than at church, dying inside as I walk past a group of upperclassmen.

My underarms are tingling and a caveman could start a fire from the friction of my thighs rubbing as I fight to remain upright on the unsteady gravel. And the church...has it moved FURTHER away?

When I'm halfway there, Brother Campbell hurries to my side— most likely because I look like a baby horse trying to take her first steps— and takes hold of my arm, guiding me to the paved sidewalk.

"Sister Thomas! Come on, now. I gotcha."

I have no shame about grabbing onto him like the life preserver that he is. If I hadn't been so out of breath from my walk of shame, he might have been able to understand what I was saying: *thankyouthankyousomuch*. Instead, I can only huff for air and pray for the moment I eventually reach the front door of the church.

Oh. And no more wedges until I'm down to at least 175 pounds.

Inside the sanctuary, I find a spot in the back of the first section. The pew is only half full and I leave a space for Victor, if he decides to come into the church and drop the childish act.

Sometime towards the end of the service, as the Pastor is making the alter call, I notice Victor is sitting across the aisle, near Stephanie, who heads the Singles Ministry.

I know of her, have volunteered in her committee a few times and participated in some of the singles outings. I also know she usually goes out of her way to get next to Victor. I've seen her watching me a little more lately, since he and I usually sit together during service. I can only imagine how happy she is to see us sitting apart today.

When I pass her in the vestibule in the way out of church, I walk right up to her.

"Hey girl! I'm in love with that bag! You gotta tell me where you found it!" I tap her arm and she reaches right over to hug me. Church folk can be petty and phony, and I'm guilty as charged today.

Victor is right next to her. Not exactly *with* her, but close enough, and I know he sees me.

"What's going on, Brother Victor?" I say it loud enough that he can't pretend not to hear and, from my peripheral, I see Stephanie's eyes glance from me to him, trying to figure out what's happening.

He tosses me a fake smile and shakes my hand, says, "What's up, Cynthia?" and continues walking.

Stephanie turns her eyes back to me and smiles, "Everything *alright*? What just happened there? I thought y'all were friends." Her voice is sweeter and more artificial than the pink pack of fake sugar Mama always dumps in her coffee.

I must give her credit for having the audacity to question me about something that clearly doesn't involve her, and I know better than to mistake her curiosity for concern.

Her question doesn't surprise me, though, and I don't miss a beat, "What? You talking about *him*,"—I tilt my head in the direction in which he has disappeared. "We're cool."

She smiles.

I smile.

Between the two of us, a million unspoken words are exchanged, though we've both run out of things to say aloud. I'm relieved when my phone rings, even though it's only Mama. Saved by the bell, I answer the call and wave a silent *see-you-later* to Stephanie before turning to escape the crowded hallways of the church.

CHAPTER SIX

That evening, after BBQ spareribs, cabbage, rice, and candied yams with Mama, I lay across the foot of her bed, listening to her latest complaints about the president.

"He's a disgrace! An idiot! He'll lead us into another war before it's all over with! Now mark my words! This man is a criminal, he ain't good for nothing. Nothing but to get all the money that he can for his businesses so he can leave us all high and dry! You better get your affairs in order, girl."

She doesn't even look at me, doesn't take her eyes off the news anchor in the screen, but I'm the only other person in the room, so I'm her audience.

"Mama..."

"I ain't gonna be here to save you when it all falls down. Imma be gone on to the glory and you gone have to be smart and fend for yourself. You gonna be on your own when I leave this place."

"Old lady, you ain't going nowhere! I'll probably be gone before you."

We lay there in silence for a bit, her propped up on about thirty pillows, me draped across the foot of the bed like her pet. The water droplet sound of an incoming text interrupts our quiet time.

I peek at the phone screen but decide not to open the message.

I can see the first few characters of the text, but more importantly, I can see the name of the sender. I won't take the bait tonight. Instead, I place the phone face down on the bed and flip myself over on my back, stare at the ceiling, and listen to the news anchor drone on about whatever.

In seconds, I can feel my boobs shifting towards my throat and the weight is enough to complicate my breathing. I shift over on my side.

The water droplet sound chimes again and the screen of my overturned phone lights up mama's bed spread. I tip the phone over, determine that a meme has been sent, and continue to ignore.

Curiosity gets the best of me, though, and after a moment, I grab the phone and tap the screen until the message comes to life. I flip over onto my stomach, realize this position is uncomfortable for my lower back, and roll up into a sitting position.

"Now look here! If you got to be doing all this tossing and turning on my bed, you gone have to…"

The messages on my phone turn the sound of Mama's rant into ambient noise.

Victor: *What's up?*

The next message was not a meme, as I had assumed, but a picture of me, taken from behind as I was being escorted from the gravel overflow lot to the church this morning.

Victor: *someone was looking sexy at church today... too bad she was on the arm of another man... smh*

"I said, you can get over there on that chair, or you can just go..." Mama's voice rises and falls in the background as I reply to the text.

Me: *You're a pervert.*

Victor: *maybe I just saw something that caught my eye.*

Me: *You didn't act like I caught your eye. You let another man come to my rescue.*

Victor: *Homeboy almost got himself messed up. I told him to get his own woman and keep his hands off mine.*

Me: *Yeah right. How r u gonna fight a man IN CHURCH over a woman who isn't yours?*

Victor: *we weren't in church. We were outside.*

Victor again: *and he knows me and you been kicking it. I talk about you all the time.*

Me: *If it's like that, why did you act so petty yesterday at fun fair park? And you wouldn't have spoken to me at church if I didn't speak first.*

"...you texting on that phone with anyway? You sitting there with the biggest grin on your face! What you need to do is..." Mama always gets irritated when my phone gets more attention than she does.

Victor: *I wasn't being petty yesterday. You were the one who said you would come to the movies with us and then bailed out. Then you were late as hell to meet us for lunch.*

Me: *You already knew where I was...*

Victor: *my baby girl kept asking where you were and she was disappointed when you didn't show up at the movie. She thought you were going to skip lunch too.*

Victor: *I don't like to see her get disappointed and that's why I'm always scared to bring women around her. I can't let somebody hurt her.*

Me: *I'm only one woman. Who else are you introducing her to?*

Victor: *see, there you go. Getting the wrong idea. I'm just trying to tell you why that put me in a bad mood. And then I had to argue with my daughter's mother this morning over some stupid stuff. Smh.*

Me: *I thought y'all were 'coparenting' what's the problem now?*

Victor: *same old stuff. She said she would pick her up this morning so I could get to church on time. Then she texted and said her car was acting up and she didn't want to drive over to my place. She wanted me to drop Empress off to her.*

Me: *Doesn't sound unreasonable. Maybe a little inconvenient, though, but not bad.*

Victor: *she was at her dude's house. She wasn't at home. Probably spent the night and was too lazy to get up and get her child. She got her priorities messed up.*

Me: *So what did you do?*

Victor: *I ended up taking Empress to her grandmother's house. I told my baby mama to pick her up from there. I'm not taking my baby to some other dude's house.*

Despite my preoccupation with my phone, Mama's incessant chattering continues, "...prune juice that won't tear my stomach up. That last one left a funny taste in my mouth. I knew something was wrong with it. Shouldn't have drank it."

I sigh, straighten my back, and lay the phone on the bed again. Then I turn to face mama. "There was nothing wrong with that prune juice, Ma. I checked the expiration date before I bought it. And, it was organic. No preservatives, no added sugar. It should have been fine for you."

"Well it messed up my stomach." She is unwavering.

"But did you have a bowel movement?" I can hear the muffled water droplets sounding off, punctuating our conversation. I glance at my phone again.

Victor: *I know that pissed her off but it pissed me off too. Empress don't like going to her grandmother's and her mama probably didn't want to drive over there either.*

Victor: *so she texted me and said that she was going to get an attorney to challenge the custody agreement.*

Victor: *just gonna cost me more money and waste my time.*

Victor: *she puts me in a bad headspace and I guess I was already irritated from you leaving us at Fun Fair Park. I wasn't in the best mood by the time you saw me at church.*

Victor: *hello?*

Me: *Hey I'm here. Had to check on mama.*

Me: *So you just decided to take your frustrations out on me. You ignored me at the park and at church.*

He sends a meme that says *I'm sorry.*

Victor: *I wasn't mad at you. I just had a lot on my mind.*

Mama's one-sided conversation is epic. "...next time, just get my prune juice at the Dollar Tree like I asked. I like the one they have there. And it's cheaper, too. Ain't no sense in spending all that money on that organic stuff at them fancy grocery stores. Aren't you supposed to be saving money anyway? Or did you quit that money club already? I swear, you don't stick to nothing for very long. I thought it was a good idea y'all had…"

Me: *So you were in your feelings. Heard that one before.*

Victor: *I gave you an apology. What else do you want? A kidney? Lol*

Me: *Don't let it happen again.*

Victor: *It won't happen again. Can't let Brother Campbell step in and make me look bad again.*

He sends a selfie, laying on the couch—or bed? I can't tell—wearing a white tank top, one arm behind his head making his bicep look as big as his head, staring directly at me, biting his bottom lip. He gets me every time.

I drop the phone.

Mama stops rambling about whatever. "What's wrong? Why you throw that phone down like that?"

I pick it up again and text back:

Me: *I cannot fool with you tonight. You so silly.*

Victor: *send me one.*

My voice is no more than a distracted whisper when I answer Mama. "Nothing, Ma. I just dropped it."

Me: *one, what?*

Victor: *a pic*

Victor: *of you*

Me: *Good night.*

Victor: *good night beautiful.*

"...why you even come in here and flop all over my bed? All you did was tap on that phone. You sure didn't talk to me. What were you doing? Facebooking? Or what? That's why you can't meet somebody. You stay up in that phone instead of speaking to people. How do people get to know each other anymore? I used to..." She's getting wound up, I can hear it in her voice. Mama can give a lecture on any topic at the drop of a dime.

I stand at the foot of the bed, blocking her view of the TV. "So you don't want me in here? Am I bothering you by being in your presence?"

She leans to the left, craning her neck to see the TV behind me, and then mumbles in a tone far less authoritative than before. "I didn't say that."

"Huh? What's that, now? You say you want me to get out of your room?" I feign hard of hearing and slide over to block the TV again.

She leans the other way, desperate to catch a view of the screen, but she won't tell me to get out of her room this time.

"That's what I thought!" I lay across the foot of her bed again, reconsider my comfort, and move up to the top to lay next to her. She hates it when I bother her but I know she loves having me around.

CHAPTER SEVEN

Victor succeeds in texting me like clockwork all week:

Good morning, beautiful.

What's for lunch?

Memes every afternoon.

Invitations for mutual selfies every night.

I seldom oblige his requests for pictures of me. Although I have mastered the perfect selfie angle to hide my stomach and chubby chin, I can't take a chance of some internet hacker getting hold of my nudes. Victor says it can't happen, that he would delete the pictures as soon as I send them, but I'm just not comfortable with it. Maybe if we were married, but even then I would be hesitant.

By Thursday, he's apparently given up on the notion I would ever send a picture of more than my smile, and he invites me on a date instead. Well, sort of.

Victor: *Do you still get discounts to Planet Splash with your credit card points?*

Me: *It's not a discount. It's a free room upgrade and a spa credit.*

Victor: *Is that cheaper than the regular price?*

Me: *yeah*

Victor: *That's called a discount.*

Me: 😐 *It's not a discount. It's perks.*

Victor: *Whatever.*

Victor: *I want to take my daughter there this weekend. Can you help me to make the reservation?*

Victor: *If it's not too much to ask, I want you to come with us.*

Me: *This weekend? I could probably find you a better rate if you pick a date that's a few weeks out.*

Me: *Why you wait until the last minute? Maybe I have plans.*

Small bubbles appear and then disappear on the phone screen. I wait for a moment and realize he isn't going to respond. Lying back on my bed, I scroll through my Facebook feed out of sheer boredom.

Ruth's daughter and granddaughter have enjoyed a girl's day out. They've posted pictures of their toes with freshly pedicured nails, shopping bags, some sushi rolls, and a picture of their hands holding matching ice cream cones.

They both look so much like Ruth, and then...they also look so much like each other. More like sisters than mother and daughter.

I heart each of the pictures individually, rather than a single heart for the post itself, to let them know I've taken the time to appreciate each one. To remind them that, although Ruth is gone, I'm still here if they need me. I haven't seen either of them since Ruth left.

Further into the newsfeed, I see my old friend Derrick has run 3.00 miles in 30:51 minutes. I like the way he posts a picture from the app to track his route and progress. I've been thinking of running again—outside, not on the treadmill—and I think the app would come in handy. I heart the post and then save it so I can remember to download the app. Plus, his dimples are getting cuter with each pound that he's losing.

Lurking through his photos, I can see he's moved to Canada, formerly played in the Canadian Football League, assists in a kid's football camp, and is possibly single. There's a little bit of a question mark around that last part. I see a lot of pictures with his sisters and mom, but no pictures of children, a wife, or a girlfriend.

I have to say, I'm a little surprised. If he's half the teddy bear he was in high school, then any woman should have snatched him up by now.

Thinking back to our high school break up, it really wasn't his fault, or mine. It was just the timing. He was convinced he had a future in the NFL, and I couldn't leave Savannah while my dad was struggling with colon cancer. He had to chase his dream, and I couldn't follow. That had been more than twenty years and 150 pounds ago—for both of us, evidently.

My cyber investigation is interrupted by a text from Victor:

Victor: *Get off of Facebook.* 😄

Me: *What are you talking about? Stalker.*

Victor: *I can see that you're online.*

Me: *Just killing time since you stopped texting me.*

Victor: *Baby mama called.*

Victor: *she going out of town with her dude and wants me to get Empress again.*

Me: *Two weekends in a row? Wow.*

Victor: *I know right. She put that dude before our daughter.*

Me: *I meant two weekends in a row you get to spend with your daughter. Thought you'd be happy about that.*

Victor: *I love anytime I can spend with my daughter. Just don't want her to feel like her mother is kicking her to the curb.*

Me: *She's not. She's just giving you more daddy/daughter time. That's a blessing.*

Me: *She won't be this little forever.*

Victor: *True.*

Victor: *So, can you do it?*

Me: *Let me figure some things out. It's short notice.*

Victor: *Never mind. I'll figure it out myself.*

Me: *Why you getting so sensitive?*

Me: *I just need to make arrangements for my mom. Can't just up and leave her alone.*

Victor: *Yeah. Call your boyfriend and tell him you had a change of plans.*

Me: *What boyfriend? What are you even talking about? You so suspicious.*

Me: *I can do it. I just have to take care of my responsibilities around here.*

Victor: *Yeah okay.*

Me: *I know you're not supposed to be mad.*

Me:?

Me: *send me a pic so I can go to sleep.*

Crickets.

I lie back on my bed for a moment, feeling as though I shouldn't even help him out at all. He's so oversensitive. But, a weekend with him and his daughter would be fun. I love that little girl and I love that Victor feels comfortable having me around her so much. And, what else do I have to do this weekend, besides watch TV with Mama?

Julene picks up on the first ring, hollering at someone who is crying in the background. "Imma end up killing one of these kids! What's up?"

"Please don't kill the children. Give them to me." I'm only half-kidding with her. I love hanging with her kids, but I love it when they go home too.

"Listen, these kids will ruin any chance you have at catching a man! They would scare the Pope away!"

"Well, in that case, never mind. I can't take any more strikes against me when it comes to catching a man! I need all the help I can get!"

"So what's up? You're usually asleep by now or watching TV with your mom."

"So, Victor called…"

"Oh Lord…wait! He actually called?"

"Let me reword that— he texted me and invited me to Planet Splash with him and his daughter this weekend."

"That's a little short notice, isn't it?"

I exhale, trying not to let the excitement fade from my voice. It isn't the most romantic gesture on his behalf, but I still think it was nice. Julene has a way of seeing through the BS, though. "Stop trying to look for something wrong!" I tell her. "I just need to ask you for a favor."

"Okay…" She sounds suspicious.

"So, do you think you can stop by and check on Mama a few times while I'm gone? She's mostly fine, but she sometimes needs help getting in and out of the shower. I'll put all of her meals together before I go. She can heat them up herself, so if you just stop by to see if she needs anything that would help me out a lot."

"I can do that for you. Not a problem. As much as you've helped me out with the kids, I probably owe you more than that!"

"Girl, I appreciate you! I need to get out every once in a while, and I feel like I can't be gone more than a few hours because of Mama."

"Well, that's your only mama. I wish I had that kind of relationship with mine."

Julene rarely speaks of her mother. I know she's had a rocky relationship with her family, but, as close as our friendship has become, most of her family life is still a mystery to me. I steer us back to a safer subject. "Will you bring the kids? She loves to see them. I know she wishes she had grandchildren of her own."

"I don't know about that." Julene laughs. "I might leave them with my little cousin and go spend the night with your mama just to get some peace and quiet!"

"She'll talk you to death! I'm telling you. I appreciate it, though. I'm looking forward to getting away for a little bit. And hopefully Victor won't be Man-struating. He's such a moody baby sometimes! And look, he asked me to make the reservation, rearrange my schedule, and ended up getting mad at me because I said I would've preferred more notice."

Julene laughs out loud. "So he asked you for a favor and got mad because you didn't jump to his command quick enough?"

I remain silent. I hadn't meant to tell her that last part. I need to vent, but I feel like I only tell her the bad things about Victor. And there's so much good. I can tell she doesn't like him. She's never said it directly, but it's clear she doesn't care for him, and I know it's based solely upon what I've told her.

She doesn't wait for me to respond. "Don't get quiet on me, now! I'm not judging. But I don't know how you can put up with that moodiness! I think I probably would have cussed him out by now. He wouldn't like me at all."

Truth be told, I know she's right. I've wanted to curse him out so many times. But, I always feel torn. He's confided in me so much, has trusted me with his deepest feelings, shown me glimpses of his sensitive side, let me into his daughter's life—I just get it. I get him. With all his imperfections. I see the Victor most people don't get to see and that allows me to tolerate his weird ways. Plus, look at me! I have some peculiar ways that would probably annoy some people too. No one is perfect.

And I think, when we look back on our time together, no matter what the future holds, I'll be able to say, '*I was there for you when you were down. I was the one who didn't walk out on you or get offended by you or try to take advantage of you.*' I'm just not the kind of person who would turn my back on someone when need me.

"And let me ask you this," Julene isn't finished, "would he be asking you to do this if you weren't getting a discount?"

"He invited me to go out with him and his daughter the other day and didn't ask me for anything in return."

"Alright. Long as you know what you're doing. I just had to ask. I can handle your mom. Just go and have a good time!"

CHAPTER EIGHT

From the second we arrive at the resort, Empress and I are inseparable. She shadows me like an intern while I sanitize our hotel room, studying the way I clean the light switches, remote control, and the bathroom.

She studies my every move and asks questions about everything.

"Miss Cindy-uh, why did you wipe that one again? Are you going to clean this one and that one? What do germs look like? Did you ever have a germ on you? What if I touch this? Are the germs on the floor? Are you going to wash the floor? Are you going to wash my shoes? Can I wipe something too?"

Her questions are endless, inquisitive, and intelligent-- she notices everything.

"Baby girl, stop asking so many questions! If you don't let Miss Cynthia finish, we won't have time to go to the pool." Victor's attempt to distract her is in vain.

"But daddy, I'm cleaning, see?" She grabs a wet wipe and scrubs an imaginary spot on the bedside table.

"She's fine. I don't mind teaching her how to clean. You know I'm OCD about this stuff." I wink at him and smile.

He shrugs his shoulders, knowing he's outnumbered against us. "Well, hurry up so we can get to the pool, then."

At the pool, Empress dives right into the kiddie pool and Victor heads straight towards the snack bar. I stand for a moment, unsure of what I should be doing—going with him or watching her—before deciding someone needs to supervise the child. I walk to the edge of the kiddie pool and smile down at Empress.

She's splashing around, squishing water between her fingers, blowing bubbles at the surface of the water. "Miss Cindy-uh! Look! I can do this!" She grabs hold of the pool's edge and kicks her feet behind her as though she's swimming.

"Wow! That was great!" I encourage her. "Can you do it without holding on?"

She tries to swim towards the center of the pool but can't seem to get both feet off the ground at the same time.

"I can't do it like that yet. Maybe when I get bigger." She grabs the pool's edge again and kicks her feet until waves slosh out of the pool and onto the deck.

"Look Miss Cindy-uh! Can you do this?" She splashes with all her might.

"No, honey. Miss Cynthia can't do that. Maybe you can teach me one day." I sit down at the edge of the pool and ease my feet into the water. It's surprisingly warm.

"Ooh...can you get in? Play with me!" She pleads with me, her eyes shimmering with excitement.

I look towards Victor, who has found a table close to the pool's edge. Empress sees him at the same time. "Daddy! Look what I can do! Miss Cindy-uh can't do it! I'll teach her! Want me to teach you?"

I sit at the water's edge for more than an hour, feet dangling in the water, while Victor splashes around with Empress. They play Marco Polo, tag, they race one another from one side of the pool to the other, stopping occasionally to invite me in or flick water in my direction.

I'm studying the way the skin on my feet has begun to resemble grayish-white prunes when I hear it: "Daddy! No! You got the water in my eyes!" Empress is in tears, hands flailing in the air like a blind person.

"Baby, you're fine. Open your eyes. I'm right here." Victor tries wiping her face with his hands, tries to convince her she isn't blind and doing his best to assure her that she's okay, but she isn't having it.

Squinting through one eye, she wades towards the edge. "I wanna get out. I don't wanna play anymore."

Victor, thinking she might change her mind, swims circles around her, teasing. "You're getting out? Just because of a little water in your eyes? You gonna leave me in here by myself?"

She's already clamoring out of the pool, ignoring his pleas for her return.

"Come here, Little Bit." I reach towards her, inviting her to join me on the edge of the pool.

She walks the few steps toward me and crawls into my lap. I cradle her there, feeling the chill of her wet, little body, inhaling the scent of chlorine that clings to her skin.

When she nestles her head into the crook of my neck, I try to wrap her a little tighter into my arms-- into my lap-- to warm her. Her sniffling subsides and I look up in search of Victor.

He's gotten out of the pool and has begun to gather our belongings. When I smile at him, he doesn't smile back. Instead he mumbles something to the effect of "Let's go," before making his way towards the elevator lobby.

I look down at the half-sleeping little girl in my lap and whisper into the top of her head. "Don't go to sleep, Little Bit. Let's go upstairs and get your bath and a snack before you get too tired."

I carry her onto the elevator and into our suite while she plays with the small curls at the nape of my neck. She won't let me put her down, and I enjoy holding her.

When we step into our suite, we're both happy and relaxed, but Victor's annoyance is palpable. "Put her down. She's a big girl. She can walk."

"I know she can, but she…" I protest lightly, not sure if he's serious or not.

"Cynthia. Put. Her. Down. She knows how to walk." He's definitely not kidding.

I set her feet on the floor and tell her to get ready for her bath.

She looks up at me, "I need help with my bathing suit."

Except for the way she pronounces my name, her speech is exceptionally proper, and I can't help but adore her. I look towards Victor, my eyes asking for permission. He nods, grudgingly, and begins thumbing through his phone.

After her bath, we paint our nails, play I Spy and make S'mores in the toaster oven, and finally she drifts off to sleep.

Victor hasn't spoken more than five words all evening and I can feel that he's bracing himself for an argument. About what? I don't know, but I've made a point not to engage him in the negativity, so I try a different approach.

"Today was nice. We had a good time with Empress..." I talk to him over my shoulder as I busy myself, putting away the marshmallows and nail polish bottles.

"Yeah, you thought of everything." His voice is flat, a contradiction to his otherwise pleasant comment.

"You're right. I did think of everything." I pull a few of my bags from the cabinet in the suite's small kitchenette and hunt through them until I find the bottle of red wine I brought. I pour glass for him and one for myself, then walk over to the sofa where he is sitting. "Here. Sit back. Chill out. I'll make us a late-night snack."

He accepts the wine, meeting my eyes with an attempted smile.

Back in the kitchenette, I pull out containers of the finger foods I prepared earlier in the morning. I've got cubes of cheese, salami, almonds, strawberries, and grapes. I'd also made a bowl of green salsa fresca from a recipe I found on Pinterest: diced feta, green tomatoes, cilantro, green peppers, onions, lime juice, and a splash of olive oil. I pour some bite-sized tortilla chips into a bowl and arrange everything on the coffee table. By the time I finish, Victor has downed his glass of wine and has poured a second.

Finally ready to relax and have an adult conversation, I sit on the couch and put my feet on his lap.

"You big mad or little mad?" I tease him, unwilling to allow our evening to be spoiled by a bad attitude.

"I'm not mad." He rubs my feet absentmindedly.

"Okay…" I reach for some almonds, grab a few strawberries, and wait. With him, there's always more.

"It got under my skin a little bit; the way Empress ran to you when I was just playing with her in the pool."

Here we go. I think to myself but allow him to continue.

"I've played with her like that in the pool before. We always splash each other and a little water never bothered her until today. And when she ran to you, it just made me feel like the bad guy. Like an outsider."

"I think she was probably just getting tired. You know kids get cranky when they're tired. She almost fell asleep in my lap." I try to change his perspective and encourage him to look at things from her point of view instead of his own.

Despite my attempt at reverse psychology, he has a different theory. "I think her mom just puts things in her head and tries to turn her against me. I pride myself on being a great father but, truth be told, the crap I put up with when I deal with my daughter's mom makes me want to sign away my parental rights and let her continue in her misery. Sometimes I wonder why the best fathers get the worst baby mamas and vice versa."

I take a deep breath before I speak. "Stay focused. Your daughter is the most important person in this equation. You can't let any situation or anyone—even her mother—disrupt your relationship with your daughter. If the mother has a new man, then that's great! Maybe she can find her happiness and hopefully things will get better for your daughter. Until then, press on and continue to love and spoil your little girl. You're a great dad and your presence is so important in her life. It's important now, but it will be even more important as she gets older."

He drains his glass of wine, reaches to pour another, and empties the bottle.

"I've lost count of how many times I've told her I'm on my way to get my daughter for the weekend and when I pull up, she tells me I can't get her because she's asleep. What does her being asleep matter if I'm getting her for the weekend?"

I sip my wine sparingly—I only brought one bottle. "There are some things we will never have the answers to. What you *can* do is what you have to do—continue to be a great parent in spite of the other parent."

I sip again and continue. "I used to think only women dealt with this, but I've come to know different. There are great parents and there are parents who choose to hurt everyone around them—even if that's their own children. I've heard lots of stories. But the truth is, children know more than we think, and they see everything. And as they get older, they begin to understand what's going on."

He grips my feet a little harder. "And I know she only let me get Empress this weekend because she was going out of town with her new boyfriend. She was bragging about it on Facebook."

I try diffusing his suspicions. "People post all kinds of stuff on Facebook, especially when they know other people are checking. You don't know what she's really doing."

He shakes his head, deflecting my suggestion. "Some lame dude tagged her on Facebook and said he had a special getaway planned. The picture he posted looked like Miami or somewhere like that, which is funny because I had planned to take her to Miami right before we broke up. That was the time that she took the tickets I bought for us and went to Florida with her girlfriends after I lost my job. Like, who does that? She just turned her back on me when I was down and she didn't give a damn."

I wag my finger at him playfully and tease, "Now, tell the whole story. You said she broke up with you because you were cheating with your supervisor."

That's when he stops rubbing my feet. "No. That's what I hate. You females always want to make something sound so…"

I put my wine glass down, keeping a smile but steadying my voice. "You females?"

"See. There you go, getting all sensitive." His voice rises to the verge of shouting before subsiding to a tone just north of defeat. "I'm just saying, that's not what happened. I was having trouble at work and she was mentoring me. When me and my baby mama started having problems I didn't have anyone to talk to for a female perspective, and I started going to her for advice—nothing inappropriate. But Empress's mother was jealous and didn't want me communicating with her. And I knew how she felt, but I needed someone to talk to! Plus, we worked together every day, so how do I not talk to her?"

I wait quietly for a moment before speaking again. In the silence, he grabs my feet and rubs them softly again.

I offer my advice: "You should have been confiding in your woman. You're supposed to turn towards your significant other, not away from her when you need to talk to someone."

He exhales heavily, squeezing my feet gently and lifts his eyes to find mine. "I know that now. Look, I was hiding the friendship and I was wrong for that. When I found out that she was starting to catch feelings for me, I should have ended the friendship, I know. But the attention I was getting from her kind of boosted my self-esteem and I wasn't getting anything like that at home." He pauses and holds his hand up.

"Again, I know I was wrong. I admit it."

"Then why didn't you stop?" We've spoken of this before, on various levels, but tonight I'm curious— sincerely curious about why men do what they do. How is it possible they can confess to love so deeply and still make the most ridiculous choices?

"Because—now I know this is wrong, I recognize my mistakes, but I'm just being transparent, here—I figured no one was getting hurt and I wasn't technically being unfaithful. I didn't have sex with her. But she started to get real clingy and she was coming at me hard. I could have done it if I really wanted too—that's the crazy part!—but me and Empress' mom were trying to work things out. I tried to let my supervisor know I couldn't communicate with her like that anymore, but she got pissed and basically got me fired." He looks towards me as though he still needs help figuring out where it all went wrong.

I piece the rest of the puzzle together. "And you had to go home and explain why you got fired…"

"Right. And she was convinced I cheated on her. But I didn't! I'm a good dude, man, I swear. I just got caught up in the attention and I guess my self-esteem wasn't where it needed to be at the time."

I shake my head, imagining how the scenario had played out. "She wasn't trying to hear that, though, huh? You messed that one up, my brother."

For some reason, his foolishness makes me laugh and I can't help but rub it in a little more. "You know you were dead wrong for that. You violated the trust in your relationship and that's as bad as cheating..."

Victor grabs my half-filled wine glass from the table and walks toward the window. "I already admitted that! I didn't cheat but it was still wrong! How many times are y'all going to keep saying that? Why do y'all keep making it sound like I'm such a bad person?"

I shoot him a hard look, daring him to say it again. "First of all, who is y'all? Are you putting me and your ex in the same category? Where is this coming from?"

He walks around the room for a moment before taking a seat on the arm of the couch, cradling my wine glass in his hands. "You're right. I was out of line. It's just been so frustrating. I feel like she just took it too far. Two wrongs don't make a right."

"You mean, because she dumped your butt?"

He stares into the glass, shaking his head slowly, "Nah, it's just the way she did it. She said she forgave me and told me we could move forward. You know, work it out for our daughter's sake. But, all along, she was pulling money out of our household and planning to leave me anyway. So, that's how she was able to purchase her condo without me knowing. And then she talked me into paying for that bogus vacation, which she ended up taking without me."

For some reason, I actually feel a twinge of sadness for him. Not because of a situation he'd brought upon himself, but because I can tell he still feels the pain. Even though it was a past relationship, I can sympathize when someone I care for is in pain. "Oh wow. She really set you up. You know, I…"

He's no longer listening to me. He gulps the last of the wine and continues rambling in a way that's starting to sound a little too pathetic for my liking. "…been so depressed lately…will never trust any female again…"

I can't look at him anymore. A pity party because he screwed up his own relationship? Because he suffered a little heartbreak? A little embarrassment?

I could write a list—no, I could write *volumes* about the times love has been unjust in my life. No one would believe the number of times it had slapped me in the face, tied one of my arms behind my back, ripped the rug from under my feet, taken off its mask…

The stories of *my* heartache, *my* embarrassment, *my* PTSD—would be enough to make his hair fall out. But he never asks, and I don't like to dwell on my past trauma. I still believe—still pray—for a true love that would make all my past struggles feel justified.

I stand up and begin collecting the food and dishes. I try to send Victor to bed so we can end this conversation. "Go ahead and lay down. Get some rest and I'll clean this stuff up."

Victor stands up, freezes for a moment to steady himself, and I turn my back.

The fact that he's clearly buzzed from the alcohol and has spiraled downward into an abyss of self-pity has basically spoiled the romantic evening I had hoped for.

Just as I bend over to put my tote bag under the cabinet, I feel him come up behind me, and I freeze.

"You scared me! What are you doing?" I spin around to face him, sucking in my stomach so that no part of my body touches his right now.

His eyes are glassy and relaxed as he leans closer, clumsy in his attempt to kiss my earlobe or maybe my neck. Something in my stomach does a flip flop.

He smells so good. The lingering smell of his body wash and cologne make me feel some kind of way, and it's been a while since we've been intimate. It's difficult to manage between his weekends with Empress and my responsibilities at home. But tonight, knowing he's drunk—or at least tipsy—I don't feel as though his arduous advances are an expression of his true feelings for me. I can't shake the feeling his attraction tonight is fueled by alcohol, depression, and convenience--not a combination that makes a girl feel like a sexy goddess.

There are times when I regret that we've been intimate at all. Sex outside the confines of marriage makes me feel guilty enough, but sex outside of a legitimate relationship? I'm not proud of it.

I push past him, freeing myself from the close confines of the kitchen, out into the open space of the living room where I can allow air to circulate into the tingly spaces under my arms and between my legs.

"Come on, girl. Stop playing." He glances towards the door that separates us from his sleeping daughter. "What? You worried about waking her up? She could sleep through a hurricane. It's fine."

I shake my head. "Not tonight. I'm just not feeling it. It's been a long day, I guess. Let's just get some sleep."

"I'm trying to *help* you go to sleep. Come *on*…"

"I'm not comfortable." I say this as evenly as I can and I wish he would just drop it.

"I'm trying to help you *get* comfortable. So what's the problem?"

"The problem IS, you're still not over your ex! And don't try to tell me I'm wrong! It's obvious! And it's *your* fault! You wasted the whole evening reminiscing about *her* and now you want to get intimate with *me*? Get real."

I leave him standing in the living room and I slip into bed with Empress. Almost instinctively, she rolls over so her back faces me and presses her soft, baby toes into the side of my leg. I lay there, in the dark, watching the silhouette of her sleeping body, wondering how my own daughter would look while she slumbered, until I fall asleep myself.

CHAPTER NINE

The next morning, I awake to the soft sounds of Empress and Victor talking outside the bedroom door. I check the time on the bedside alarm clock: 8:57. I hadn't planned to sleep this late. My hope was to wake up early to make breakfast for Victor and Empress.

When I emerge from the room, they're both sitting in the breakfast nook, eating sausage biscuits from the resort cafe and grinning at me.

"Did you have a good sleep, Miss Cindy-uh?"

Victor nudges her arm and gives her a secretive, encouraging smile. "I mean, Miss Sin-Thee-Uh."

She grins at Victor, so pleased with herself for pronouncing my name like a big girl.

I walk over to the table, kiss each of them on the forehead, and begin to rummage through my bags in the kitchen. "Are y'all already eating? I was going to make breakfast for you."

Victor jumps up from the table. "Not today! I went down to the cafe and got you coffee."

"And we got you some spa, too!" Empress can barely contain herself.

Victor shoves her playfully and hands me a cup of coffee. "Go get dressed. You have an appointment for a massage and a pedicure in the spa today."

I open my mouth to speak, but he won't hear of it. "Go! Your appointment is at 9:30!" He ushers me toward the bedroom. "We'll be down at the pool when you finish."

In the bedroom, I grab my phone on the way to the shower and notice I have a new text message from Victor.

Victor: *Sorry about last night. Sorry I made you feel uncomfortable. Will you forgive me?*

He's also sent a meme of a donkey with the caption: *I know I've been an ass. Please forgive me.*

Yes, he'd been an ass. How could I not forgive him?

After the spa, I clean our room and pack up our things, then meet Victor and Empress at the pool. Still unable to drum up the courage to reveal my body in a swimsuit, I dangle my feet at the pool's edge and watch the Daddy-Daughter Show. They play and race and tease. They strike ridiculous poses so I can take pictures.

They beg me to get in. *Not this time. The water is cold. Can't get my hair wet.* I remind myself of the reason I have to get this weight off. I should be comfortable enough to get into the pool with my—with Victor and his daughter.

When they finally pull their shriveled, dripping bodies from the water, I greet them with towels and flip flops. I'm helping Empress into her cover-up and Victor is taking candid pictures of us when a woman stops by to admire our cute "family." *Would we like her to take a picture of all of us together? It wouldn't be a bother.*

Awkward glances are shared between Victor and I, but Empress grabs our hands, pulls us closer to her and shows off her snaggle-toothed smile.

"Okay, now let's do our funny faces!" She's shouting this as she sticks her fingers into her ears and nose at the same time, transforming her baby face into something that elicits giggles from the woman who is snapping our pictures.

"Okay, I took a few good ones," she says, handing the phone back to Victor, who tosses her a giant smile of appreciation.

When she turns to rejoin her own family—is it her family? How can you really know the dynamics of any group of people, anymore?—he shrugs his shoulders in my direction and snorts. Empress runs a route in the shape of a figure eight around our legs, weaving in and out of the space between us, singing a made-up song.

My phone buzzes and a message from Mama appears:

Mama: *Where are you? This girl been over here all day!*

I begin to text her back and then think better of it. I text Julene instead:

Me: *how's everything going?*

She replies right away.

Julene: *I think I'm getting on her nerves! Lol!!* 😆 😆 😆 😆 😭 😭 😭 😭

She includes a picture of Mama sitting in the bed scowling directly at me. At least, it feels like she can see me.

Victor walks closer, glances over my shoulder at the picture and laughs. "I guess it's time for you to go home, huh?"

I slide the phone back into my purse and turn to him. "I should have known she wouldn't let me stay away for too long. I'm going to head back and I guess I'll see you later. It was fun."

As we hug goodbye, Empress squeezes herself into the space between us and attempts a group hug. She manages to wrap a small arm halfway around my thigh and pulls the three of us closer together. "I love you and you and you love me too!"

Her baby voice is muffled from the close contact, but I definitely heard her say she loves me, probably not understanding what love means.

I pray one day I'll hear her daddy say the same.

That night, while I'm lying at the foot of Mama's bed listening to her captivating observations about politics, corporate corruption, bowel movements, and cancer, a text message makes my phone vibrate.

Victor: *ieirhrhshsfsfa hjhbsbsbpokm*

Me:?

Victor:) *:$:"&:;;;()8573!:/*

Me: *Empress? Is that you?*

I send her a selfie.

I receive a selfie of Empress in return, with a glimpse of Victor in the background.

Moments later, my phone vibrates again. Mama drones on with her stories of indigestion and dry scalp.

Victor: *What's up? You text Empress more than you text me! Lol!*

Me: *She started it.*

Victor: *I can't do nothing with that girl! Her mama was supposed to pick her up 2 hours ago, but you know how that goes.*

Me: *shame.*

Me: *so she's just staying up late, huh? I know it's past her bedtime.*

Victor: *taking advantage of daddy, as always. What can I say?*

Victor: *what are you up to this week?*

Me: *was supposed to have a doctors appointment tomorrow but I had to push it to Tuesday because I have to take mama to an appointment tomorrow.*

Victor: *Doctors appointment? Is something wrong?*

Me: *same old thing, she thinks she has stomach cancer or something.*

Victor: *not her! You! Why do you need a doctors appointment?*

Me: *oh! Lololol!*

Me: *I have to get my lady parts checked out.*

Victor: *what's wrong with your lady parts? Everything was fine, last time I checked.*

Me: *you don't know what to look for!*

Victor: *I could've been a doctor. Tell me what the problem is, I bet I can diagnose it right now. Won't even charge you a copay.*

Me: *yeah right. Ok.*

Me: *it's my annual exam. Gotta make sure everything is working properly.*

Victor: *is your doctor male or female?*

Me: *his name is Dr. Matthew Turner. A man.*

That's a lie. My doctors have always been female. I just feel more comfortable that way. But he doesn't need to know that, and since I can see he's concerned, I decide to give him something to worry about.

Victor: *well let me know if he says anything to you.*

Victor: *as a matter of fact, tell him to keep his hands to himself.*

Me: *and how is he supposed to examine me if he doesn't use his hands?*

Victor: *exactly. I'll examine you myself and I'll let him know if something is wrong.*

I can't help but laugh out loud when I read his text. Victor's concern about my gynecologist's gender is a joke of course, since my decisions about my health are beyond his jurisdiction. It's cute though, his part-time possessiveness, so I let it slide. In fact, since he's feeling so vulnerable tonight, I decide his message is undeserving of a response.

Clicking the phone off, I kiss Mama goodnight, and busy myself with my nighttime routine.

CHAPTER TEN

O n Tuesday, while I'm driving home after the annual exam with my gynecologist, I call Julene. "So, I go to the OB/GYN and she tells me if I want to have kids then I need to go ahead and start making moves for it. She said, 'Cynthia, 'I'm not beating around the bush with you anymore. If you want to have a baby, go ahead and do it soon.'"

Julene's gasp is audible. "What kind of doctor says something like that? Why would she say it like that? It's not like you can snap your fingers and just have a baby!"

Her reaction makes me laugh a little. Julene knows how badly I want to be a mother, and I knew she would defend me—even against my physician.

"Well, I asked her to be straight with me, and I've been going to Dr. Gandhi forever. She knows me. It started with a conversation about my skin. Since I have PCOS, it's harder to control my acne and I wanted to know if she thought I should try a prescription but the one we talked about is known to cause birth defects and I wanted her opinion on how long it stays in your system after you use it."

"Mmhmm." I can hear an echo in Julene's voice and I know she's hiding out in her bathroom. It's her favorite place to take phone calls.

"She recommended an IUD while I'm on the acne medicine for six months, just to prevent an accidental pregnancy and birth defects for the short term, but she said it's safe to get pregnant once I stop taking it. She also said I need to set a weight-loss goal before I even try to get pregnant."

"You already knew that, though." The faint sound of swirling water echoes behind Julene's voice.

"I said, if the risk of birth defects is *that* strong, then I don't know if I want to take it at all." I know this next chunk of information is the most important. "She also asked me if I have considered artificial insemination, but she said I would need to make that decision by December of next year, depending on the results of some tests she ordered. If my numbers are normal, I might be able to buy a little time, but not more than two years, tops…"

Julene is whisper-shouting into the phone. "She doesn't know! She can't tell you that for sure!"

"Well, she even said she wasn't God. She said 'If you get pregnant after forty that's definitely your right, but if you want to have the best chances, then now's the time to do it'. She went ahead and ordered a panel of bloodwork just to check my hormone levels."

Julene is quiet, taking in this unexpected information, allowing me the time to spill all the details.

I continue, "She knows I'm not married, and I told her that my relationship status is complicated at the moment, so she had one more suggestion."

"Okay…" I can almost hear the thoughts running through Julene's head.

"She said she could refer me to an infertility specialist to figure out if I can freeze my eggs or if I'm past that age and…she gave me a donor list…"

"Oh…okay…okay." Julene's voice is barely audible. She speaks slowly, in a way that tells me she's choosing her words delicately. "A donor list, huh? Who put that option on the table? You or Dr. Gandhi? What about Victor? Does he know you want to start a family ASAP?"

I'm shrugging my shoulders as though she can see me through the phone. "Victor is so hot and cold. He always says he doesn't want to be tied down, but he's blowing up my phone every day and making plans for family vacations and everything. I would love to do this with him, but I'm afraid of waiting on him. Girl, my eggs are running out!"

Julene calms her own voice. "Okay, let's think this through. Are you prepared to be a single mother? Because I can tell you, there are no guarantees. You could have a baby with Victor, and he might be a great guy, and things can still go wrong. You can still feel overwhelmed and alone, even with the father in the house. Or the relationship can break up. And of course, if you have a donor that means you're voluntarily choosing to take everything upon yourself, both a child and your mother.

"And my InVest babies…"

"Right. So that requires a lot of energy and you wouldn't want to neglect anybody because of your responsibilities to a newborn baby. Or you'd hate to feel like you're neglecting the baby because you're trying to manage everything else."

"Gotcha." I wait for the 'but.'

"But, I can say, if you're serious about having a family, you have to start by taking care of yourself. You are a grown woman! You're free to have the love life you want, you know? You should be out dating! Living! If Victor would rather text somebody to death instead of spending actual time together, then let him do that to someone else! Hell, if all he wants is a friend, then he's wasting your time and keeping you from meeting a man who might want a wife."

"True."

"So maybe you don't need a donor. Maybe you can do it naturally. You just need to give yourself the freedom to date. But first you gotta cut Victor loose. You can't let him take up anymore of your time."

"Well, Dr. Gandhi is talking about doing it in the next year or two. There's no way I can meet somebody new and get pregnant that fast. It's different with Victor. We already have history. Like, I already know he's a good man. He has a good career, he loves the Lord, I know his family...he doesn't make me feel self-conscious about my weight..."

Julene interrupts me, vetoing my excuses. "No, that's a lie. That is a lie. On my one-year anniversary of meeting Andrew, I was lying in bed with an infant in my arms. So..." she laughs out loud as she recalls the start of their relationship, "It can happen. It can happen fast. Making a baby don't take nothing but nine months."

We both burst out laughing. It's true. Just a year after she had kicked out her drug-addicted baby daddy, she had met an amazing man, gotten pregnant, and had her fourth child. Then, eight months after the baby was born, they got married. I was in awe. When it happened, I was overjoyed for her and her family, but I was envious too.

"I know, I know. But that's your story. It might not be mine."

"Well, my question for you is, what do you want most?" Julene's voice is steady and calm, as though she were sitting on the beach rather than running a bustling household.

"My whole thing is this: I definitely want a husband to share the experience with. But you know, it just seems like it isn't happening the way I hoped." I exhale heavily, my inner turmoil neutralizing the joy of potential motherhood.

"Okay, so, here's a thought: your doctor is saying you're not a candidate for an ideal pregnancy at this time, anyway, right? Because of the weight?" Julene sounds as though she's had an epiphany.

"Well she said it could be either the weight or the PCOS. She also said we need to figure out how to regulate my cycle because I've gone for months with no period, but she said weight loss is a good place to start." I hope I'm explaining this correctly; there's a lot I still don't understand myself.

Julene seems to have a grasp on it though. "And she's saying, whether you want to do artificial insemination or get pregnant naturally, you would want to have made a decision by next year, right?"

"Yes, depending on my hormone levels."

"So basically, in her professional opinion, you have about a year to make some decisions and get some things in order."

"Mmhmm." This is why I love talking things out with Julene—she's a problem-solver. I feel my excitement coming back.

"I'm thinking, if next December is the deadline, go ahead and start putting things in place for it. Lose the weight, monitor your health, date some nice men. Maybe by the end of next year you will have met a man who you want to have that type of relationship and a family with. That's a win-win situation! Either way, you'll be healthier to carry the baby regardless of which path you choose by this time next year."

"That's basically what Dr. Gandhi was saying."

"Yeah. So, whether you do it naturally or artificially, you'll still want to take this next year to optimize your health, focus on yourself, and date with the understanding that you're looking for a serious relationship, not pressuring anybody, but also not wasting your time. Just see what happens."

"Mmhmm."

She's on a roll at this point, talking faster, sounding confident that this could really happen for me. "You never know. It only takes one connection with someone, and you do have a year. You're not pressuring anyone, but if you meet a man around your age, between thirty-eight and forty years old, and he wants to have a family, then his clock is ticking too!"

"Right."

"And at the end of the year, if you haven't met someone, then that's okay! You'll have everything else in order that you want to do with your life: you'll be healthy, the artificial option is still on the table, and you'll have your head in the right place to seriously consider it."

"You're right. And I was thinking of getting a second job so I can put money away for daycare." My mind is racing now, planning, always planning.

Julene keeps rolling, hardly able to organize her thoughts. "Well, don't jump ahead of yourself! I just think, irregardless…"

"Irregardless is not a real word." I have to correct her. She hates when I do it, but I can't resist.

She accepts the correction. "Okay *regardless*, without regard for whatever may come, make this a year for yourself. A Year of Selfie! The doctor, she's not God either, she's only giving you her professional opinion. Anything can happen, but you have to go on the information you've been given. You're making an educated decision for yourself. So, take good care of yourself, figure out how you want to approach the dating life, and don't let yourself wimp out or punk out. Go on some dates, meet some people, try some new things, it could be a really fun year for you." She makes it sound so easy.

A nervous chuckle escapes from my lips. "I'm going to do better for myself. I promise. I just want to make sure I have a game plan."

Julene's voice sounds like a hug, if that's possible, and it makes me want to cry when she says, "Seriously, I'm excited about the possibilities, and I don't judge anyone. If this is something that could happen for you in your life, and it's something you want to experience, I don't think there's anything wrong with you getting your ducks in a row to make it happen."

"True, but it's all preliminary information at this point. I'll know more when I see her again for the follow-up appointment. It sounds like this journey is going to cost me a whole lot of money…"

"Don't get hung up on the financial aspect! Focus on your health too. Get serious about where you want your health to be a year from now." Julene is my tireless cheerleader.

"Yeah, I met with Vito this week. I'm going to try to be more consistent."

I can hear Julene talking to her daughter in the background and I know she'll have to get off the phone soon. "Give me a minute, I'm trying to talk to Miss Cynthia."

And I can hear her daughter saying, "Oh! Miss Cynthia? Mommy can you tell Miss Cynthia I hope when her husband comes, her treats her like love? Tell her I said that, Mommy!"

When Julene comes back to the phone, she's laughing. "Did you hear that? Where do these kids get this stuff? Are you sure you're ready for this madness?"

It makes me laugh too. "Tell her Miss Cynthia said thank you!"

"Yeah, I'll tell her. But anyways, good luck with the working out stuff! Remember when we did bootcamp that time with Vito? And he had us doing those cross-body mountain climbers and burpees and toe touches and squats? I think I died that day!"

Before I can respond, I hear her talking to her family in the background again. "Are y'all watching this TV now? Who left these lights on?'

She attempts to return her attention to our conversation. "I haven't been working out too much since then. Just walking and jumping jacks and planks…"

We could laugh for another hour at the way we must have looked at Vito's bootcamp, but I know her family needs her, so I tell her I have get off of the phone. "Well I gotta go because …"

But she's fussing at the dogs and she doesn't hear me.

I try again, "Hey! Just call me back later, okay?"

"Okay, I will." She pauses before saying goodbye. "Cynthia? One more thing."

"Hmm? What is it?"

She laughs out loud, unable to contain the joke. "You might want to let Victor know he's about to be a baby daddy again!"

"Girl! Bye!"

No sooner than I hang up with Julene, Victor texts me.

Victor: *How was your appointment?*

Victor: *Did he ask you for your number? LOLOLOL.*

Me: 😌 *Not funny. My doctor is a female and she said my chances for ever having a baby are decreasing.*

Me: 😌 😖

Victor: *what does that mean? Are you sick or something?*

Me: *it just means it's not as easy for women my age to get pregnant.*

Me: ⌛. *It means time is running out if I ever want to be a mom.*

Victor: *You better start looking for a baby daddy then.* 🔍 💀.

Me: *Get real. I'm a grown woman. I don't need no baby daddy. I want a husband. A real family.*

Victor: *Good luck with that.*

Me: *What's that supposed to mean?*

Victor: *I'm just saying. Sometimes the family thing ain't all that. At least not in my experience. You couldn't pay me to have another kid. I'm not trying to get tied down again. I'm trying to chill and just enjoy life.*

Me: *you can't enjoy life with a wife and a family?*

Victor: *just saying I want a peaceful simple life. No drama.*

Me: *I want peace, too. And a simple life with no drama. And a family.*

Victor: 👆 *Don't let me stand in your way.* 😆

CHAPTER ELEVEN

The problem with text message conversations is there aren't enough nonverbal clues to clarify a person's statements. Emojis aren't enough. They're a disguise. A diversion. Personally, I have mastered the art of using friendly-looking symbols to hide my true feelings via text.

Maybe that's why that last text conversation with Victor just continues to nag at my consciousness for the rest of the day. Did he want to be alone for the rest of his life? Could he honestly believe casual relationships would be enough to sustain him?

He's damaged, I know, but I can't accept he has given up. Maybe the relationship with his daughter's mother is over, but it's so easy for me to see he and I share something much different-- so much better. I'm so much better for him. He's told me he sees it, too.

He's easily the best man I've ever dated, which is why I know he's as good for me as I am for him--even with his flaws and pain and issues. On the inside, he's a good person. As a bonus, he's also fine, he's smart, he's clean. Plus, he's manly which is an attribute that most reminds me of my daddy.

While I wait for them to drop some fresh fried chicken at the Chicken Coop, I think about my position in life. I'm independent. I can handle things on my own, but I don't want to live life alone. Who would want that?

The thing is, sometimes I just can't tell what he wants. If it isn't a future and a family with me, then what are we even doing?

The not knowing is eating me up, so I call him. I have to hear his voice. I need to figure out a casual way to broach the subject again, because, for some reason, the resoluteness of his words—even through the text, worry me. A lot.

He texted me earlier, as he normally does, but I had just walked in the door from work, Mama was already calling my name, I was trying to cook, and I just couldn't keep looking at my phone to carry on a decent conversation.

I figured after I'd settled down I could talk to him in peace. Then I'd be able to hear the words come out of his mouth—that he doesn't want a family with me or anyone else. That he's satisfied with our half-in-half-out friendship for the rest of the foreseeable future. That if I continue this journey with him, it might never lead to motherhood. So, I finally call him, and as soon as he answers, here comes Mama chattering away.

I'm covering the phone with my hand, whisper-shouting at her, not wanting him to overhear. "Mama! I'm on the phone!" It seems as though she's only getting louder!

I mute the phone for a second so Victor can ramble on about child support and custody arrangements while I try to corral Mama. "Mama, I am cutting the watermelon up just like you asked me to! What is wrong?"

She moves in closer to the counter and studies the chopped fruit. "Well make sure you…"

I drop the knife. "Come on! I'm on the phone! Can I just have a moment to myself?"

She eases onto the stool across the counter from me. "You think imma use the bathroom tomorrow?"

I just stare at her, like…

Seeing my expression, she scoots off the stool and begins to make her way back to her room. She's mumbling. "I guess you just don't want to talk to me, then. I can take a hint."

Oh my gosh. I unmute the phone and offer Victor a few *mmhmms*, though he doesn't seem to notice my distraction. At the same time, Mama suddenly seems so small, hobbling away from me. *This lady…* I shouldn't have yelled at her.

I cover the phone with my hand and call after her, "Mama. Listen! I…you know what? Just hold on a second." I return to my call with Victor. "Let me call you back, please."

My interruption is abrupt, and I can hear him pause before he says, "Okay", but I end the call before he can object. Then I turn to her. "Mama, I sat in that room with you for about an hour and talked to you about bowel movements, arthritis, pain, cancer, everything! You don't have any of them! You had a great bowel movement the other day. You didn't go today. Okay, maybe you'll go tomorrow. You're eating the right foods. But Mama, if I'm on the phone, you can't just accuse me of not wanting to talk to you! I'm on the phone! You've gotta give me at least two hours to myself!"

She doesn't say anything. She just glares at me for half a heartbeat and then disappears down the hallway.

Should I feel guilty about the way that I treat my mother? Maybe. But enough is enough! Right now, I have more serious issues to worry about.

I scoop all the watermelon into a container and shove it into the refrigerator. Just before the door closes, I grab the slice of cheesecake Mama had asked me to bring her on my way home.

Sitting at the kitchen counter and nibbling on the cheesecake crust, I call Victor back. When his voicemail picks up I consider leaving a message, but change my mind and hang up instead.

By the time I finish two rounds of Cookie Scramble, the cheesecake is gone and I drift into the bathroom to conduct my nightly routine: Candle, shower, shave, suck tummy in, lift butt, lift boobs, face mask, moisturize, and then bed.

Just as I wedge myself into a comfortable position between my three pillows, my phone lights up with a text.

Victor: *So now she won't let me speak to my daughter.*

Me: *What? Why? Since when?*

Victor: *Since we got back from the resort.*

Victor: *She said she didn't know you were spending the night with me and Empress.*

Victor: *now she wants to go back to the lawyer and have the agreement amended.*

Me: *to say what?*

Victor: *she wants to be notified when I plan to have other women around our daughter.*

Victor: *I cannot win with this chick!*

Me: *you are a great father. Just stay focused on your daughter.*

Me: *she was probably just trying to get under your skin with all the lawyer stuff. She doesn't mean it.*

Victor: *I can't keep dealing with this stuff!*

Victor: *I never want to have another child.*

Victor: *on my daddy's grave, I will never get tied down like this again. Period.*

And, as if by the power of suggestion, at the mere mention of the word period, a familiar pang courses through my back and it feels as though my ovaries are doing a slow roll. With PCOS, my cycle is unpredictable, but when it's on, it's on. My body begins preparing to dispose of another unused egg.

I lay the phone on the nightstand and plug in the charger. Then I trudge to the bathroom and fortify myself with feminine products. I pause as I consider taking some ibuprofen for the pain but decide against it. I don't like taking medication. Even when the cramps feel like I'm about to give birth, I tell myself someday I'll have a baby without any pain meds. No epidural. So, the pain of a monthly—relatively speaking, thanks to the unpredictability of polycystic ovarian syndrome—is nothing more than a warmup for the real thing.

Back in my room, I lay on my bed and reflect on my two-year history with Victor. What do we really have? He's a good guy, even with his issues. Does he take advantage of my generosity sometimes? Maybe. Does he like to text more than call? Probably. Does he take me out on dates without Empress? Not really. Would he stick around if I demanded he treat me better? Something inside of me is afraid to know.

Morning comes earlier than I'd like, and I'm greeted by my daily Sprinkle of Jesus message: *Blessed is she who believed the Lord would fulfill His promises to her! Luke 1:45.* There's nothing from Victor. No 'Good morning, beautiful.' No funny meme.

He's still feeling sorry for himself, I guess. I'm used to the moodiness. I'll give him space.

By the time I get home from work in the evening, I have sent him two inspirational text messages, a selfie, and a link to a new spa that has opened in town for little girls. Still, there's no response from him.

Okay then, Crybaby.

The next day, another Sprinkle of Jesus: *Givers have to learn to set limits because takers don't have any.* Another day of silence from Victor.

By the third day, I'm realizing he's truly ignoring me, even though I've only tried to encourage and uplift him, and I'm annoyed because his behavior doesn't even surprise me. When he's feeling down, he'll shut me out and have me feeling like I've done something wrong, and then he'll be blowing my phone up again when he needs to vent about his baby mama or something.

For the next few days, I ride the mythical rollercoaster of emotions. I'm mad, I'm sad, I'm worried, I'm pissed off. I tell myself that he's just going through a tough time. I tell myself he's an opportunist. I remember he never reimbursed me for the night at the resort.

I text him again:

Me: *Just wondering when you were planning to give me the money back for the resort reservation? Or should I stop by to pick it up?*

No reply.

Me: *Hello?*

Me: *Ok, then.*

Me: *I'll just send you a PayPal invoice and you can just pay me back like that.*

No response. I can't even tell if he's opened my messages.

Now, I'm worried. It isn't like him to completely ignore me for this long. I mean, we are friends, first and foremost. At least, I thought we were, and I'd like for us to be more. In many ways, we are more. What if he's sick? Or hurt? Or clinically depressed?

My stomach feels sick at the thought that something is seriously wrong. I call his phone and his voicemail picks up. I hang up and call back, thinking I should leave a message. When I hear his voicemail message again, I freeze…and hang up. What is wrong with me?

Sitting for a moment, I decide to send him a message from Facebook, but first I check to see if he's been active online since we last spoke.

I can see he's been tagged on some memes of Lebron James and Michael Jordan over the last few days by friends, I guess, and he has thumbs upped a few, but nothing more. I send a Facebook message, and wait. Nothing.

I sit there, trying not to think the worst, contemplating jumping into the car and driving to his house. And then I see a Facebook suggestion for someone who I might know. It's his mother, her profile picture a close up of Empress kissing her cheek.

I make the half-baked decision to send her a message—just to say I'm a church member who is concerned because we have not seen Brother Victor at the ministry leaders' meetings lately. It's not an actual lie because I have not seen him at the meetings, although I'm not a ministry leader and don't typically attend their meetings anyway…

I wait. Within moments, I can see she has viewed the message, but she doesn't reply and I feel foolish. I wish I could retrieve the message and delete it. She wouldn't tell me about his whereabouts, anyway.

My phone vibrates in my hand and startles me so much I drop it.

Victor: *What's wrong with you?!? Are you crazy??*

Me: *What are you talking about?*

Victor: *Why are you blowing up my phone like that? I was with a client!! Over some money? I'll give you your money today, since you want to play me like I'm some lame dude.*

Me: *It's not that serious. I just needed to put the money back on my credit card. Stop acting like I was trying to play you. I was actually worried about you. I know you saw my messages all week.*

Victor: *so you contact my mother?*

Victor: *hello??*

Me: *I told you, I was worried about you. I thought something happened to you. Not hearing from you for almost a week is not like our normal routine. If someone cares about you, then they should be worried if you just fall off the face of the earth.*

Victor: *Look, I have a lot going on in my life. I'm not happy with some aspects and that gets me down sometimes, so I just need time to process this. You already know my pet peeves because I have expressed them to you on more than one occasion. I hate having people in my personal business when I'm stressed. I tell you all the time that I sometimes just need to not be bothered and we don't have a "normal" routine. I know we're friends, but it's like if you don't hear from me then you start thinking I'm dead or I'm on suicide watch. CALM DOWN. This is just what I do to cope. And that's why I told you I don't want to be on a routine, I don't want to be obligated to anyone or anything right now. I'm sure I'm not the only friend that you have and I'm sure that you don't start calling their family or freaking out whenever you can't get in touch with somebody. I don't think we are on the same page as to what our "friendship" is because I feel like you're treating it like we are together as boyfriend and girlfriend or husband and wife and I'm just not even close to that level right now. You led me to believe that you understood how I feel.*

I stare at the phone, absorbing the epic-length text message, reading it slowly, then skimming it quickly. I study it, wondering who is on the other end. Who is this man? He had always referred to our relationship as a "friendship", and it did begin as a friendship. I would have even considered him to be my best friend, aside from Julene, since Ruth had gone.

But we had moved past that basic designation a long time ago. We have shared things, sexual and otherwise, that exceed the boundaries of "friendship."

As for a normal routine, we do have a normal routine. I can set my clock around his good morning, his lunch breaks, his commute home, and his daughter's visitation schedule.

I want to replay immediately. I want to call him and ask him why he's tripping? I want to ask him why he pushes me away when I'm always on his side, no matter what he's going through. But I wait, and I think, and I take a cleansing breath before I text him back. I type and delete four different responses before I settle on the simplest reply:

Me: *Hey at least I know where I stand. I'll just step back from everything and stay out of your business.*

Me: *And just to avoid crossing the line of friendship, don't send me anymore pictures of you biting your lip or showing off any of your body parts because I don't communicate with my "friends" in that manner.*

Me: *And I probably shouldn't know so much about your baby mama problems. That's your personal business.*

About forty-five minutes later I get a response.

Victor: *what   was   all   of   that?*   😵 😵 😵 😵 ☝ ☝ ☝ ☝ 👇 👇 👇 👇

I don't respond.

Victor: *I transferred the money to your account.*

Me: 👍

Victor: *are you supposed to be mad?*

Me: *nope. There's nothing to get mad about. You told me how you felt.*

An hour later, he responds.

Victor: *I was a little harsh. I'm sorry.*

Me: *you're always sorry.*

He sends the jackass meme again and I ignore it.

Later that night, while I'm watching the Weather Channel with Mama, my phone vibrates to announce a new message.

Victor: *hey.*

Ignore.

Victor: *hey.* 👋

Ignore.

Victor: *I said I was sorry. Dang.*

Victor: *today was rough.*

Ignore.

Victor: *there were some things you and I needed to talk about. I didn't know what I was feeling. And you know what I've been going through. Plus, I was with a client.*

Victor: *But instead of giving me a chance to talk to you, you want to blow my phone up and interrupt me at work.*

Victor: *the Bible says be slow to anger and quick to forgive.*

Me: *I don't need you to forgive me.*

Victor: *that's not what I meant.*

Victor: *hoping you can forgive me. Because I have something special planned for us.*

Me: *For who?*

Victor: *For us. Me and you and Empress. I'm working on getting us tickets to see The Lion King when the play comes to Atlanta. They just went on sale today. I was going to surprise you.*

Me: *Your baby mama don't want me around her.*

Victor: *See, there you go trying to worry about everything. I got this under control.*

Me: *No thank you. I don't want no drama.*

Victor: *No, for real. I talked to her. I told her you are somebody I really care for and Empress loves you to death. And if you're going to be in my life, then you can also be around my daughter. She needs to learn to accept that.*

Me: *Wow. I'm impressed.*

Me: *So you see me in your future?*

Victor: *She don't want me to say nothing about that bum she been dating.*

Me: *Get back to us...*

Victor: *You know I don't do labels. Don't get any ideas. I'm just saying I like to chill. With you. My daughter loves you. Don't mess it up.*

Me: *What's that supposed to mean?*

Victor: *I just want peace. I just want to keep things simple. That's it.*

Me: *Quit trippin! Ain't nobody trying to lock you down! Lololol! Don't nobody want your funny acting behind, anyway!*

Him: *I don't see you trying to run away from me...*

If we were playing a game of chess, this would be a check-mate moment. He's right and he knows it. He makes me so angry, but he always manages to draw me in again. Unable to think of a good comeback, I click the phone off, roll onto my side, and ask Mama to turn the TV up a little so I can hear.

She casts a slideways glance my way and hits me with a harsh truth. "You coulda heard the TV just fine if you weren't over there grinning and tapping on that phone. I'm going to sleep now, so you can just go watch it in your own room."

For emphasis and out of sheer spite, I'm sure, she turns the volume down a little more, snaps her bedside lamp off, and pulls the covers over her shoulders.

Lying next to her in the dimly lit room for a few minutes, I stare at the TV, but my mind is on Victor. Why is he so complicated? How long will it take me to undo the damage from his past relationship?

My mind is filled with more questions than answers, and then my phone vibrates with yet another question. This time, it's a text from Julene:

Julene: *are we still going out with the singles ministry tomorrow? bc I gotta get a babysitter lined up. Hubs has to work late shift.*

The light from my phone makes Mama's room glow and she flops around in the bed with enough exaggeration to let me know I'm disturbing her.

After a quick response to let Julene know I'll be there, I make a graceful exit from Mama's room.

CHAPTER TWELVE

I don't know why I continue to show up for the Singles Ministry functions. Most of the attendees aren't even single. And the men usually schedule their own separate outings, so it's basically just a girl's night out for the women of the church.

The pastor's wife heads the group and her favorite restaurant is TGI Friday's, so that's where we assemble for dinner.

I usually drag Julene along for moral support, even though I know most of the women in the ministry. I've seen enough pettiness and fickleness in the church to make me leery of a few of them, but I'm trying to stay active, get out of the house more, and stay in the church, so I show up.

By the time Julene and I walk in, the ladies are seated in the back of the restaurant, deep in conversation.

"...so, girl, as soon as I stopped catering to him and putting him up on a pedestal, he changed his whole tune. Started breaking his neck to spend time with me." It's Stephanie. I recognize her voice before I even see her.

Something about her voice just grates on my nerves. And based on the way she looks at me—especially when

I'm near Victor—I know she doesn't like me. To be honest, I've never been too fond of her either, but I keep it cordial.

The pastor's wife, always trying to put a biblical spin on the conversation, offers her advice. "The only way to get a man to move closer to the altar is to stop walking in the spirit of a wife if you are only a girlfriend! Stop cooking and cleaning for these men! Stop taking care of them. There are certain benefits and services you should only reserve for your husband."

Stephanie cosigns on the idea. "That's exactly what I had to do. I just told the Lord, 'I don't want to be a girlfriend for the rest of my life!' And the Lord told me to change my approach."

When First Lady tries to interject, Stephanie refuses to relinquish the spotlight. She continues with her success story. "He tried to act like it didn't bother him. But when I stopped being so 'available,'" she winks at her friends, "that's when he started getting serious. He started taking me on real dates and he even planned a little getaway for us."

She rambles on and on about how she had expected him to propose, but he hadn't. She isn't discouraged, though, she informs everyone, because she feels quite certain the proposal is looming in the very near future.

"Where did he take you?" One of the few ladies who is actually single tosses the question from the far end of the table.

"We went to the Biltmore Estates, up there in North Carolina. That's why I thought he was going to propose. Everyone gets engaged at the Biltmore! But he told me he just wanted to see me enjoy myself. He sent me breakfast in bed, scheduled a massage for me, arranged a private wine tasting…" Her eyes shine as she recalls the way he had pampered her.

First Lady chimes in again, "Oh, the Biltmore? It is so beautiful up there! Pastor and I went there for a…"

She can't regain control of the conversation and Stephanie cuts her off again. "It is! Girls! He didn't propose to me there, but when he does—" she stops mid-sentence and looks around the table at everyone, "you see how I just claimed my destiny? *When he does propose*—I would love to have my wedding there!"

She pulls her phone from her purse. "Look at this place! I took pictures. Just look at the view from the mountain! I took this picture from our hotel room." She passes her phone around the table, inviting everyone to have a look.

"Y'all can flip through. I took pictures of everything!"

As the phone migrates around the table, someone asks a question. "Wait! Isn't this Brother Randall?"

Someone else peers into the phone to see the man more clearly. "He's over the Youth Ministry, isn't he?" All eyes dart towards First Lady, who shoots a glance towards Stephanie, who smiles demurely before responding.

"Yeah, girl. We weren't really trying to put our relationship out there like that. You know how messy things can get in the church. No offense, First Lady. But yeah, he's such as sweetheart. Very respectful. A true gentleman."

Someone across the table laughs and stage-whispers, "I bet he wasn't a gentleman when you got to that hotel room!"

Stephanie sits back and crosses her arms, grinning. "What happens at the Biltmore, stays at the Biltmore, right? I'm not saying anything! Just believe me when I say he has really stepped his game up since I stepped mine up!"

Sweat springs from my underarms and underboobs at the same time. As I wait for the phone to make its way to my end of the table, I instantly regret wearing the bright pink blouse that will make it impossible to hide my pit stains.

When the phone is in my hands, Stephanie's face is smiling into the camera while Victor stands in the background of her selfie, trying not to smile.

In another picture, a side profile picture, he stares out of the window of the hotel room, no shirt on.

In the next, the two of them are nested together in a winery.

In another, he covers his face, not wanting to have his picture taken.

I stare at the screen, unable to swallow or breathe, until Julene pries the phone from my sweaty fingers and passes it back to Stephanie.

I hear Stephanie's voice directed towards me, "Cynthia! Girl, you better promise to give me a heads up before he proposes! I need time to make sure my nails are done so I can post a picture of my ring on Instagram!"

She's flashing an imaginary ring, laughing and posing for her imaginary social media post and I cannot swallow my shock. I feel Julene's hand gripping my leg under the table and I try to play it cool. "Why, what…why would I tell you? How would I know anything?"

I want to think she's being genuine, but something in her reply tells me she's aware of the knife she's twisting into my gut with assassin-like accuracy. She smiles at me as she answers, "Well, you're his homegirl, right? He tells me all the time how you're such a good friend, like a sister to him. He said he tells you everything, so I just assumed he'd tell you when he was ready to pop the question."

My mouth falls open. Stupefied.

Stephanie keeps right on talking, as though she and I are the only ones at the table. "He loves you to death, Cynthia. He worries about you, with your problems losing weight and everything going on with your mother. He's always talking about hooking you up with someone, because he doesn't want to see you alone, but I told him no one likes being set up on blind dates. I told him the Lord will send you the perfect man when the time is right."

Everyone at the table is eating it up, glancing from her to me, whispering. Giggling, perhaps. I can't be sure. What do they know? The insides of my ears feel wet. Can you sweat inside of your ears?

Next to me, Julene is suddenly fumbling with her phone, taking a fake phone call, saying she needs me to take her home…something about her kids…something about the babysitter needing to leave early.

I allow myself to be pulled from the table, led towards the front of the restaurant, and placed into the passenger seat of my own car. Julene drives us home, and though I am silent, she is not.

"What you wanna do? Ride by his house or what? I can't believe him! And don't let him try to deny it! She had receipts! That was him in the pictures! And then she gonna try to put you on the spot in front of everybody? Oh no! Oh, unh-uh! I could have snatched that fake smile right off her face!" Julene glances over at me. "I'm sorry! I just can't stand petty-acting chicks! I feel like she knew exactly what she was doing. Ugh!"

She grips the steering wheel of my car and then exhales. She sits back in the driver's seat and looks over at me. "I'm sorry, girl. Don't let me get you all hyped up. Do whatever you need to do. I'm here for you."

She's right, of course, about everything: Stephanie's motives, Victor's propensity for evading the truth, her allegiance to me—but I don't know what to say to her right now. I only know I need to see his eyes when I ask for answers.

Chapter Thirteen

I wait until I see Victor in person to ask him about Stephanie. He'd invited me to his house for dinner with him and Empress, and I'd agreed, but I didn't mention anything about Stephanie. Instead, I gave myself time to calm down, time to think about what she'd said, and time to pick through the inconsistencies of her story.

If she was in a real relationship with him, how had he been able to spend so much time with me? How had we spent weekends together? How come Empress had never mentioned time spent with another woman? I'm no fool. I have definitely 'questioned' the baby about who she knows and who she likes to play with. Empress has never mentioned women other than her mother and grandmothers.

I'd be lying if I said I've never stolen a glance at his phone, skimmed over his text messages, or scrolled through his pictures. Other than a few benign text messages and Facebook tags, I've never found anything to be concerned about. He has a handful of female friends, many of them I know personally, and he has made no attempt to hide them.

He's a handsome man—he's more than handsome, he is *fine*—and as a leader in the church and a single father, he could certainly be viewed as an eligible bachelor. More than a few women in the congregation have hinted about their interest in him. Some have blatantly thrown themselves at him—he's shown me the text messages to prove it. But I didn't see any clues he was leading them on. If anything, he ignored the advances and tried to push them away without hurting any feelings.

I can say I was never one of those women. I hadn't pursued him, hadn't even taken him seriously the first time he called me on the phone. I remember thinking there must have been so many women fighting for his attention and I'd prefer not to be part of the crowd.

But the more that we got to know each other, the more openly he interacted with me—especially at church—I could clearly see how his attention could garner some jealousy from the sisters in the congregation.

Why else would Stephanie have made those comments about my weight and my dating life? Just to get a reaction out of me? I wouldn't give her the satisfaction. It's one reason I prefer not to offer my personal life up for public consumption. Regardless of what anyone sees or thinks, I'd only tell them Victor and I are good friends and allow any other information to remain private.

I have calmed down considerably by the time I settle onto Victor's couch to ask him about his self-proclaimed almost fiancé.

Although there is no conviction in my voice when I ask him about it, it's obvious I've gotten under his skin by bringing it up at all: "Are you serious? I'm not dating that girl! I'm not doing anything with her. It was her birthday weekend and she already had the trip booked but somebody backed out I guess, so she asked me to go with her and she said I didn't have to pay anything. I had my own room! I swear!"

My mama always says 'a hit dog will holler,' and Victor is definitely hollering like a hit dog, so I sit back and watch as he puts on a fiery and dramatic performance.

"See this is what I'm talking about. This is why I don't want to be in a relationship. It's too much drama. I can't even take an innocent trip with a friend. And why would you investigate behind my back by asking her about me?"

I exhale slowly. He is a master manipulator, but I'm determined not to award him for playing the victim. Maybe Stephanie had inflated the story, but he certainly isn't innocent in all of this. "Wasn't nobody checking up on you! Get over yourself! She was at the table in front of everybody—even the First Lady—talking about how she was getting engaged to this guy and all about this romantic vacation they took. She was passing her phone around and pictures of you were all up in her phone. I don't even know her like that! But apparently, she knows a lot about me. You told her all of my business."

Victor stops pacing and speaks calmly, keeping his back to me. "Right, I mentioned you and I are friends. I didn't hide anything. She knows I kick it with you and I told her I'm not interested in her like that. I told her I'm just trying to keep it simple."

I take note of his slumped shoulders and wonder if he'll ever get tired of saying those words. I've heard them quite a few times, myself. "Okay, right. Same thing you told me. I get it."

He whips around to face me directly, "There you go, trying to twist my words. You know it's different between me and you. Sometimes I do feel like you could be the one, but then we go through this kind of stuff and it just doesn't seem worth the headache. I can't. I'm done."

I observe his one-man show and find it to be over-the-top. "Calm down. You're so dramatic. Talking about no drama and you bring all the drama. I was just asking. And I feel I have a right to ask these questions."

I wait for him to sit down and take a deep breath before I continue. "You can't be leading her on. Who goes on an overnight trip to a romantic place with someone they're not interested in? I'm just saying, think about it. Watch out for these chicks. She's got your name all in the streets, passing your picture around at a table full of church-folk. She's literally telling people that you're about to get engaged."

This entire conversation sounds ridiculous and I can't believe I even need to explain why this is an issue. I take a deep breath and bring my voice down to a conversational tone before speaking to him again. "You know what? You're a grown man. Let's just drop it. But I wish you would use better judgement."

I stand up and head towards the kitchen to peek into the refrigerator. "What are we eating tonight?"

Victor shrugs his shoulders and laughs with an edge of sarcasm. "Whatever you want. You can choose, since my judgement is so bad."

While I would typically defer to him and eat whatever he chooses, I'm taking his sarcastic words literally, and I peek inside Empress' room to ask her what she'd like for dinner.

Empress wants pizza, I want a salad, and he wants chicken wings, so we decide to place a takeout order at the sports bar and tavern down the street.

When Victor leaves to go pick up the food, I light a candle and start tidying up the living room. Reaching into the couch to fluff and straighten the cushions, I almost break a nail on a hard object wedged into the crevice. That's when I realize he has left his cellphone.

I grab the phone and head towards the door, thinking of flagging him down before he drives away, but I'm stopped by another thought.

Fingers trembling, I try punching in the passcode to unlock it. I had watched him key in the code a few weeks ago and I try to recall the pattern I'd seen. With no luck, I sit for a moment and then have a brilliant thought.

"Empress! Come here, baby!"

She trots out of her room wearing a princess costume and plastic high-heels, one half of her face covered in play makeup. "Yes, ma'am?"

I smile at her and wave her closer. "Let me see your finger." When she extends her tiny hand, I grab it and place the tip of her index finger against the home button on his phone. The screen springs to life and I kiss the back of her hand. "Thank you, Pumpkin."

She giggles when I kiss her hand and then looks at me curiously. "Whatcha need Daddy's phone for?" Then she looks around, realizing he isn't around. "Where is Daddy?"

I walk away from her, already investigating the contents of his phone. "Oh, he went to get the food and I wanted to play Candy Crumble, but my phone was dead."

This explanation easily satisfies my little friend, and she disappears into her room again.

Searching through the phone, I don't know what I expect to see or not see. I remember a life hack tip I heard recently: *"When faced with two choices, simply toss a coin. It works not because it settles the question for you, but because in that brief moment when the coin is in the air, you suddenly know what you are hoping for."*

Do I want to see that he's been lying and confirm my suspicions or do I want to find nothing and feel foolish for not trusting? I scroll through his text messages and find nothing. There's also nothing in his email and nothing in his social media direct messages are empty. For a man with so many female friends, his phone holds no secrets.

The banging sound near the front door startles me so much that I jump, and I'm horrified to see him watching me through the window. I drop the phone and kick it under the couch. I don't know how much he's seen, but my mind scrambles to think of a plausible excuse for my actions. When he walks through the front door, shaking his head, I feel hot and nauseous. He walks right up to me. "Where's my phone?"

"I don't have it." My voice is weak with guilt.

"Yes, you do. You know I saw you! You just couldn't help yourself, huh? I knew you didn't trust me. This is why I can't get into a relationship with you, because of this kind of drama and insecurity."

"Insecurity? Drama? Are you serious?" I'm guilty, I know, but I'm also exhausted by his martyrdom. "Do you know how loyal I've been to you? How I sit here and listen to you cry about your baby mama and all of your other problems when you never ask to listen to mine?

How I pull out my credit card whenever you ask me? How I communicate with your daughter better than you do? If I'm insecure, then it's your fault because you keep me guessing.

"Sometimes you want me and sometimes you don't, and you make me feel like something's wrong with me. And then I find out you're entertaining these other chicks, making them feel like they might have a chance with you. You take up all of my time and keep me hanging on just enough that I can't spend time with anyone else, but you don't really want me either. So, hell no, I don't trust you! You don't give me a reason to trust you! For all I know, you just keep me around to entertain your daughter and listen to your problems."

I realize I'm screaming at him. In an ironic twist, I have become the hit dog hollering, and I see his eyes dart towards Empress' room, but I've come unhinged. "Maybe you *are* dealing with that crazy girl from church and maybe you *did* go away on a romantic weekend with her. You sure did tell her a lot about me! But did you tell her I know all of her business too? I bet you didn't tell her I know all about her legal problems and everything, did you?"

He steps closer to me, his voice eerily friendly. "Like I said, this is why I can't do this with you females. You can't just chill and enjoy life. No! You have to ruin it with your jealousy and insecurity and pettiness. You run your mouth to your girlfriends and then you want to come and try to handle me like I'm doing you wrong. I have been upfront with you from the jump. I didn't try to lead you on. I told you what I've been through and I'm just not ready for that kind of pressure yet. So, this is *your* fault. You said you were fine just chillin' with me, but I guess that's not enough for you because you keep trying to pressure me into something I said I didn't want. I can't believe you have the nerve to make it seem like I'm hurting you."

He cuts me off before I can respond. "You're too bossy, too bitchy, and you can't get over your control issues and that's why you're never gonna get a man. You want to wear the pants in the relationship and you wanna get mad because I won't wear the skirt. I won't bow down and lay down whenever you bark—and you can't accept it."

I'm stunned. "I'll never get a man? Let me tell you something: If I'm going to grow old alone, then so are you! Maybe that's why you're alone. You're an opportunistic narcissist and you might be bipolar too. While you're strutting around the church acting like you're holier than thou, you should really get some help for yourself."

I grab my purse and jacket, and head towards the door, but turn around before I open it. "And that's why your baby mama left your sorry, bipolar behind! She was fed up with you and honestly, I don't think you have ever gotten over her. Well, baby, you're gonna have to deal with it on your own. You won't spend another moment of my time using me as your personal therapist or your daughter's playmate! I'm reclaiming my time and you can just move on to your next victim."

I think, as I slam the door on my way out, I hear Empress, "Miss Cindy-uh…"

Outside of church, the days and weeks without Victor are tolerable. I feel empowered by what I said to him. He tried to text me after a few days and I ignored him, of course. I stayed busy with Mama, babysat for Julene, got caught up with things at work, and checked in with my personal trainer more often.

I'd be lying if I said I don't miss his friendship, but I want to free myself from the hold he had on me—the mind games, the hot and cold, the pity parties. I realize he had become my bad habit and Julene always reminds me it takes the brain only twenty-one days to break a bad habit. I convince myself I need twenty-one Victor-free days and I'll be able to move on with my life.

Julene's rationale is skewed, apparently. Either that, or God has a comical sense of timing.

On the twenty-first day of the Victor cleanse, I'm awakened by a text. He's texted me a few times since our argument—the run of the mill good morning messages and such. Those aren't too hard to ignore. But this particular text rouses me shortly before one in the morning from the foot of Mama's bed where I've fallen asleep, and leads me into my own room where I can read and re-read the message out loud:

Victor: *How stupid are you?*

Victor: *You're not slick. I know what your car looks like.*

Victor: *the next time your crazy ass wanna drive by my house and stalk me, do me a favor and don't!*

Victor: *you can't take a hint. I don't want to be with you. Accept it you crazy ass stalker! If you come by here again, I'll call the police!*

Maybe I shouldn't, but I text him. His messages are too wild to ignore.

Me: *this is Cynthia…*

Me: *who did you mean to text?*

Victor: *don't play dumb. I know who it is! You drove past my house trying to check up on me and I caught you!*

Me: *why would I drive past your house? I'm at home.*

Me: *I was sleeping.*

Victor: *I saw you! I know what your car looks like!!*

Victor: *I was looking through my front window when you went by. Now you feel stupid.*

Me: *are you hallucinating? My car hasn't left my driveway all night.*

And then, because the whole scenario is so bizarre, I get out of bed and walk down the hall to the kitchen window to see if my car is still parked under the carport. It is.

I take a picture of it and text it to him.

Me: *my car is parked.*

Me: *it was probably one of your other 'friends' creeping by to check on you.*

Me: *you can't keep your women straight, I guess.*

Victor: *just stay your crazy ass away from me.*

A man can only call you crazy so many times.

I change his name to "Do Not Answer" in my contacts list…again. It's been a long time since I've had to ignore him, and it hurts. It hurts because I was doing so well without him, but I never wanted him to be completely absent from my life. I was learning to move on and I'd hoped we could be adults about it. Maybe even 'friends' as he'd always wanted. But he had to go and disrupt my progress with his drama.

He was adamant that I had driven past his house to spy on him, and maybe someone had done it, but it wasn't me. Maybe it was some other woman whom he'd sent on a head trip because he'd given her the silent treatment or gaslighted her in some way.

However, I know him well enough to know he didn't believe me. I know he'll have everyone in the church looking at me sideways and thinking I'm some lunatic or a jealous, desperate female. That's exactly what he'd told me about all the other women who were constantly offering themselves to him.

I lay back on my bed and close my eyes, but falling asleep is an impossibility. I wander back into the kitchen and peep through the window again. My car is still there, covered in a layer of condensation from the dewy, middle of the night air.

I dig a bag of hot Cheetos from the deep recesses of the pantry and sit at the kitchen island to scroll through Facebook.

One of my cousins has tagged me and forty-two others on a post about a woman who had made history as the first black female to own a NASCAR team.

Tiffany, the pregnant girl from work has posted a list of baby names she's considering.

Ms. Irene's son shared a rap video that he's been featured in.

Derrick, my old high school crush, is training for a mud run. He's coaching a pee-wee football team, and he's also trying to go vegan, according to his meal prep pictures.

The First Lady posts a string of 'inspirational' messages for the Singles Ministry. Scrolling through the most recents, there seems to be a subliminal message lately.

This will be the year God places your heart in the hands of your husband.

Be happy being single.

You deserve a man who will go out of his way to make it obvious that he wants you in his life.

Remember that you can remain pure as a single Christian woman.

Be wise enough to let go and strong enough to wait for what you deserve.

A direct message from Julene pops up, interrupting my scrolling.

Julene: *what are you doing on Facebook this time of night?*

Me: *lol. I should ask you the same question.*

Julene: *couldn't sleep. One of the kids has a cough. Upper respiratory something so I'm up every 4 hours giving meds.* 😕

Me: 😌

Julene: *I figured all this drama in the singles ministry would be keeping you awake.*

Julene: *aren't you glad he's not your problem anymore?*

Me: *what are we talking about? I didn't hear about any drama at church.*

Julene goes radio silent. I can see bubbles as though she's texting a reply and then they disappear. The bubbles reappear and disappear again.

For some reason, it makes me feel weird inside, and a wave of anxiety floods my chest.

Me: *you have to tell me.*

Me: *?*

Julene: *ugh. Apparently there was a big thing bc Stephanie was telling everyone that she was in a relationship*

*with Victor and he was denying it. So she started going
around to some of his friends on the deacon board and the
security ministry trying to get through to him.*

Me: *where was I when all of this was happening? I
haven't heard anything!*

Julene: *well girlfriend…idk.*

Julene: *anyways, I guess he blocked her on everything
and told his boys that she was crazy.*

I can feel myself getting red in the face. He really
loves to call women crazy. I dump the empty Cheetos bag
into the recycling bin, find a pack of 100 calorie fudge
stripes cookies in the pantry, and return to the kitchen
island.

Julene: *So I guess she got tired of trying to hunt him
down and she went to the First Lady and told her that she
is pregnant by one of the deacons and felt that she was being
shunned.*

Me: *by who?????*

Julene: *girl! By him!!! By Victor! And he's saying he isn't
the father bc she was free to date whoever she wanted and it
could be anyone.*

Julene: *how is he gonna put her out there like that????
Like she's just a hoe?*

Julene: *girl aren't you so glad that you dodged that bullet?
Good thing you didn't end up making a baby with him! He
won't even be a man and own up to his responsibilities!!*

Julene: *ok now you're caught up on the latest. Get some
sleep so we can get to church early enough in the morning
to get a front row seat for the next episode of Sanctified and
Salty! Lol!* 😆😆😆😆😆

I reply with two rows of laughing until crying emojis
even though I'm not really laughing. I text her a lie, even

as the tears run down my cheeks and collect beneath my chin.

On Sunday morning, it's nearly impossible to drag myself from bed. I have a pounding headache and my throat feels a little sore. I contemplate not going to church at all, but as soon as Mama starts in with all her questions and complaints, I decide to throw on some slacks and a blouse and get out of the house.

Julene texts me multiple times before I pull into the church parking lot to tell me she's saved a seat for me up in the church balcony where we can see everyone.

I sit in my car, not wanting to walk in. I don't want to be involved in Victor's relationship scandal and I don't want to witness it explode either, but I do want to see for myself if he's with her.

How could another woman—if she's telling the truth—be carrying his baby when I'd been preparing to do the same thing? And I was trying to do it the right way. Thanks to my habit of trying to plan and control every moment of my life, someone else is walking around carrying my baby? Why couldn't I have let loose and been more spontaneous during my twenties and early thirties?

Another thought crosses my mind: the person who drove past his house at an ungodly time of the morning must have been her. Why had he assumed it was me? Who knows?

While I sit in the car, stalling for time, an email notification pops up on my phone. When I open it, I see it's a message from the church administrator's office, informing me that I may no longer attend the single's ministry events. The reason, it states, is that I have 'aged out' of the group. The single's ministry is reserved for church members who are between the ages of twenty-five and thirty-eight. I'm thirty-nine. The email comes at an oddly coincidental time, given the apparent drama in church and my unfortunate connection to Victor and Stephanie, but I'm battling a headache and I can't deal with this right now. Plus, the Singles Ministry was a waste of time anyway. If it had been a worthwhile ministry, I wouldn't still be single, would I?

I take a deep breath, collect myself, and walk into the church as casually as I can manage. I'm late, but that's okay. I don't think I could have handled the church announcements and forced fellowshipping with the choir singing and the congregation standing to shake hands and hug one another.

I stand in the vestibule while the choir finishes a song and then enter the sanctuary just in time for the tithing and offerings. I make my way up to the balcony and take a seat beside Julene.

"Hey girl! Thanks for holding my spot!" I whisper towards her as I slide into the pew.

She just smiles and pats my knee like an old church mother, then she opens her purse to show me gum, mints, and other hard candies.

I mouth a quick, 'No thanks' and turn towards the pulpit but think better of it and lean in to choose a piece of gum from her purse.

"You're such a mom." I whisper to her and she smiles in return.

The choir takes their seats and the First Lady takes to the pulpit. She is a minister, but she rarely preaches the main Sunday sermon.

The air inside of the church feels constricted, and from where we sit, looking down over the sanctuary, I notice it's at capacity. Around us, the balcony continues to fill, so much so, that the ushers are asking people to squeeze together to make room for more parishioners.

The First Lady opens her sermon with a scripture from Colossians: "Since God chose you to be the holy people he loves, you must clothe yourselves with tenderhearted mercy, kindness, humility, gentleness, and patience. Make allowance for each other's faults, and forgive anyone who offends you. Remember, the Lord forgave you, so you must forgive others. Above all, clothe yourselves with love, which binds us all together in perfect harmony. And let the peace that comes from Christ rule in your hearts. For as members of one body you are called to live in peace. And always be thankful."

A chorus of Amens float through the church and First Lady swipes her iPad on. A large white screen floats down from the ceiling and the title of her sermon appears in bold lettering: HANDLING A BREAKUP IN CHURCH

Julene makes googly-eyes at me and I reach over to squeeze her hand. Here we go.

There is nervous chuckling down below and the First Lady laughs too.

"Okay, Family, we can talk about this, right?" She smiles brightly and walks around to the front of the pulpit. "Sometimes, in a family, things happen that can cause hurt feelings and mistrust. Amen?"

A deacon near the front row shouts an amen in response.

"Okay, now this church—this family—as the living body of Christ, must govern ourselves accordingly when it comes to those situations which stand to divide us. Because, we know the devil will be creative in the tools he uses to bring down the kingdom of Christ."

She looks out into the congregation and laughs again. "Come on, now! Y'all stick with me. Follow me on this. Now what is the devil's mission? He's not lurking around for no reason! He has a job to do! What does he come to do?"

The congregation, in one voice responds, "*To steal, to kill, to destroy.*"

She uses the microphone to point towards the congregation. "There you go! So, watch me now— I'm going to bring you back to the scripture in a minute. One of the ways the devil comes to destroy is through our RELATIONSHIPS! So, we, as Christians, have to arm ourselves with the right weapons to fight back. Because we know our individual relationships with each other are not more important than the work we do corporately to glorify the Lord."

She pauses and hums the melody of an old hymn as the organist plays a short rift and a few members in the front row encourage her to continue.

She moves back to the pulpit and taps her iPad screen again. A list of bullet points appears on the overhead screen. She reads and explains each one:

"'Stay calm and be kind.' Watch your words. Don't explain your side to anyone or get offended. You don't want to devastate the whole church by letting the drama spill over into the body of the church.

"'Don't make it weird.' If everyone gets quiet or uncomfortable when you come around, then maybe you've been making it all about you and your drama lately. Take the focus off yourself and focus on something else.

"'Don't make excuses.' You don't have to explain your side of the story to everyone. Just let the dust settle. It'll be okay. I promise, it will! Just don't feed into the negativity.

"'Don't talk about it.' Don't go around talking to his friends or bringing it up amongst others in the congregation. Don't make it your talking point with all your friends. Don't add fuel to the fire."

"'Don't leave the church.' Be grown about it. You can still stay in ministry. If he moves on with someone else, regulate your emotions and don't make the other person your enemy. You can still be kind, still say hello, still go feed the hungry together." She laughs out loud as she explains this point. "Remember that you are here to do the Lord's work, not to find a date!"

"'Even if your heart is broken, it's okay. It will mend.' Trust me on this one. It will get better.

"Finally, grow up! Don't make it weird. Just get over it! Let it go! Keep growing, keep going to church!"

The organist plays an energetic rift and the rest of the church band begins to play a lively tune, signaling the end of her sermon. There is rustling and commotion down below and I can see that Stephanie has gotten up and walked out of the church. Is there a baby bump? Is she crying? I can't quite tell from this angle.

The morning service concludes with a call to the altar, a few final announcements, and then the First Lady takes her place at the front doors of the church for the recessional.

Standing in line to shake the First Lady's hand on the way out of the sanctuary, my mind is reeling. I don't want to see her, but Julene's hand is on my shoulder, so I take a deep breath and dig deep down into my soul, but I know my smile is nonexistent.

I can hear the people just ahead of me in line congratulating her on a great sermon. *Amen,* they're saying. *Get things out in the open,* they're whispering.

But when it's finally my turn, and she grasps my hand just a little longer than I'm comfortable with, asking me how I enjoyed the message, I become unglued.

"Frankly, it was bullshit." Her gasp is audible and I can feel Julene's hand pushing me forward, trying to force me out of line. But I'm bigger than she is, and I hold my ground. "That was TRASH ADVICE and it did not come from the scripture. There are predators and opportunists who take advantage of vulnerable women who believe themselves to be in a safe place in this church and no one is talking about it!"

I am hollering. I know I am because the pastor himself appears at my side and wraps his giant arm around my shoulders.

I shake him off and turn to address them both. "The Church is spending so much time telling women how to conduct ourselves, how to be wife material, but no one is teaching these men how to become husband material. That entire sermon was directed at the single women of this church, and that's bullshit! You want us to be quiet and let the men of this congregation slide from woman to woman with no consequences."

A crowd has gathered, but I am so incensed I can't even see their faces. I keep going. "How about taking a look at the men in this church who are playing the women against each other. How about one man of God holding another man of God accountable for his actions? This is disgusting and misogynistic, and you both know it!"

Only then, when they look thoroughly deconstructed, do I allow Julene to walk me to my car. She's silent and so am I, but at my car, we hug. It's a hard hug and we both know it means we'll talk later.

With trembling arms, I steer my car out of the church parking lot, careful not to look in the rear-view mirror at the mess I've left behind. Lord knows I hadn't planned on saying any of those things, but they'd slipped out of my mouth, they couldn't be reeled back in, and at this point, I'm not sorry about it.

On the way to the house, I stop by the local barbecue joint and order two plates for Mama and me—a feast of stewed turkey wings, pulled pork, macaroni and cheese, spicy yams, potato salad, greens, cornbread, and banana pudding for dessert. As an afterthought, I order an Arnold Palmer for each of us.

That meal marked the beginning of my downward spiral for the week, because I skipped my workouts for the next two days and left the gym to throw up on the third.

CHAPTER FOURTEEN

By Thursday, feeling fully disgusted with myself, I try to start a smoothie cleanse, but break down and have a milkshake and fries on the way home from work, a choice which causes me to throw up again.

All of the puking, coupled with my public outburst at church gives me reason to consider that I might be pregnant, which is crazy, I know, because that would make Victor the father, and he's already put a bun in someone else's oven. But, it's been a little over a month since I was with Victor, and, with the irregular menstrual cycles of PCOS, it's hard for me to read my body's signals.

Just to be sure, I pick up a few pregnancy tests from the drug store and use all of them on my first pee of the morning on Friday. They're all negative, and I'm flooded with a sense of sadness so deep that I cry over cheese toast and bacon before work.

As I'm reapplying my makeup and heading to work, I receive a text from Julene informing me she has the weekend off and wants to take me out for drinks.

Me: *thanks but I think I'll pass on your offer. I haven't been feeling so good this week.* 😞

Julene: *the medical term is Depression.* 👑

Me: *you are not a doctor.* 😆

Julene: *maybe not. But I am a healthcare professional and a mother and your friend. So my diagnosis stands. The appropriate course of therapy is a night out. Just me and you.*

Me: *k*

Me: *Fitzgerald's?*

Julene: *sounds good.*

Julene: *7?*

Me: *sounds good*

When we walk into Fitzgerald's, we find a high-top table near the back of the bar area and Julene enlightens me with her thoughts on relationships: "Everyone has to decide what they can deal with. You say you couldn't deal with a man who cusses you out. You know my husband and I will pop off on each other in a heartbeat, but I know how deal with it. We might yell and cuss, but we get everything out in the open, and then we move on. What I don't know how to deal with is a man who plays games with my mind. For me, mind games and manipulation are too much to handle."

It's true. I've heard Julene curse her man out on numerous occasions. It doesn't matter if the kids are around and it doesn't matter if we're in public. When she unleashes, everyone takes cover. It's hard to tell whose wrath was worse, hers or his, because he's cussed her out quite a few times too. I've witnessed a few incidents myself, but she hasn't been shy about confiding in me about their private blowouts, either.

"Right, right, but..." I sip my wine carefully, not wanting to smudge my lipstick, considering her perspective.

"I know I'm right! Different strokes for different folks. Pick your poison." Julene stirs her Manhattan with the tiny straw and then takes a quick sip.

"Right, but what if you don't want either? What if you want a healthy relationship with no mind games and no curse words?" The words seem childish, coming out of my mouth, but the truth is, I still want to believe.

She chuckles with such kindness, I can't tell if she's making fun of me or not. After another sip, she says, "Okay. Well let me know when you find that! Oh yeah, and when you do, I'd also like a unicorn for my kids."

She waves the waitress over and orders another Manhattan for herself and another glass of Moscato for me.

I laugh unexpectedly and Julene looks at me suspiciously. "What's so funny?"

"What is a Manhattan? Sounds like something Frank Sinatra would drink."

She laughs too. "Why do you drink Moscato? It's like wine for babies! When are you gonna step up to a nice, bold red?"

I turn my glass up and drain it. She does the same, then looks at me. "I guess I drink Manhattans because it's what my mom always drank at social events. I used to think it was so sophisticated." She shrugs her shoulders and I almost miss the shadow that flickers across her face. I can count on one hand the number of times she's talked about her mother. I decide not to press the issue tonight.

I think about my own choice of beverage. "My parents never drank anything stronger than Pepsi, so I figure Moscato is a step up from there."

The waitress returns with our drinks and I stop her before she leaves. "You know what? I'll take a—" I glance at Julene. "What should I order?"

She stops, mid sip, and thinks for a moment before answering. "A cosmopolitan! No! A margarita!" She looks at the waitress. "Can you make that two?"

The waitress laughs and reaches for our drinks, but Julene stops her. "No! We'll keep these, but you can go ahead and bring the margaritas for the next round."

As the waitress turns to leave, I stop her again. "And some queso and chips?"

She smiles at us, "Certainly. I'll be right back with that."

After a long sip of her Manhattan, Julene has a confession. "You wanna know why I cuss my husband out? Or anyone else, for that matter?"

She sounds so serious, I'm afraid of what I might hear. I sip my drink and raise my eyebrows.

"It's because I was raised in a fake family with people who only cared about impressing other people. I hated it, and I decided to stop caring about what everybody else thinks. I stopped trying to be a people pleaser and I was tired of trying to live up to everyone else's standards." She pauses for another sip.

"When I moved here, I promised myself I wouldn't keep my feelings bottled up anymore. I try to treat people right and I try to live right, but when someone crosses me, I'm letting them know, right then! My husband knows it, too."

I raise my eyebrows again as I watch her over the lip of my glass, and she continues speaking.

"It's like this," she sips slowly, her eyes searching the corners of the bar for the right words. "Basically, if something happens between me and my man, even if we fuss and cuss, we love each other afterwards. Once the argument is dead, then it's dead. Sometimes things are messy and ugly, but we don't bring it up again and we both know we'll do anything to protect each other."

It sounds beautiful and liberating. Maybe it's a little dysfunctional, but hey, it's working for them. I know it would never fly with someone like Victor. Tip toe, tip toe—that's how I had to move when it came to him. His feelings could be hurt way too easily for me to let loose the way Julene could. It doesn't matter anyway. With all that has happened, if he's about to be a daddy, then it's really over between us, I guess.

We both sit back a little so the waitress can place the cheese dip and chips on the table. I taste it before she leaves, just to make sure it's hot enough. I realize I feel warm inside, and I can't tell if it's from the queso or the alcohol, but it doesn't matter. This is the most relaxed I've felt in a long time.

I swirl a chip in the dip for a second while I think about how to ask Julene the question that has played at the edges of my mind since she first joined our book club a few years ago.

"So, what happened?" I decide to just blurt it out.

She stops, tiny straw stuck to her bottom lip, and looks across the table at me. "Huh?"

Empowered by liquid courage, I press her. "What happened before you moved here that made you..." How do I say this? If our friendship was a house, then the part of her life that happened before she moved here is a room she keeps locked at all times. As close as we've become, and as open as she is, this is one area that has remained off-limits. "What happened when you lived in Chicago that made you…"

"Oh! How come I don't give a damn anymore?" She interrupts me with her own supply of words. "Because I realized I only have one life to live and ain't nobody gonna live it for me."

I grab a margarita glass from the center of the table and salute her. "Let's drink to that."

Julene, with a glass in each hand, salutes me in return. "To living life on your own damn terms."

The next morning, I awake with aching feet and a kaleidoscopic memory of the previous night's events— lots of laughing, some singing…an argument? Did I get into an argument with someone? Tears? Seems like I remember crying at some point. My eyes feel swollen.

My feet are aching. Not aching like after a long day of wearing heels, aching like tender and sore to the touch. Sliding one leg from beneath the sheets, I peer down at my feet. They're filthy. They're dusty and black around the edges, bringing to mind the days when I was little and loved to race in the street with no shoes on. If I had gotten into bed without showering, then I must have really tied one on last night.

My pedicure is ruined, the paint has almost completely peeled from my toenails- all except the big toe which is still pink.

In the fog of my hangover, I remember I despise pink polish. I like glitter, but I hate pink nails. It makes me think of pig feet for some reason.

Pulling myself into a sitting position, I wobble uneasily, waiting for the swirling and pounding inside my head to fall into a singular rhythm, and then I pull my foot as close to my face as I am able. My flexibility is minimal and think about the progress I'd made when I used to take yoga.

When I realize there is no pink polish, there is only the tender pink tissue of my nail bed, fully exposed in the absence of my big toenail, I puke down the front of the unfamiliar T-shirt that I'm wearing.

"Mommy! She's awake. But I think she's sick!"

I hear the tiny voice behind me as I run into the bathroom and hurl in the toilet. Then I peel the T-shirt off, toss it into the trash can, and wrap myself in the towel that hangs behind the door. I'm rinsing my face and mouth in the sink when Julene appears behind me with a cool cloth and a bottle of Pedialyte.

"I ran out of Gatorade." She offers this as an apology as she pushes the Pedialyte into my hand and guides me back towards the bed. "Just rest for a little bit. I already went and checked on your mom. I told her your phone died and you were watching my kids for me while I took care of something."

I look up at her, wanting to say something, but too overcome by nausea to speak. How can people just drink like this every weekend?

"She has eaten and taken her meds. She's fine. You can sleep here until you're ready to go home."

I pull the covers up to reveal my feet and wiggle my toes. I manage to whisper, "What happened?"

She stops to peer down at my feet, and I'm embarrassed by the filth.

She looks embarrassed too. "Well…what happened was—" then she bursts out laughing. "Girl, you were on 100 last night! You sang karaoke, you danced with somebody's uncle! You kicked your shoes off! I was right there, partying with you. But neither one of us was in any condition to drive, so I called my husband and his buddy to come and pick us up. You needed help getting to the car and I guess you couldn't really pick your feet up because they were just dragging along every few steps."

A few weeks ago I had seen the number 283 on the scale, so I don't fault the guys for not being able to carry me to the car. I'm more horrified by the thought that I had danced barefoot on that disgusting barroom floor.

"I guess when they dragged you to the car, the toenails kinda scraped off." She gives me a handful of Ibuprofen and I settle back into the pillows.

I want to laugh, picturing myself being dragged from the bar, but I feel too weak. I don't know if I've ever been this hungover before.

"Was I crying about something? Am I a sad drunk?" I look to Julene for answers.

"Girl! We were both a hot mess! You were crying about being older than all of the other mothers when you take your future child to kindergarten and I was crying because my son said my boobs look like puppy dog ears!" She's laughing just hearing herself say it out loud. "My husband said we can't ever go out drinking again! He said we need to stick to the book club and stop trying to be young.

"And here," she tosses my phone onto the bed. "This thing was ringing and dinging all night…well, all morning, technically, so I turned it on vibrate. I was going to turn it off, but I figured your mama might call, so…" She stops smiling and her voice becomes very even. She's suddenly hard to read. "It was Victor, drunk texting and calling you until about 5:30 this morning. What the heck is his problem?"

She's right. When I look at the phone, there are back-to-back calls, voicemails, blurred pictures, memes, and I know she's seen them. As much as I want to read his messages, look at each picture, *call him*, I don't. Not now. Not in front of Julene. I just thank her and slide back under the covers.

Chapter Fifteen

S omething about my drunken night with Julene snaps me out of my food spiral and resets my attitude—sort of. When I get home, I peel off my clothes, take a steaming hot shower, and then soak in the bathtub. I know it's weird, but I always have to shower before I sit in the tub.

Afterward, I stand in front of the bathroom mirror and study myself. I lift my heavy boobs, turn sideways and suck in my tummy, use my hands to pull my tummy in even tighter, turn around, cup my butt and lift it upwards.

Then, I drop everything and let it sag. I look over at the basket in the corner which holds an assortment of tampons and pads. I wonder when I'll need them again. With PCOS you can never tell what your body will do next.

Next, I step on the scale and the verdict is 286. That's a healthy weight for an eight-foot-tall woman, but it's far too much for my five-foot six frame, and I begin to wonder if I have a food addiction.

I get down on my knees then, to ask the Lord for help. I hate what I see in the mirror, not because I don't love myself, but because I *do*. I *do* love myself and I want someone else to love me too. What I *do not* love is what I've done to my body, the body that I will depend on to carry a baby one day. This body will need to run at the playground and swim at the beach—well, I probably won't get in the filthy water—and trek from one end of Disney World to the other.

I need this body to do great things and I need the Lord to help me find my way. I pray for the strength to break the bonds of my food addiction and the compassion to treat my body with more love.

I don't eat the pizza Mama requested for dinner tonight. Instead, I pour a sensibly sized bowl of bran cereal and tell myself the grumbling in my tummy is just the sound of the Lord doing a great work inside of me.

Overcoming the food addiction doesn't take nearly as long as it takes me to overcome the Victor addiction. However, I have often been told that most addicts tend to replace one addiction with another, and I think that's what makes me start spending money.

For every French fry and every milkshake I reject, I reward myself with a trip to TJ Maxx. This is wrong given all I've learned about wealth building and self-control, but I swear with each shopping bag I stash in my room, the number on the bathroom scale inches downward.

"What are you doing? Sounds like you're in the car." Julene is like a detective, using clues to determine my whereabouts.

"I gotta stop and get my mama something to eat and some stuff to make my smoothies and then I'm going to get a run in before it gets too dark." I say all of this, even as I steer my car into the parking space at TJ Maxx.

"Good! I'm proud of you for sticking to your plan! How's your mama been doing?"

I exhale. I've tried not to complain about her so much lately. "She's doing good. I felt bad the other day, 'cause I was like 'Mama, you are not in a nursing home. You are able to take your medicine. If you can tell me what medicine you have to take, then you're able to take it.' So, I ordered some new bottle tops to make it easier for her to open up her medicine, and she can set her own medicine in her pillbox. That kind of activity is good exercise for her brain.'"

"Yeah."

"The thing is, I don't mind helping her, but it's like she has an infantile syndrome. She doesn't want to do anything for herself, but I'm not running a nursing home!"

I pick up a candle, sniff it, and continue. "As far as me sitting in the house staring at her, listening to her aches and pains and moans and groans…she doesn't have anyone else to talk to. I get it, but I want her to do things for herself. She's my mother, not my child. If she was eighty-four years old, then yes, I could see that she would need more help, but," I sniff another candle and then sniff the first one again before putting both in my cart.

I hear a murmured sound from Julene, so I keep going.

"Last night, about 11:00, I was still trying to get things ready for today. And girl, by the time I finished my paperwork, it was 1 A.M. Then I got up at 5 and finished the rest of it, so I didn't go to work until about 9 this morning and then I went to the gym afterward."

"Girl, you can't keep going like this."

"It's preparing me for motherhood. The other day, I didn't get home until 6:30 and she's ready to eat, but she wants me to prepare it for her so she had been calling, asking me what time I was going to be home to give her dinner. If I go work out, I have to be back by 8:00 to give her a shot, which breaks up my evening. I'm like, why can't you get your shot at 6? And when I start making suggestions for her, she acts like she's hard of hearing or like she can't understand me!"

Julene laughs with me and then hollers something at her kids in the background. She returns to the phone. "So, wait. Motherhood? Are you really going through with it?"

We haven't spoken about the fertility thing very much, and honestly, the statement had just tumbled out of my mouth.

I realize I've accumulated a cart full of scented things, loungewear, stationary, and a pair of shoes. Satisfied with my findings, I head towards the checkout counter.

"I don't know, Julene. I'm thinking seriously about it."

I hear Julene exhale. "Well, you know I support you 110%. I just worry about all the pressure you'll be under. How are you going to care for a baby, your mama, and your man?"

This makes me laugh. "WHAT man? As for Mama, I'm seeing people out in the community who are ninety something years old, pushing it! I'm like Mama, please. Yes, you have stents in your heart, you had a heart attack, but at least they didn't have to crack your chest open!"

"But could it be some level of dementia? Cause if it is, you can't really compare her to other people her age…"

Julene's question is reasonable, but I know my mama better than she does.

"Yeah, that's true, but if you're talking about money and stuff, then she don't have no damn dementia!"

"Oh! Its selective!" Julene's laughter echoes faintly, and I know she's hiding in the bathroom again.

The light blinks and a computerized voice announces the cashier is ready for me. I attempt to camouflage the sound by coughing, but she hears it. "I thought you were at the grocery store. It sounds like you're in TJ Maxx and you've been doing a lot of shopping lately."

"No, I, hold on, hold on a second." I put the phone on mute while I swipe my TJ Maxx rewards charge card for $187.31.

Walking away from the register, I return to my phone call. "I'm not going to rush out and do something crazy. I'm going to give it a year, like the doctor said and then go for it. I'm excited and scared at the same time."

"I'm excited for you!" She's definitely in the bathroom.

"But sometimes I worry about whether I can do it, what kind of parent I could be."

"Well, I can tell you, nobody ever knows how to be a parent. You just do what you think is best. You adjust when you can adjust. Lots of people come out of some really bad situations and they do fine, by the grace of God, even with terrible parents. And you have some other people who have everything handed to them and no reason to fail and they turn out to be a mess."

"Mmhmm."

"And you also have to think about the logistics of raising more than one child at a time. You know, your risk of having multiples is higher if you have any kind of fertility treatment, but you have to raise them individually. I didn't realize how serious sibling jealousy is. That's what my kids are going through. My daughter had a meltdown the other day because she said she felt like I favored her little brother over her."

I reflect on Julene's family dynamic. With four children and a relatively new husband, it must be hard when one child demands more attention than the others. "And you probably do. In one way because he's probably easier to deal with. And on the other hand, he might feel like his sister gets all of the attention because you spend so much energy trying to rein her in, and that probably makes him feel like his sister is being favored."

"That's exactly what I think. She feels like he is favored because he's always the good kid and I think he tries not to rock the boat. But the reason he doesn't is because she raises so much hell! It's always something with her sports, her behavior, her attitude, or her weight. We spend so much energy on her, until I think he just doesn't want to be a bother. He feels like she gets all the attention with all her issues, and she feels like he's the golden child because he never has any issues. Meanwhile, I have a baby who's still cutting teeth! When you're a parent, you don't know all the answers. Everybody's trying to survive, and most days, I don't feel like I know what I'm doing." She's laughing at herself, but I know she's serious.

"Oh, so you're like, let me just try this and see how this kid turns out." I tease her.

"Yeah and you don't know how it's going to turn out down the line. You think you're doing something for one reason and it turns out it might have contributed to some other issues! I'm sure my kids would tell a totally different story." Her echoing laugh makes it sound like she's in a tunnel.

"I think you're an awesome mom and I'm sure your kids would say the same."

"Girl! Everything I know about parenting, I learned from watching the Fresh Prince of Bel Air! So, there you go!"

Julene is the one who came up with the idea I should devote an entire year to caring for myself, but I'm fully committed to my Year of Selfie so I buy myself a car. It's a pearl-toned Audi with a creamy peanut butter interior and digital everything. I haven't driven it, though, other than the one time I drove it to take Mama to the doctor.

For the most part, I've been driving my old Toyota, even though it's on its last leg. My plan was to buy a new car so that I'd have something more reliable to drive, but this is my first time ever owning an almost brand-new car and I realized I want to save it for special occasions or times when I'm all dressed up.

Maybe it's totally unrelated, but the scale said 247 on the day I came home with my new car keys.

Even though I definitely did my research beforehand, the car buying process was still a learning experience for me. I should have asked for more perks when I bought it, and I can't help but wonder how things would have gone if I had a husband to go with me…

When I brought it home, Mama looked the car over for a second, but she looked me over for what felt like an eternity. "Well congratulations. You grown now."

Her statement was so flat, so matter of fact, that I felt guilty. But why? I deserved to treat myself! I work hard. I shake the guilt away and walk around my car, demonstrating all of the features for her. I sit in the driver's seat and lean out the window, "Is this what grown feels like?"

She sits down on the seat of her walker and says, "Yeah, especially when you make them damn payments."

On the day the scale reads 241, I sit on the floor in the den while Julene twists my hair. I decided to try a twist-out style and was having a hard time getting it just right. After watching a few videos with me on the internet, Julene said she'd take a shot at it.

"Your hair is so soft! I wish I could get mine to…" She pauses mid-sentence and hollers at her daughter to get out of my closet. I lift my eyes just in time to see Julene's daughter emerge from the far corner of my coat closet, clutching a slew of Kate Spade and Robert Wayne bags.

"I'm shopping, Mommy!" She pulls the bags onto her miniature shoulders, holding as many as she can, while prancing around the room.

There is something about the way a child says 'mommy', I'm realizing. It's as though they know you are all they have in this world. You are their entire universe, the beginning and the end of everything. It's an innocent vulnerability and it wrenches the strings that hold my heart together, but the sweetness of the moment doesn't distract Julene from the real problem at hand.

She drops the comb and jumps to her feet. "Unh uh! Unh uh! What is this?" She grabs bag after bag, peeks into the closet, and sees there are more. She turns and looks at me. "You shopping like this?"

"Girl, it's not that much. I was going to return most of it anyway."

Julene side-eyes me. "Come on now, no you weren't. What else did you buy?" She disappears into the closet and crawls out dragging Michael Kors, Cache, and Tom Ford shopping bags. "Girl! What are you doing? It looks like an outlet mall exploded in your closet!"

She tosses the bags back into the closet and then sits down on the ottoman. "I'm not your mama, you're a full-grown woman, but what the hell? What's our book club motto? You should know it, you wrote it."

I walk towards the closet and stare at the mountain of shopping bags. "I was just browsing around the mall. I wasn't shopping for anything, but then I saw the earrings at Kate Spade, and I've never had any. And something said, what are you saving money for? For your kids? Looks like I'm not having any, so what else am I supposed to do? Live life for today, right? I'm treating myself this year, just like you recommended."

Julene pulls a tattered copy of the first financial book we'd read after she had joined the book club from her purse. I'm both impressed and envious that she actually carries the book in her purse after all of this time.

The familiar pain of Ruth's memory passes through my heart and I wish she was here.

"What does it say here?" Julene flips through the pages and begins reading aloud. "'Positive self-talk.'" She flips a few more pages. "'What the mind can conceive, it can achieve.'"

She looks at me over the top edge of the book, her daughter is busy trying to cram both of her feet into one of my new shoes, and I fidget with my cuticles.

Julene continues. "You can't be feeding yourself those lies. Talking about you won't have any children! You don't know that! You have options and you're supposed to be working towards your goals."

"I am working towards my goals! I've lost over forty pounds…"

She interrupts me. "And you look damn good…"

I appreciate her compliment, but don't stop to acknowledge it. "And I'm going to keep dropping these pounds, but that's the easy part!" I never thought I would say losing weight was easy, but lately, weight loss has been the least of my worries. "You have no idea how it feels to sit in this house with MY MOM! You don't know how it feels to go through an entire day without someone to call and say I've been on their mind-- no one waiting to hear from ME. Victor wasn't the best—I know you probably want to strangle me every time I say his name—but at least he showed me love sometimes. Without him, even when he gets on my nerves, I'm missing a huge hole in my life. It's lonely and it hurts."

I pick up the items Julene's daughter has strewn across the floor and stuff them back into the bags.

"I know shopping isn't the best use of my money, but it keeps me from eating French fries and it keeps me from texting Victor."

Julene wrestles a brand-new lipstick from her daughter's hand and tosses it to me. "I know you're struggling. It's not easy, but you made a healthy choice by cutting him out of your life, and I support you, girl. However, I'm telling you from experience, it takes a lot of money to have kids and I had to learn it the hard way. So, keep praying, keep trusting the Lord, and save your money. When your baby needs formula and diapers, I can promise you, those Kate Spade earrings won't do you any good!"

We stand amid the mess, surveying my haul, and I hold the earrings up to my ears. "Should I return these?"

After a moment, Julene smiles and says, "Girl, you can buy a pair just like that from my cousin Rashanda for five dollars! As a matter of fact, she sells all her jewelry for five bucks and her stuff is cute."

Julene leans over to pick up my new pair of boots. "Now these—keep these. You can treat yourself to a little treat, but don't go overboard."

We abandon our plans for my new hairstyle and start separating my shopping bags into two piles: keep or return.

When we finish, we hug at the door, and I wish I could tell her she's been my life-preserver lately. I'm out here, drowning in an ocean of self-doubt, loneliness, and shopping bags, but she helps me to keep my head above water and I don't have the words to express the depth of my gratitude.

Instead, I tell Julene I love her. She says she loves me, too—she always does, and I blow her daughter a million kisses until they buckle themselves in the car and disappear down the street.

Chapter Sixteen

I have an addictive personality. When I searched online, I found at least three of my recent behaviors on a list of addictions: overeating, overspending, and hoarding. Maybe I'm not a full-blown hoarder yet, but my closet full of shopping treasures looked pretty hoard-like when Julene's daughter exposed it.

And, although there may be some truth to Julene's twenty-one day theory, everything I've read online says addicts can't typically quit one behavior unless they substitute another one in its place. I'd replaced Victor with food and food with shopping.

When I woke up this morning, I sat on the couch with a steaming cup of coffee and let the morning sunlight warm my face. Perhaps I prayed, or maybe I meditated—but I forced myself to be still until I knew what I needed to do. I made the decision to replace shopping with something else: living. The Year of Selfie had been a good idea on Julene's part, but if I'm honest with myself, I only used it as an excuse for reckless behavior.

Today, I give myself permission to try again.

My first task is to reenergize my InVest group. I know it's fallen to the wayside in the wake of my personal issues.

Back when we first made the decision to groom our youngest family members for financial independence, I set up a Facebook group for the younger beneficiaries. It's been several months since I've posted anything, so I begin posting a quote from a financial book every evening. I add pictures to make the posts more interesting to look at, and I even include a few YouTube links because I know most kids prefer videos and cartoons when they're on social media.

The frustrating thing is, no matter what I do or how often I post, I don't get a single like. Not a smiley face or a heart—nothing. The kids just aren't interested. It's a closed group, but there are thirty-eight members, so, where are they?

After two and a half weeks of one-sided Facebook posts, I launch an experiment. Instead of posting another philosophical tip on wealth building, I post a video clip of the custom Range Rover a popular YouTube personality recently received as a push gift from her husband.

In the video, the adorably pregnant mother-to-be is blindfolded as she is led to the wildly expensive SUV she's always wanted. It's fully loaded, her husband explains from off camera, with a limited edition pearl finished paint job, deep dish, low profile rims, a diamond encrusted push-to-start button, built in coolers in the front and back consoles, and a surround-sound tv system in the backseat—for the baby, he says.

The video has 6.3 million views and 430 thousand likes. My videos have had no more than thirteen views and zero likes. It's got me worried.

Even as I work to figure out how to connect with the young generation who will one day manage the assets held in our trust, I resolve to practice self-care in at least one way every day, so I grab my earbuds and go for a walk every evening—no excuses.

The earbuds are actually a decoy—I don't listen to anything. I know most people listen to music and podcasts while they walk or run, but I need to be fully aware of my surroundings, and how can I do that if I have music blasting in my ears? However, I don't like to be bothered by the neighbors as I walk the neighborhood, and I've found the earbuds are a great deterrent. People don't try to stop and talk to me if they think I'm listening to something. That is, until Glen shows up.

I've seen him going in and out of his house from time to time since he moved across the street from Mama's house about a year ago, but I haven't made any effort to get to know him. From a distance, he seems friendly enough as a neighbor—waving when he sees me or Mama, pulling our trash bin from the curb and such—and he seems to be maybe forty-ish, if I had to guess. Truthfully, the old me would have scoped him out by now. I would have found out where he works and how many baby mamas he has, but I'm just in a different headspace these days.

The new me only cares that he doesn't make a lot of noise, he keeps his yard clean, and I never see a bunch of cars parked in front of his house. Some people in our neighborhood insist on keeping cars parked along the curb, blocking the streets and sidewalks, which annoys me to no end when I'm taking my daily walks.

Recently it seems, since I've made a regular habit of walking the neighborhood, I'm crossing paths with him more often. On most days, I can get away with a quick wave or smile, but today he's waiting at the bottom of his driveway as though we've had made plans to walk together, which we haven't. And I have my earbuds in. He doesn't care.

"I see you out here walking almost every day, but you never stop to speak." He pauses as though he expects an answer from me, but I keep walking. He falls into step beside me.

"And I knew I needed to take some time to get myself back in shape." He pats his barely-there tummy.

I glance at him, see that my stomach is still bigger than his, smile a reasonably polite smile, and pick up my pace.

"So I figured I would get out here and walk with you. Your husband or boyfriend won't mind, will he?"

I wag my naked ring finger in his direction and smile, but I keep walking.

"I heard that! So, tell me about yourself. Why aren't you taken?" Clearly, he won't take the hint that I don't want to talk, so I give up the tough-girl routine and answer rhetorically, "Why aren't *you* taken?"

He launches into a thorough explanation of how he was a virgin in high school and college, how he had planned to wait until marriage, as he had been taught by his parents. To overcome peer pressure, he became actively involved in the Christian Athletes Association through his high school. His vow of celibacy changed when he got engaged to his college sweetheart and decided to have sex with her before they were married.

It was a mutual decision, he clarifies, because they were already committed to each other and knew they would be married after graduation. His voice is strained as he tells me the love of his life had contracted an aggressive strain of meningitis and died before they could consummate their relationship.

The tragedy had rocked him so badly he'd had to withdraw from school, return home to his parents, and seek counseling.

When his epic story concludes, I look over at him and pluck one earbud from my ear. "So you're a virgin?" It's rude, I know, but he has divulged so much unsolicited information that I feel it's a fair question. Plus, I've never met a grown man who has never had sex—even in the church.

He laughs and for some reason, I laugh too. "No. That was over twenty years ago! I'd be lying if I said I haven't sown my royal oats since then. I've been in a few relationships since then, but none that felt as right as that first one."

He tries to slow our pace to a stroll, and I can tell he wants to just stop and talk. I won't let him, though, so I keep moving swiftly, glancing at him over my shoulder, forcing him to keep up.

"So that's why I made the decision to move out here. The job opportunity was right and the cost of living is so much cheaper than San Diego. Even though it's just me, I figured I might as well buy a house instead of throwing my money away on rent."

"'Make thy dwelling a profitable investment.'" I recite a lesson I learned from one of our club's early reading selections.

He offers me a fist-bump. Its awkward, fist bumping a man, but I don't want to leave him hanging. "Whatchu know about The Richest Man in Babylon?"

"I actually know a lot about it. I do my reading." I stop just short of telling him about our trust. After Victor, I promised myself I would never give another man enough information to take advantage of me again.

Glen doesn't seem to notice. He just keeps right on walking and laughing about who knows what. As we walk, I steal a few glances at him. I've never really looked at him closely, but I can see he's a little goofy—in a cute way, I guess—if I close one eye and squint through the other.

His skin is basic brown, his teeth are okay, his T-shirt and shorts are whatever, the hair at the crown of his head is a little thin—I imagine he'll probably have a bald spot one day.

By the time I've worked up a decent under boob sweat, we're already back on our street.

"Whew!" Glen offers me another fist bump. "That was a good walk! I don't think I push myself enough when I work out by myself. Are you walking tomorrow?"

"Most likely." I smile at him. "Why? Are you planning to invite yourself again?"

He laughs, easy and comfortable. "Well I got tired of waiting for you to invite me! You just breeze past here every day like you don't see me! That's not very neighborly, so I figured I'd have to invite myself."

I shrug my shoulders. "Hey! When I'm out here walking, I'm on a mission. What can I say?"

"I hear you." He punctuates this with another fist bump. Then he says, "Take my number," and waits until I pull out my phone. "Let me know when you're walking again, or if you go to the gym, and I'll link up with you."

I type his number into my phone and wait for him to ask for mine. I don't want to give it to him and my mind races to find an excuse to blow him off if he asks. I don't want to be rude and I didn't pick up on any bad vibes from him while we were walking, it's just…he seems very friendly and I'm not currently accepting applications for new friends at this time.

"Okay, sis! It was nice hanging with you! See you tomorrow?"

We're at the bottom of my driveway and he is clearly waiting to see that I get inside safely, so I walk up to the front door and toss him a quick wave before I disappear behind it.

In the shower, I replay our evening in my mind. Sis? Multiple fist bumps? Didn't ask for my number? And he reads? Have I met my future husband or my long-lost brother? Just as quickly as the thoughts enter my mind, I shake my head to erase them. I've got no space in my life right now for a friend, husband, or brother.

We walk, night after night. Well, most nights, anyway. I finally give him my number, but I've also made a commitment to myself to stick to my own schedule and not alter my routine for him. If he can join me, fine. If not, also fine. Most nights, he joins me, and he's typically sitting on his front porch, ready, waiting for me to step out of the house. If he can't, he calls to let me know in advance. He got on my nerves a little, at first, with his peppy personality and fist bumps and questions:

How do you keep your hair so neat while you work out?
What's your favorite holiday?
What's your top five list of movies?
Do you have siblings?

What CD is in your car right now?
What's the last show that you binge-watched?

He tells me a lot about himself, too, even though I don't ask. Things like how his parents have only been married for twenty-eight years because they didn't tie the knot until he was ten, how he loves cookies of every flavor, he doesn't have any social media accounts, and he works as an IT consultant mostly from home but sometimes travels. He's self-conscious about his back fat because it won't go away no matter what he does, he owns every Jay Z CD but also loves classic reggae, and he has every episode of Sanford and Son on DVD. I even get the more personal stuff, like how his twin sister left home at twenty-two and never came back, and how the traumatic football event that paralyzed a friend in college led him to decide he would never let his future son play tackle football.

Despite my independent attitude and occasional irritability, our time together morphs from something neighborly into something stronger than I'm willing to admit. Two months fly by, filled with evening walks, jokes, and fist bumps. I'd be lying if I said Glen hasn't grown on me. If I'm honest, I'll admit I have a crush on him, as goofy as he is. In fact, I don't think goofy is the right description anymore. It was mean of me to label him when we first met. I now realize he isn't goofy at all. He's genuine and unapologetically imperfect, and I find it to be a pretty cool attribute. He puts me at ease, he makes me laugh, and he laughs at himself, too. It's a positive, masculine energy that has a way of drawing me in, even as I remain committed to keeping my distance.

Here's how I do it: I resist the urge to go over to his house and make dinner. I don't offer to pick up a last-minute item from the store for him. I allow the Amazon boxes to stay on his front porch when he works late. I don't give too much of myself. I won't expect anything from him. I've learned to hold back and save a little bit of me for me.

He tells me his work requires him to travel from time to time, but I still glance at his house when I pass by on my walks. I'm committed to walking, no matter what, so I never call and ask him to join me, but I'm bummed on the days when he isn't out there.

"Girl, how do you know if he's really out of town for work?" Julene voices the thoughts that flooded my brain from the moment he first told me he'd be away for a while. "I saw a Lifetime movie about a dude who had two families. His wife didn't know what he was up to, but she was suspicious—you know how we have a sixth sense sometimes? And girl, his wife followed him one day and confronted him at his other house in front of his other wife! Then he tried to play her off like she was delusional! It was crazy!"

"Well, he's not my man, so there's no need for me to take it that far, but you never know what really goes on in people's lives."

"You like him, though, and I can see why—he's a cutie, in a dorky kind of way. And he seems like a nice guy, from what you tell me. Plus, he's almost forty years old and doesn't have any kids? By definition, he's actually a mythical creature."

That's why, after walking alone for three days in a row even though his car is parked in the driveway, I give him a call. Just one, and no text. He doesn't answer, so I convince myself to let it go. But I start feeling guilty about jumping to conclusions, and I pray he isn't sick or hurt. Living alone like that, he could have fallen in the shower, and who would know?

On the next day, I can see signs of life at his house: a porch light that is on in the morning is off in the afternoon and on again in the evening, the recycling bin is at the curb, a pizza delivery car idles in the driveway just as I'm getting ready for bed. It's almost 10:30 at night, and yes, I did stand there, watching through the kitchen window to see if he looks like he's near death when he opens the door to get the pizza.

But he doesn't come out to get the pizza. *She* comes out to get the pizza.

I'm over it. No, I'm pissed. I shouldn't be mad, I know, because we didn't have any commitments to each other. It's not like we're in a relationship, but we have grown closer. We really liked each other, at least I thought we did, and he had not once mentioned he was dating. We talk about everything. How could he have confided in me about the time he broke down and ordered a pair of men's Spanx to wear to a job interview, but fail to mention he likes to stay up late at night and order pizza with strange women?

If I say this isn't a punch in my gut, I'm a liar.

When the phone rings around lunchtime on the next day, and the caller ID says *neighbor glen*, I silence it. The subsequent voicemail, I ignore, and the after-work text message, I leave unopened.

CHAPTER SEVENTEEN

The scale has been stuck on 236 for a few weeks now, so I change my exercise routine and purchase a treadmill. It's not that I don't want to bump into Glen, but obviously the neighborhood walking isn't working anymore. From what I've been reading on my old friend, Derrick's Facebook and Instagram pages, it's normal to hit a plateau once your body gets accustomed to a particular routine.

Ruth always swore by the treadmill as long as she had her earbuds and her Motown music, so I adopt her habit.

Instead of listening to music, though, my preference is to peruse Facebook. I can prop my iPad up on the treadmill's small console and catch up on everyone's lives, to take my mind off the fact I still don't like to run.

I notice Derrick seems to be running around the same time as me on most days, according to his social media updates. Each time I step onto the treadmill, I tag his status update with a thumbs up and then I update my own status: *Cynthia Thomas is* feeling motivated *and* running.

Lately, he's tagging me on his posts, inviting me to a game of fitness cat and mouse: *@CynthiaThomas Catch me if you can.*

I follow the links on the pictures he posts to find the name of the app he's using to track his workouts. I download it before I step onto the treadmill and share my results on Facebook with a tag I know he'll see: *@ DerrickWoods Can you keep up?*

He replies with a selfie of his face, drenched in sweat, and I can tell from the background he's in the gym, judging by the mirrors and weightlifting equipment in the behind him.

I give his picture a thumbs up and comment: *you're not running today?*

In moments, a direct message pops up in the lower right corner of the screen accompanied by a thumbnail picture of Derrick.

Derrick: *why? Did you miss me?*

I wait exactly fourteen minutes before I respond

Me: *I almost missed your message; I was too busy crushing my workout.* 😃

Derrick: *somebody's feeling pretty cocky! You wouldn't be so confident if we were working out in person.* 😉

His grade-school threat makes me laugh out loud, and I send him a reply:

Me: *is that a challenge? ain't nothing between us but space and opportunity.*

Derrick: 😆 😆 😆 😆 😆 *don't let your mouth write a check your a** can't cash! Lol!*

Me: *lol! Just name the time and place. I can show you better than I can tell you!*

Derrick: *how about two weeks from Saturday?*

Me: *what about it?*

Derrick: *I'll be in town for a youth football clinic and I was thinking maybe we could hook up.*

First of all, I don't "hook up" so I definitely need to clarify that for him. And secondly— more importantly— I'm not ready to see him. Yes, I have lost fifty pounds, but there are still lots of lumps and bumps I'm not proud of yet. I'm not ready to be around someone who's preaching the health-conscious jargon all day: eat this, not that; low carb, high protein; vegan this, organic that; shred, burn, cleanse, juice.

Me: *what're you trying to do, challenge me to a foot race or something? Lol! Aren't we a little old for that?*

Derrick: *lol! No I don't want to race you. I know you're grown and sexy now. I was thinking I could take you out to dinner or something while I'm in town.*

Me: *When will you be here?*

Derrick: *I fly in on the 16th and the camp is the morning of the 17th. Maybe we can meet for an early dinner after the camp. I fly out early the next morning.*

I catch a glimpse of myself in the mirror next to my treadmill. My chicken wing arms still jiggle and my backfat rolls form deep creases above my butt. I increase the incline and intensity settings on the treadmill and wonder how much weight can I lose before he gets here.

He messages me again, and the sound of the notification interrupts my self-evaluation.

Derrick: *no reply? If you already have a date or something, I understand.*

Me: *Lol! I was just finishing my last sprint on the treadmill! Dinner with you sounds nice. Just let me know the time.*

I spend the next two weeks trying to make the best of a smoothie cleanse I found online. The day before Derrick is to arrive in town, the scale is still stuck at 236, so I give up on the smoothies and go to the mall to buy a pair of Spanx. It's the only way I can think to tighten up the sagging places so I can appear as trim as possible in my jeans. I also pick up a cute pair of boots, a casual V-neck tee shirt, a tailored blazer, and a new pair of earrings.

I might not be the skinniest girl in town, but I'm almost back to where I was when Ruth passed, and it's been a long time since I've been out with someone as athletic as Derrick.

Ordinarily, I might think he's a little out of my league, but I've known him long enough to still consider him an old friend. Seeing him again will be nice, and it'll be good to be taken out on a date by someone who actually wants to be in my company.

When the doorbell rings and I open it to see the delivery guy from the local florist standing there holding a funeral spray, my breath catches in my throat.

"...have a delivery here for..." He cranes his neck around to read the name on the card. "Cynthia Thomas?"

Mama, who had been watching TV in the den, has wheeled herself out into the hallway to see who was at the door. "Cent? Who done died?"

"Nobody, Mama. It's for me." I mumble this as I nod a *thank you* to the delivery guy, juggle the awkward floral arrangement, and push the door closed with my foot.

"He don't have to slam my door like that!" Mama wheels herself closer to inspect the delivery.

"He didn't slam your door. I closed it." I can barely finish my sentence as I lay the flowers on the coffee table in the front room and pluck the card from the toothpick holder. It's no surprise Victor's is sending me flowers— narcissists will do anything to get your attention if you ignore them—but his taste has definitely slipped.

The flowers he'd bought when we spent the night at the resort were much more appropriate, but I guess he must have ordered these online, and maybe he couldn't really tell what kind of arrangement he'd chosen. I'm still pissed at him, and I did make a vow to cut him out of my life, but what can I say? I'm a sucker for flowers.

I slip the card out of the envelope and try to read it privately, although Mama has literally wheeled her chair so close to me her foot rest has bumped into my shins.

Just a little something to keep a smile on your face until I see you tonight. ~Derrick

"...I said, who died? And why they sending the arrangement to my house? The Lord ain't signed my name yet!" Mama's voice rambles along, creating a soundtrack for my reeling thoughts.

Derrick? Derrick. A funeral spray? Funeral flowers. Surely, he could have selected a simple bouquet of... anything! Tulips. Roses. What can be easier than roses? I'm irked with myself for thinking the flowers could have possibly been from Victor in the first place.

"Mama, nobody died. I have a date tonight with an old friend from school and I guess he just wanted to send me something nice. It's a sweet gesture."

Mama studies the bundle of flowers for a second, lets out a judgmental humph and wheels herself back into the den.

Stuffing the card into my back pocket, I study the flowers as they lay on the coffee table and try to find the good in the situation. It's sweet, but it creeps me out, looking like we're about to have a sitting up right here in the front room.

In an instant, I have an idea. I search through the kitchen cabinets, find a vase, and get to work dismantling the floral arrangement. I rearrange the flowers in the vase and step back to assess my work. Satisfied with my work, I take a picture of the new arrangement with my phone and send it to Derrick.

Me: *so beautiful! Thank you! I love them!*

Derrick: *Don't thank me. You deserve flowers every day.*

Derrick: *that doesn't look like the arrangement I picked out though.* 😬. *Glad you like them.*

We end up at the local soul food spot for dinner, but it wasn't my choice. I'd suggested some other options: a new vegan restaurant that offers a full menu of raw and fresh foods and juices, a Thai restaurant known for the best lettuce wraps and curries, or a clean eating spot that creates custom meals for the local high protein-low carb-organic-only foodies.

Derrick: *Where do we have to go to get some real food around here?*

I stare at the text message he'd sent me and tried to figure out what he meant. Real food? That's what I was trying to give him. I was at a loss as to how to meet his expectations.

Cynthia: *What's your idea of real food?*

Derrick: *it's my cheat day, so...* 😺

Cynthia: *I'll meet you at Burtons. Do you remember where that is?*

Derrick: 😆 *I haven't been gone long enough to forget about Burtons.*

Derrick: *they don't have food like that up in Canada.*

Cynthia: 😆 *Maybe you should come home more often.*

Derrick: *why? Are you gonna cook 4 me?*

Cynthia: 😑 *Nope. But I'll make sure you don't eat alone at Burtons.* 😆

Derrick: *lol! I hate eating alone. I'll see you there at 7?*

Cynthia: *sounds good! See you soon!*

Clicking the phone off, I wander into the bathroom and spend a few moments studying my skin, hair, and belly before treating myself to a long, hot shower. A night out and dinner with a handsome man is exactly what I need.

Chapter Eighteen

Burtons has always been a lively, bustling, turn sideways to squeeze between the tables type of establishment. As well-known for their fried croaker as they are for their legendary sweet tea, it's the kind of place you send out-of-towners when they're only here for one night and want to know where to get the best meal.

If this is where Derrick wants to spend his cheat day, I can't really blame him, but I have the kind of arrangement with my Spanx and jeans that will require me to refrain from ordering any of the usual stuff. Maybe Derrick is the kind of guy who can eat whatever he wants tonight and sweat it all out tomorrow, but I know my body better than that-- it's not so easy for me.

At the hostess stand near the front of the restaurant, I scan the dining room for him. Although the place is full, a big football player should stand out easily enough, but I don't see him.

Just as I pull out my phone to call him, a hefty man extracts himself from a booth near the back and waves at me. The beautiful, white smile with the small gap between the two front teeth, I recognize immediately--

the neck rolls, additional chins, and jiggling beer belly, I do not.

By the time I've moved within arm's reach of the table, he's grabbed me and pulled me into a smothering bear hug.

"Derrick?" I can't free myself from his robust embrace, so I turn my head to the left, just enough to speak without smearing my lipstick on his shoulder.

Releasing me from the hug, he grabs my hands and holds me away so he can look at me.

"Dang, girl! You looking *good*." Instantly, the moist heat from his fat fingers makes me feel clammy.

I laugh and shrug my shoulders, unable to return the compliment. He looks like himself, and yet, he doesn't look anything like the pictures he's posted online.

Even as I try to erase the shock that must surely show on my face, he seems to be oblivious. He ushers me into the booth, carefully squeezes himself into the space across from me, and smiles. I hold my breath as he scoots the cheap wooden table towards me a little more to make room for himself, opposite me.

"Cynthia! Man! You really look nice. You dropped a lot of weight. Not that you needed to lose any weight because I always thought you were fine. But you know…" he shrugs and pats his belly. "I know how hard it can be to lose weight. What do the old folks always say? I'm still a work in progress."

I watch him for a moment. He's so sincere and sweet. He's still such a cute man if you ignore the many chins and mountainous belly.

"Derrick, we're all works in progress. The work is never done."

He smiles at me again. Our connection feels vaguely familiar, but I still feel as though I'm seeing the man in front of me for the first time.

Our server appears with a small basket of hush puppies, cornbread, and honey butter. Burtons has perfected the craft of hush puppy and cornbread making like none other. Just from looking at the basket, I can see the crust is the perfect combination of crispy and crunchy. The oil is still glistening in the nooks and crannies of the bread, and I know when the bread is broken open, a soft and sweet steam is guaranteed to rush out as the honey butter is slathered from edge to edge. It's impossible not to salivate, but I put my hands in my lap and fight the temptation to touch the bread.

"Y'all know what you gonna be having tonight?" The young waitress stands, waiting for our order but she doesn't have a notepad or a pen, so I wait. She glances from Derrick to me, and as neither of us volunteers to go first, she selects me. "What can I get you, babe?"

"I'll have the grilled chicken tenders salad, no cheese, no croutons, and the vinaigrette on the side."

She nods. "That it?"

"Aren't you going to write it down?"

She taps the side of her forehead. "I've got it right here, don't worry." She glances at Derrick again. "What you having, big fella?"

Instantly, I'm embarrassed, but he just smiles like a giant panda bear and flips the menu over, stabbing his chunky finger into the center of the page.

"Give me that Admiral's Platter with fries and…a loaded baked potato. Extra cheese. Extra bacon." He smiles at me. "Potatoes are vegetables, so don't judge me."

The waitress looks at me again. "You want me to bring you an extra plate so you can share? The Admiral's platter is enough for two people."

I haven't even formed my lips to the word 'no' when Derrick speaks up, jokingly but something about the way he says it bothers me, "Share? I'm not sharing with her! She could have ordered her own platter, but no...she wanted a *salad*." He waves his hands in my direction like I have the cooties, and I'm not amused. Neither is the waitress, who says something sympathetic to me with her eyes before turning to walk away.

"So, you're completely off the wagon, huh?" I ask this because there's no way I'm going to ignore the glaring conflict between his online persona and the man currently sitting across from me.

He's in the process of grabbing a handful of hush puppies from the basket, knocking a few onto the table in his haste.

"Come on, now. I told you, it's my cheat day. This is supposed to be a judgment-free zone." He plucks the stray hush puppies from the table and tosses them into his mouth.

I raise a brow. "You ate off the table? Do you know what kind of germs…"

"Oh no! You still bougie, huh? You were always kind of 'can't touch this, don't touch that'…unless we were behind closed doors." He winks at me and I remember our high school days. They weren't all that.

"I'm not bougie. I work in a hospital and I don't have time to be getting sick off all the germs people are spreading around."

"You told me you some kind of secretary." He looks at me quizzically, his tone is as though he's caught me in a lie.

"I run the insurance verification component of the hospital's back office team. So no, I'm not *some kind of secretary*. I work in an environment where I'm exposed to all sorts of germs and I know something about disease transmission. Also, you don't have to be the head of the Centers for Disease Control to know you need to wash your hands before you put food in your mouth and not eat off this nasty table that's been touched by everyone in Savannah."

He tosses the last hush puppy into the air and catches it with his mouth, chews it for a moment and then grins at me. "You still feisty, I see. It's cool. That's one of the things I always liked about you. I love me a spicy, southern, bougie woman. You can't find women like that up in Canada."

I laugh out loud and wonder to myself: *what am I doing, sitting in front of this clown?*

Our server appears, balancing five hot plates on her arms. She holds my salad in her barely-free hand.

Once she's placed the salad in front of me and five platters of various sizes in front of Derrick, she waits to see if we need anything else. Derrick has a grocery list: Ketchup, hot sauce, ranch dressing, extra sour cream, a cup of ice, and another sweet tea.

As though he's eating alone, he begins consuming his meal, shoveling fries and shrimp and fried oysters into his face at a frenzied pace. I lean back in my seat to observe, my attitude oscillating between disgust and intrigue. Mid-gobble, he lifts his eyes to meet mine. "You're not eating? Don't tell me you're one of those females who doesn't like to eat in front of a guy." He narrows his eyes. "I know you can eat."

I allow a long pause to hover over the table before waving the waitress down and motioning for a take-out box. I return my attention to Derrick. "So what brought you back down South? Seems like you could have put together a football clinic somewhere a little closer to Canada."

He licks the French fry salt from every, single one of the fingers on his right hand before replying. "Well, I'm thinking of moving back home. I mean, my mama needs my help around the house and I always planned to come back and help out in the community. One of my line brothers is putting a good word in for me at the middle school. They've been looking for an offensive coordinator assistant and I wouldn't mind doing something like that. I love working with kids."

"You want to move back down here to be an assistant coach at the middle school? It seems like you'd be moving your career backwards instead of forward. And what about all of the personal training and big things you were doing up there with the CFL?"

He pulls the straw from his cup and begins chewing it like a teething ring. "That's the thing: it was cool, but I got tired of the politics and favoritism. It's just like the NFL, it's all about who you know and who owes you a favor. If you rub someone the wrong way, you can't get ahead in the league. I just didn't want to put up with it anymore. I'm too old for the games."

He flips the straw over and gnaws the opposite end. I cross my legs and bounce one foot gently, remembering when we were kids, he always chewed on something when he lied.

"Plus, I'm looking forward to spending more time with you. My goal is to start a nonprofit youth football organization down here and, I don't know, just see where things lead me."

He shovels a fistful of ranch-drenched French fries into his mouth, drains the last of the sweet tea, and waves the empty glass in the waitress's direction, signaling for more. Watching him, I have to suppress the urge to gag.

"You got fired, didn't you?" I hadn't meant to blurt the question out without softening the edges first, but it happened.

A long and uncomfortable pause stretches between us, heightening the sounds of the bustling restaurant around us. The waitress appears with my take-out box and a pitcher of sweet tea, but fills Derricks glass in silence, as though she can sense the level of tension at our table.

When she leaves, he grabs the bottle of hot sauce, douses the fried fish on his platter and pops it into his mouth before straightening his back to address me.

"No." The tone of his voice is thin and defensive. "Ain't nobody got fired. It was a mutual decision."

I slide my salad into the Styrofoam container and wave off his excuse. "Nah, brother, them people let you go. I don't know what happened, but something went down. They let you go, and you're depressed. Fried food? Sweet tea? Carbs? Come on, now. I can spot an emotional eater from a mile away."

I laugh as I nudge the empty hush puppy basket closer to him. If there was any hint of a spark between us prior to today, it has been thoroughly extinguished—at least from my perspective. Without any sexual tension between us, it feels good to joke with an old friend, except he doesn't laugh at all.

Instead, he cracks a hard smile and swirls a piece of fish in a pool of ranch dressing. "And that's why females like you are single. Instead of supporting and encouraging a man, you want to crack jokes and put him down." He won't even look at me, but he continues. "Yeah, I'm going through something. I know I'm not where I need to be, but I'll figure it out."

"So, you just walked out?" Julene is laugh-crying into the phone, peppering my commentary on the date with her own hysterical adlibs. "You just got up and left the table? You dropped the mic. Exit stage left." She can barely breathe.

"Yeah, I left. I had already boxed up my salad. I lost my appetite just from watching him eat. And he was already on thin ice, calling me bougie and talking about '*I know you can eat…*' Okay, that's bad enough! But when he started lying to my face about what happened to him in Canada and then he made that comment about '*that's why females like you are single?*' I was so done."

Julene is cracking up. "But did you at least tell him he sent you funeral flowers?" She cracks up laughing again, her words getting chopped up as though a DJ is remixing them.

I can't help but laugh with her. She's the first person I called when I walked out of the restaurant. I'd been so angry at first, but now, rehashing the evening's events with my best friend, the whole fiasco seems more comical and less disastrous.

At least the laughter can keep the monsters at bay for a little while—the monsters who live in the pit of my stomach, gnawing at my insides, reminding me that I might be single forever and never get to be someone's lady or someone's Mommy. They're like the monsters who lived under the bed when I was a little girl. They stayed hidden as long as it was daytime and as long as my daddy stood in the doorway of my room with the light on. They crept out of the shadows as soon as he kissed me goodnight, clicked off the light, and left me alone in my room.

It feels good to laugh with Julene about the funeral flowers, the big man in the little restaurant, the table hush puppies, the straw-chewing, the mic-dropping—for the moment. The monsters will wait patiently, though, and I'll have to deal with them as soon as I hang up the phone.

Once I'm home, I feel… relieved. The date with Derrick was terrible, but somehow, I'm not personally offended. Had this occurred with Victor, I'd have come home wondering what I'd done wrong or I'd be kicking myself for being so outspoken. But it was Derrick, not Victor, and I know for sure, the problem definitely wasn't me.

When I peek into Mama's room, she's sleeping soundly, and I'm grateful to have the rest of the evening to myself.

I peel myself out of my Spanx and shower again even though I had one before I left to meet Derrick, just

to wash away the restaurant smells, and curl up on the
couch to watch a movie.

CHAPTER NINETEEN

When Monday rolls around, I've reset my intentions for the week and put in a full day of work. Afterwards, I drive to the gym to try a Zumba class, but quickly realize I'll need a sturdier sports bra for such a high impact workout. It's already past dinner time when the class ends, and I head home.

The moment I turn onto my street, I see Glen. Actually, I see him even before I turn onto my street. He's standing at the corner, near the stop sign, waiting to cross, but pauses to wave at me when he notices my car.

I avoid coming to a complete stop at the corner, hoping to avoid making eye contact with him, so I slow down to a roll and turn my car towards home. I can see him in the periphery, waving and smiling as though I might stop—too goofy to know I've cut him off.

I don't know why it bothers me so much—him entertaining other women in his home. I'm old enough to know any man can be a dog, but he still surprised me. Maybe it's because he comes off as sort of dorky—no swagger, no slick-talk—he's the opposite of suave. I guess I just figured he wasn't cool enough to handle multiple women the way Victor could. Truth be told, that's sort of why I gave him a chance— thought I'd try a nice guy for once.

At least I've learned to spot a player and immediately excuse myself from his team. I'm getting better at being the first to say goodbye. I'd wasted too much time on Victor, Glen had caught me off guard, and Derrick never stood a chance. I'm still single, but I'm giving myself some credit for being a little wiser, too.

The house is pitch black inside, but for the blue glow illuminating the edges of Mama's half-open bedroom door. The light from her tv travels down the hall towards the front room where it simply fades to black. Words like 'baby mama,' 'rent,' 'agreement,' 'car,' 'property,' and 'loan' drift down the hall and I know she's watching one of her judge shows again.

"Ma! Why are you sitting up in here in the dark?" I toss the question down the bluish hall, only half-expecting a response, knowing she tends to fall asleep in front of the TV.

I click on the front room lamp and drop my bags on the armchair. The girls at work teased me today about all my bags—my work bag, my purse, my lunch bag, and my gym bag. I smile to myself, thinking of how they'd started calling me Bag Lady—teasing me about how my bags would slow me down and cause me to miss my bus. It was a throwback to an old song about a lady with too much baggage—a metaphor for the emotional baggage we all carry on our daily journeys. Maybe I do have too much baggage…

"Turn that light off in there! Why you come home and just turn on all the lights? That's why the light bill is always so high! You trying to light up the whole neighborhood?" Mama is awake.

I click the lamp off and walk down the dark hall to her room.

"Hey Ma." I place perfunctory kisses on both of her cheeks and return to the doorway. From there, I can see a plastic tray on her nightstand and I deduce she's eaten a Lean Cuisine recently. "Did you eat anything?" I ask her this anyway because I know she'll throw it in my face later if I don't.

"Yeah, if you can call it that. Tastes like some old mush from a nursing home. I shouldn't have to eat no nursing home food at my own house."

"You shower?" Her room smells fresh and she has on a different nightgown than the one she was wearing when I left this morning—but again, I have to ask.

"Well yeah I showered. I waited for you to help me, but looks like you didn't make no effort to get home on time so I had to do it myself. Could've broke my neck trying to get in and out of there! And who was going to help me? You didn't get here until late!"

Exhale. No conversation is easy with this lady. "Mama, you know the doctor wanted you to try the frozen meals because you can fix them yourself and you don't have to worry about portion control."

"Well, Hell! The little portions they give you don't amount to nothing!"

"And the occupational therapist made sure you had everything you need to get in and out of the shower safely. Plus, she wants you to continue doing these things for yourself because you are able."

"Them people don't know what I'm able to do! Only the Lord knows and He's my doctor. When He says it's time for me to…"

I drift out of her room, leaving her to rant and ramble on her own.

Then I move as quietly as I can through the dark house and into my room. I click on my bedside lamp and light a coconut-scented candle. No sooner than I can blow out the match, I hear the faint sounds of mama fussing from down the hall, almost certainly complaining about the smell of something burning. Before I can respond to her, my phone makes the water droplet sound and the screen illuminates.

Glen: *U up?*

He has got to be kidding. I haven't spoken to him since he left for his so-called "work trip." I frown as another text comes through.

Glen: *how come we live across the street from each other and haven't spoken in two weeks?* 😵‍💫

I flip my phone over so it's face down on my bed and grab the iPad. It's my turn on the word game I started earlier, and I study the available letters, trying a few different combinations. My phone chimes like a water droplet and a silhouette of light appears between the phone screen and the duvet cover. I flip it over, peeking at the message preview, careful not to actually open it.

Glen: *i see ur light on.* 😀

I power the phone off, and then, as an afterthought, click my lamp off, too.

CHAPTER TWENTY

I went to the doctor today." I'm on the phone with Julene while I lie on my bed, scrolling through Weight Watchers recipes on my iPad.

"I know! I remembered you had it scheduled for today. Didn't you see I called you earlier?" Her voice is muffled and I can hear the faint sounds of dishes clattering and children babbling in the background.

"The doctor was walking into the room with me when you called so I couldn't answer." I save a few recipes to my virtual recipe box as I speak.

"The call went straight to voicemail, so I figured you would call me back." The sound of dishes and children fades away and then a door slams. Her voice takes on a familiar echo that lets me know she has locked herself in the bathroom. "Okay, so let's start over: how did your appointment go today?"

I grab the remote control and click up the volume a notch just in case Mama is within ear's reach. "Well, she confirmed my hormone levels are too low, which means my egg count is also low. She checked for a hormone called AMH, which helps her to estimate how many egg follicles are in my ovaries. She said you're only born with a certain number of eggs—that's all of the eggs that you'll have in your lifetime."

"Mmhmm."

"She also said the whole process of conception is like an equation: you need enough eggs, your ovaries need to function properly so the eggs can mature, and the quality of the eggs needs to be decent. She wants to refer me to an infertility specialist for more testing when my cycle starts again."

Julene goes into Primary Care Physician Mode and it crosses my mind that she would have made a fantastic doctor. "Okay and is your cycle regular? Do you know when it starts again?"

"It's getting better, but I wouldn't say regular. It's been a little more consistent since I started getting back on track with my workouts."

She's quiet, listening, so I continue.

"The thing is, my AMH level is dropping. She told me it's dropped six points since last year."

"Okay…hmm. So, your hormone levels are down. That means the number of viable eggs is dropping faster." She pauses, processing my information as though I were her actual patient. "But we already knew that. Isn't that what she told you the first time? Tell Dr. Gandhi, we ain't paying her to tell us what we already know! What's the solution?"

"Well, that's why she wants me to get to a specialist— to figure out what can be done."

Julene makes a sound I can only assume signifies her understanding.

"She said it's up to me if I want to do it now or if I want to wait until I get married or whatever. She did say it's amazing how many mature women come into her office wanting to explore artificial insemination like it's no big deal."

"I think that's probably true. There are probably a lot of women who are interested in it, but it's obviously such a sensitive subject, you're not going to hear about it all the time. Who would run around telling everyone they're going to pay to get pregnant? The decision is so personal, you might hear about it on TV or something, but not from anyone we would know personally or socially. But, please believe, they're doing it or at least strongly considering it, even if they don't tell you."

She's warming up, which means it's my turn to listen. "Mmhmm."

"Don't you remember when it was taboo to talk about getting a boob job? Nowadays, people are openly getting boobs and butts and lips and lashes—and it's no longer a secret. It's just a matter of time before DIY babies become the norm!"

She's laughing and it makes this entire conversation a little less weird.

After a moment, she's back on track. "Do you like her as a doctor?"

I think about her question for a second. "I do. She's very straightforward with me. She did tell me I need to lose some more weight."

I can hear her exhale. "But that was already part of the treatment plan. We already knew that."

"Yeah. I know. She just wanted me to understand the miscarriage rate is higher with obese women, and I'm like 'I know, I know.'"

"Sis, if that's what it takes to reach your goal, then set your mind to it and stick with it."

Now, I'm the one to exhale. "What the mind can conceive, the mind can achieve, I read the same book as you." I try to laugh afterwards, because I know I sounded sarcastic, but she doesn't join me, so I move on.

"It's crazy. When I was younger, I never would have thought I would be in this position. I spent all my time trying not to get pregnant, and now, I'm hoping I'm able to get pregnant."

The toilet flushes and I can hear water running in the sink, then the sound of a door opening and closing. I can tell she's covering the phone while she says something to someone in the background and then she returns to our conversation. "It might sound crazy when you think of it like that. But, at the end of the day, it's science, you know what I mean? It's not about feelings or ideas. This is just how the human body works and this is where you are in your life."

"Right. My numbers are my numbers, I guess."

"That's should be comforting because you're a person who likes the facts. You like stuff that makes sense. You're a person who can come to your own decision when you have the proper information. You just need the team that's going to help you map it out."

I give her words some thought. She knows me so well, it's as though we've been friends for much longer than we really have. "You're probably right. But I keep asking myself, is this my plan, or am I trying to play God?"

"Who really knows? Maybe you're just trying to come to terms and get comfortable with what you've decided.

And if you believe whatever you're doing is God's will, then what's the problem? I mean, wait—have you prayed about this?"

And there it is. I sigh as though it's possible to deflate myself, and then I answer honestly. "Not yet, I haven't. I won't lie and say I did."

I listen for any hint of judgement in Julene's voice. There is none, and I'm thankful. "So, if you haven't prayed, then start there."

"You're right. I'm getting ahead of myself."

The ambient sounds of Julene's life fade away again and I wait while she finds a quiet place to talk.

"There's something about faith that can be a little confusing. At least for someone like me who just started studying the Word. On one hand, you're supposed to ask God what His will is and listen and do what He would have you to do. On the other hand, if you want something, you're supposed to ask for it, and you're supposed trust Him to provide it. I don't know exactly how to reconcile that, but I would say if you have not prayed and asked him to show you what to do, then you can at least pray and ask for what you want. If you haven't done either, then you're in trouble!"

She laughs at herself, and I laugh, too, for a second, and then she's back to business. "We're laughing, but seriously, if you haven't taken this issue to the altar then you're just really out there, hustling on your own. You need to ask Him for guidance or ask Him for what you want, and then you'll know what direction to take. Who knows? That could change everything."

"You're right. I've been going to doctors and searching the internet, and you asked a very simple question: Did you pray? Ugh! What am I doing?"

"Girl, you're just doing the same thing we all do. I've lived my whole life trying to figure everything out for myself. I mean, I love the Lord, I feel like I'm open to Him, and I'm thankful, but I know I don't actually take the time to stop and literally ask, pray, or listen as often as I should. I just be going through life and hoping I catch the sign as I go along."

When we hang up, I call Dr. Stovall, the infertility specialist Dr. Gandhi recommended, and schedule an appointment.

CHAPTER TWENTY-ONE

Months later, as I step out of the house, heading to work, I'm dumbfounded by the sight of Glen walking down the street with a very pregnant woman. I get into my car but sit in the driveway, watching them in my rear-view mirror, trying to read their body language, wondering when this could have happened.

I haven't bothered speaking to him in a while, it's true, but—wow. Pregnant? Meanwhile, I'm sitting over here, watching TV with my mama as my little eggs dwindle down to nothing.

When I see them disappear into the house, I shift my car into reverse and try to make a quick getaway, but I slam on the brakes when it feels as though I've run over a boulder in the driveway. Stepping out of the car, I immediately recognize the problem: a flat tire. I stand there for a moment, wanting to just turn around and go back into the house, climb in bed, and pull the covers over my head. But the flat tire won't fix itself, so I pop the trunk and get to work trying to change it. I've never done it, but I've seen it done before, and it doesn't look that hard. You just put the jack under the car and crank the handle until the tire lifts off the ground. Then you unscrew the lug nuts and pull off the bad tire, replace it with the spare and screw it back on.

Here's what I find out: they only give you a short little metal stick to wind the jack up. There's no way to do it without literally getting down on the ground, and there's no way I'm getting down on this filthy ground. However, the cramp I catch in my thighs from trying to squat down to tire-level without actually touching the ground causes me to panic and jump back up before I can even turn the little-handled jack one full rotation.

I'm bracing myself against the side of my car, trying to rub the burning sensation from my thighs when Glen appears at the bottom of the driveway. I hadn't even seen him cross the street.

"Why are you out here trying to change a tire by yourself?" He squats down and runs his hand across the tread—that's when I glimpse the ring on his finger. His hand disappears into the wheel well, and he looks up at me. "I can feel something stuck in the tire. You probably had a slow leak."

There's a lump in my throat, and I swallow hard. "That's what I figured. I'm trying to call roadside assistance right now," I mumble as I look around for my phone.

He scans the area around my car, taking note of the abandoned jack, the lug wrench, the spare tire and smiles at me. "Girl, quit trying to be so independent. Let me help you! I can have the spare on in two minutes, I'll put the bad tire in your trunk, and you can just stop by the tire shop up the road to get it patched." He pauses and glances back towards his house. "Nope. You don't even have to do that. I'll get it done for you and I can put it back on when you get home this evening."

As sweet as his offer is, as willing as he is to help, the whole scenario is causing me pain. I just want him to leave. "Don't you need to get home to your wife and baby?"

He is undisturbed by my sarcasm. Instead, he holds up his left hand and wags his fingers. "Ain't no ring on this finger! Anyway, I told her I was coming over here to help you. As a matter of fact, she's the one who saw you out here trying to change the tire, and she asked me to come over and help you. What kind of man would sit here and watch a single woman change her own tire?"

I blink my eyes, wondering what I'd seen to make me think there was a ring on his finger. It doesn't matter much. With or without a ring, I don't care if she's the wife or the Baby Mama—I don't need someone else's man coming to my rescue.

Though I would protest, I need to get to work, and I'd rather have Glen's help than God-Knows-Who from roadside assistance, so I step back and allow him to take over.

Working quietly for a moment, he finally asks, "Why did you shut me down? You went stone cold on me."

I attempt to answer as lightly as I can, hoping he can't hear the disappointment in my voice. "You had a lot going on over there. There were always cars coming and going, and I know you work a lot, but you didn't even bother to call me when you were in town."

His mouth opens and closes, but I can't read his expression. If he's going to try and lie his way out of it, I won't give him the chance. I continue, "I can see your house from here. I could see when you were home. I could see when you had company. I just didn't want to compete with anyone else for your time."

His facial expressions run the gamut in real time: confusion, surprise, and then realization. "I wasn't here! I do Airbnb when I'm out of town, just to keep a little extra money coming in. You thought…oh man! Dang, what kind of man do you take me for?"

He stands up and dusts his knees off, wipes his hands on his shirt. "I tried to reach out to you and you ignored me. Every man knows when he's been ghosted, so I took the hint and stopped bothering you." He turns to walk away but pauses to bring one more thing to my attention: "You know, I never lied to you. I liked you. You just never gave me a chance to tell you."

The day the stork appears in Glen's yard, I lay across the foot of Mama's bed to watch TV with her. I'm not necessarily interested in the TV program, I just don't want to be alone.

When the news goes off, she turns to a reality show about a family of deer hunters who've gone off the grid, living off the land, and supporting themselves by hunting. I prop myself up on my elbows and crane my neck in her direction. "When did you start watching this? Isn't it time for your judge show?"

"That idiot in the White House is going to send us all back in time! He's crazy! I figure we better start trying to learn how to live in the woods like these people.

Leave it to him, and we'll have no choice but to live in the wilderness."

I can't argue with her about politics. Instead, I roll over again to face the TV. After a few minutes of watching the father teach the son how to bait and kill the deer, I roll over again and face Mama. "Sometimes I feel like I'm the deer and men are the hunters. It seems unfair and I'm so tired of it."

For a second, I'm not sure if she heard me, but after taking a sip of her Arnold Palmer, she grabs the remote and turns the sound down a notch.

"The thing you need to know is this: sometimes in relationships, you will feel like the deer. You will feel like the man is the hunter and you are the prey. But don't forget God gives us the same survival instinct as the deer. The difference is the deer is much more observant and careful in the face of danger. If the deer sees something or hears the slightest sound, the deer gets out of there fast! Sometimes they don't make it, or the hunter sets a really good trap, but most times, the deer understands by instinct—when it's time to run, it's time to run!"

She pauses to sip her drink and swirl it around in her mouth in a way that typically irks my nerves before she continues, "Now, we as women have the same instinct, but tend to ignore it. It's called your gut." She pats her belly for emphasis. "The problem is, most of us don't know how to listen to it—or we're afraid to listen to it! We're human. We want to love and be loved, but at what cost?" She clicks on her bedside lamp and studies me. "You scared, girl."

I can't tell if she's asking a question or making a statement, but I shrug my shoulders and she continues.

"Yeah, that's the first thing-- you scared. Of what? Of being alone? Of not having babies? And then you gone let fear fool you into making desperate decisions, or spending time with some old rascal who just wants to hump everything he sees."

I sit up on the edge of her bed and turn to face her. "It's not…"

She interrupts me. "Oh! It's not like that? It's not that bad? You can look past his flaws? We all have flaws?" She raises an eyebrow. "Baby. I done been round this block a few times! I done seen all the games! I done seen nice and decent and beautiful woman go down in the dumps over a man who wasn't worth keeping." She smiles a little and it makes her look mysterious.

"Back in the day, I would go out with any guy who had a car. I loved those old cars—the muscle cars with the big engines—and I would accept a date with most anyone who could drive me around in one. I liked to eat too. So, take me on a drive and feed me—I'm yours for the afternoon, but I wouldn't put out!" She holds up her finger and wags it at me. "I wouldn't let no man use my body. If he couldn't just enjoy my company, then he could just hit the road Jack.

"And some of them did hit the road. They found out they couldn't get in my pants and they would move on to the next girl. Some of them even took to dating my friends." She pauses for a second and searches her memory. "I remember one girl—we grew up right next door to each other, went all through school together— she took to dating a boy I had let go." She smiles, the memory of her teenage drama coming back into focus after so many decades. "I just had a bad feeling about him, so I cut ties with him just like that!" She snaps her fingers to emphasize. "And she was right there, telling me how he wasn't no good and he was trying to court every girl in town. As soon as I let him go, she swooped in and cleaned up my leftovers." She chuckles to herself. "Problem was, he was exactly what she said he was. He was a womanizer and a manipulatizer. He would…"

"Ma…" I can't let that slide. She is forever making up words. "Mama, he was a what?"

"He was a manip—manapl—he knew how to get your head twisted around until you didn't know which way was up!"

"He was a manipulator." I offer the correct word.

"Well! Whatever you want to call it! The point is, he wasn't no good and he played with that girl's mind for so long until she couldn't even have kids by the time she unloosed herself from him! Some people said she was sterile because she had caught the Clap from him…"

I cringe at Mama's use of the term for a sexually transmitted disease, but I have questions. "The doctors couldn't do anything? She just gave up?"

Mama thought for a minute, considering my questions. "You mean, like, baby stimulation, or something?"

"Artificial insemination."

She doesn't care about the pronunciation. "Far as I know, nobody could afford that kind of stuff. If you couldn't pray about it, lay hands on it, or sprinkle some anointing oil over it, then it wasn't meant to be. Now, I can't say for sure if she really had the Clap, some people said she was just an old maid by then, just too old to make babies anymore, but that old dirty rascal of a man,

I heard tell he went and had five or six kids with some other girl from around town."

I pick at my manicure. "That's what bothers me about men. She wasted all her time on him and then missed her chance to have a family. It isn't fair. Men don't have a biological clock and they don't care about ours."

Mama takes another sip of her drink and raises an eyebrow at me. "Well that's the kind of wrong thinking that had her chasing him for all those years. Had she listened to her gut from the start, she wouldn't have wasted more than ten minutes on that sucker. Anybody could see he wasn't worth a squat! But also, there are lots of women who don't have children, well they don't have natural children, but they are still mothers. They are the Aunties and Godmothers—in the Black community, they are the shirro... sirro..." She glances at me, knowing I'm armed with the word she seeks. "Whatchu call it when somebody else has the baby but you raise it?"

"A surrogate."

"Well, yeah. In our community, just because you don't push the baby out, don't mean you're not a mother, and that's what happened to her. She ended up with an older guy—a guy with four children and his wife had passed away when the last baby was born. He needed a mother for those babies, and she needed some babies to mother. She ended up stepping into their lives—he was decent enough to marry her—and she was the best mother to those children! Always had them dressed to the nines, healthy, good manners, and active in church. That's all she ever wanted, and I believe she was happy after that. Might not have happened the way she thought, but it happened the way the Lord saw fit."

Mama's words give me something to reflect upon. For all her made-up words and orneriness, there are some nuggets of insight in there. What if the lady had listened to her gut and ditched the boyfriend from the start? Would she have married and had a chance to have babies? What would have happened to the older guy and motherless children if she hadn't been there? What if I had listened to my gut and chosen not to give my heart to Victor? How much time had I wasted? How would my story have turned out?

I lay on the foot of her bed and think about mama's story—her perspective. She had met and married my daddy at a young age by today's standards—she was twenty-three and he was twenty-six—but she'd had a string of miscarriages and hadn't given birth to me until she was thirty-six. Was she really so wise to marry him at such a young age? Or did she just get lucky? How could she have known he'd stick around during a time when the inability to conceive held such a stigma? My daddy was an amazing man.

"Mama. What did your gut tell you about Daddy?"

She doesn't answer right away and I roll over to see her expression. She's asleep, the remote dangling from her fingertips like a lit cigarette.

I ease myself off the bed and make my way to the door, hoping not to wake her.

Lying on my own bed eating popcorn-kernel sized bites of frozen, yogurt covered strawberries, and bananas, I try to convince myself they are as good as the Pinterest video had made them look. They're not good, though, and I can't convince myself otherwise.

Giving up on the snack, and not really hungry anyway, I slide the container onto my nightstand and lay staring at the ceiling, trying to image what kind of scene is taking place across the street. A new baby is in the house, probably fresh from a bath, smelling of baby lotion and milk. Glen has probably set up a portable crib in his home office, next to his desk so he can work at his computer and watch the baby while *she* tries to get some rest. Because, you know, the baby hasn't gotten on a good sleep schedule yet and was likely up all night, fussing and whining about whatever bothers newborn babies. *She's* keeping the baby clean, dry, and fed, while hoping Glen still finds her post-pregnancy body attractive.

I'm sure life with an infant and a new relationship isn't pretty or fun, but Lord, when will I have a chance to find out? Even in the chaos and stress of it all, it must be worth the trouble. When will it be *my* turn?

The weight of my breasts and the pressure in the lower part of my back signal that it's time to find a more comfortable position. I roll onto my left side and stare at the books lined up on my bedside shelf. The one I got from Ruth's home after she passed catches my eye—it's the first one we read as a group. More specifically, the slip of paper sticking from the top, serving as a bookmark, is what catches my attention.

I reach over, pull the book from the shelf, and open to the page she had marked. *Oh Lord, it smells like her.* I close my eyes for a second and breath in the barely-there scent of her perfume. Elixir. I still remember the name of her favorite fragrance.

Sitting on the floor next to my bed, I let the book fall open to the page that has been held by the bookmark for more than two years.

The chapter is all about fear. How fear can prevent us from attaining our goals and how fear shows up in our lives wearing various disguises.

Ruth had highlighted and underlined and circled most of the sentences in the chapter— surely for herself, though tonight, it seems to have been written just for me.

I don't *feel* afraid of anything—except maybe germs and bugs—but maybe I don't really know how to recognize fear any more than I can recognize a good and decent man. Somehow, Mama had taken one look at me and had seen it for herself.

And Ruth, in all her small and mighty strength, must've had the same realization on the day she had read this chapter. I had read it too, we all had, and these very same words were printed in my copy of the book—I just hadn't been able to receive it back then.

Tonight, I read it again, sitting on the floor of my room, propped against the side of my bed until my legs feel numb, no matter which way I turn. I sit there until I can hear Mama hollering from her room, wanting some random item from another room, until the sound of her requests dies down and is replaced by the voice of the TV preacher who comes on after all the regular shows go off.

When I awaken at some odd hour to find I have fallen asleep with the book still in my hands, I place the bookmark back in its place and sleep again—more soundly than I have in some time.

At work the next day, when I should be using my time to sift through piles of rejected insurance claims and the verification sheets my team couldn't figure out, I use sticky notes to copy down all the Ghosts of Fear listed in Ruth's book. Fear of criticism, poverty, growing old, loss of love… I write them all down.

Then, I use another batch of brightly colored sticky notes to list all the ways my fears show up in my life according to the book's definitions, and there are many:

1. Procrastination
2. Criticism of other people
3. Self-consciousness
4. Extravagance
5. Hypochondria
6. Experimenting with diets
7. Overspending
8. Inferiority complex
9. Indecision
10. Doubt

It's painful and embarrassing realizing so many of my issues have been spelled out in an old book in such a matter-of-fact manner. But here it is. Here *I* am and here's where Ruth saw herself. If I'm honest, aren't most of us snagged and bound by the web of fears that ensnare us, almost from birth?

Sitting back, I survey the sticky notes around me and realize these aren't merely bad habits. If Life is a buffet, these aren't the foods I can just avoid to lose weight. These aren't chips and French fries and queso and cake.

Some of these, most of these, are the threads that—woven together—make up the fabric of my very being. And how do you pull the bad threads out of the fabric without the whole outfit simply falling apart?

There was a church member once who had been diagnosed with breast cancer. It was a lump, technically, and she had been hopeful—we had all been hopeful— that, since it had been caught early, she could be cured with a simple lumpectomy. We expected the doctors to just take the lump out.

But the doctors, when they studied the breast tissues, found the lump had little fingers— stringy little cancerous fibers that had woven themselves all through the breast tissue. They could take out the lump, but the stringy pieces were invasive and far-reaching.

The unhealthy breast tissue had become so deeply intertwined with the healthy tissues, the doctors were unable to separate the good from the bad. To confidently eradicate the cancer, to get rid of all the cancerous little fibers, they'd have to remove the entire breast.

These fears of mine, these cancerous little fibers that have permeated my whole life, have defined me. Though they aren't pretty under this microscope and I know they need to be eliminated what will remain of me, if anything, when they are gone? Is it too late to separate the good from the bad?

This chapter, the one, in my opinion, that is the most profound, comprises the last few pages of the book. And it leaves me, as I flip the back cover closed, with more questions than answers, so I think for a moment, and I do the one thing that the book doesn't suggest.

I get down on my knees and pray.

But the Bible says 'prayer without works is dead." And that's why I bust out a fresh pack of sticky notes and get to work, listing the thoughts and actions that are the opposite of my current fears and symptoms. Because there's one common factor that I can see from my list of fears and symptoms: they are all conceived in my mind. Doubt, worry, superstition—I think them and I believe them, therefore they exist.

Stand back, ladies and gentlemen, I'm about to perform my first fear-ectomy.

It takes some time to adjust, but I adopt the habit of starting and ending my day with prayer, meditation, and exercise. I study my sticky notes, both positives and negatives, until I have most of them memorized.

I find a cute, zippered pouch at the Dollar Store and toss the stickies in there when I'm not reading them. Sometimes, I reach into the bag without looking, like I'm grabbing a raffle ticket, and I concentrate on selecting a positive one.

The Laws of Attraction say I will attract the right sticky, but that isn't my goal. Mainly, I'm practicing a habit that is essential for my happiness: believing in a positive outcome, making a decision, and taking action. There's no more reaching into the bag and feeling around blindly, hoping, but unsure if I'll choose the right card.

I'm getting better at fixing my mind on it, reaching in, grabbing the card I want, and *expecting* it to be great. Funny thing is, the pressure I once felt on my chest, that I always blamed on my heavy breasts, it doesn't bother me so much anymore.

CHAPTER TWENTY-TWO

The ribbons from the deflated balloons have wrapped themselves around the neck of the wooden stork in a bizarre fashion that makes me stop and stare— forgetting for the moment that I am running late for the Trustees meeting. No one would know the flaccid blobs hanging from the ends of the ribbons had once been buoyant and iridescent balloons had they not seen them the day that they were placed on Glen's front lawn.

The whole display should have been pulled from the yard after the first week—at the most. It's like leaving your Christmas decorations up after January 1st. It's become an eyesore that greets me every time I leave the house or return home.

It's a symptom, I guess, of the haggard life new parents live. Things start falling by the wayside—lawn maintenance, personal appearance, anything associated with the outside world—until the concept of caring for another human being can be mastered.

His house looks sad. To be fair, aside from the strangled, faded stork and scraggly lawn, it looks the same as it always has, but it makes me *feel* sad. I imagine the little family adjusting to life with the new baby, but I never see them, and I never see friends or family members stopping by to visit.

I know he doesn't have a big circle, but surely, *she* must. She must have girlfriends and coworkers, right? Besides the occasional movement of the car and a light on or off in one window or another, you'd barely know anyone lived there at all—much less a new family. I would think—although I can't say with certainty—that if it were me, the aura of joy would be far more evident around my home.

When I step outside, a police car pulls up and parks in Glen's driveway without flashing lights or sirens. It's a non-emergency, I deduce. When an unmarked car pulls alongside the curb in front of Glen's house, I stand in my driveway, staring blatantly. The front door of the house opens and closes, and the officers disappear inside.

As soon as I get into my car and reach for my seatbelt, my phone chimes with the tune of the water droplet and my mind snaps back to my present concerns. I'm late and don't have time to worry about my reclusive neighbors. Clicking my seatbelt on, I glance at my phone before starting the car.

Victor: *Wyd.*

I drop the phone in my lap as though it's on fire. I don't open the text message but I can gather more than enough information from the preview screen alone. Victor. I can hear his…

Another droplet sound and the phone vibrates in my lap.

Victor: *I miss you.* 😍

Another droplet and a picture of him, biting his lower lip, staring at me as though he can see through me.

And today, for the first time, as I take the time to look closely at his face, his eyes, his lip-biting swag, I have to ask myself:

What grown man randomly sends lip-biting pictures of himself to old female friends while he's disputing the paternity of a baby with another woman?

Today, it doesn't feel like flattery. It doesn't feel like we have a special connection. It feels like he's crazy as hell and it feels like he'll keep doing it as long as I entertain it-- and then he'll find someone else to manipulate. *Oh Lord why did I waste my time waiting for him to love me?*

Now, the phone rings and I almost decide to reject the call, when I realize the caller ID says Julene.

"Hello?"

"Where are you?" She gets right to the point.

I hold the ignition button down with my finger and shuffle the phone around a little, hoping to camouflage the sound of the car starting. "I'm on the way. Almost there."

I ease the car out of the driveway. Procrastination is the reason I'm running late today. I'm getting better with my issues. Not perfect, but better.

"Well don't waste your time! Nobody's here. I'm here, and Ms. Irene was here, but she said she couldn't stay. Ms. Emma Lee said she probably won't make it, either-- something about her grandkids."

I give the gas pedal a little more pressure. "No! We haven't had a meeting in so long! People can't just start picking and choosing when they want to show up. We made a pact."

"But *you're* not even here, so…" Julene laughs. "And I know you very well. If you say you're *on your way*, then it means you just pulled out of the driveway."

Slowly, I steer the car towards the curb in front of a neighbor's house, check my mirrors, and, seeing there are no cars coming, make a U-turn in the middle of the street and head home.

Pulling into the driveway, I can see the frame of Mama's glasses reflecting through the slats of the window shade in the front room window and I know she didn't expect me back home so soon. There's a commotion in our house, I imagine, because the space between the slats grows larger as I pull up to the house, and then the blinds close completely. The glasses disappear and the blinds swing towards the window pane and then away erratically by the time I step out of my car.

Mama.

I walk into the house and look around. There's a small bowl of Vienna sausages and saltine crackers on the sofa table near the window. Otherwise, the room appears to be untouched.

I grab the bowl of unauthorized snacks and walk towards her bedroom.

"Hey, Nosey. Since when did we start eating in the front room?"

She doesn't look at me. She just presses the buttons on the remote casually and tosses a flippant comment in my direction. "Ain't nobody been eating in no front room. I'm trying to watch my show."

I slide the food onto her bedside table and take my usual spot at the foot of her bed. "So, what's going on across the street?"

She drops the remote and perks up. "Well, it looks like that young gal done up and left your friend with the baby. She been gone for a few days, now, and this the second— no third! — this is the third time the police done been over to the house. I guess they trying to find her. Probably gone have to put her in a mental hospital or something if they find her. Cause I don't know *who*— what woman in her right mind would leave a precious, innocent baby like that? Unless you got post-parnaman or you by Polo. That's the only reason I can see."

I sit up too fast at the foot of the bed and feel a wave of vertigo. I don't even address her abuse of the words *postpartum* and *bipolar*.

"Mama, what are you talking about? I haven't seen any police over there, except for today."

"Baby, you just haven't been paying attention. Them folks been back and forth to that house, trying to find out where she went. Because she's his sister, you know, so…"

I jump to my feet, then, to face her directly to make sure she isn't spiraling into dementia. "Are you trying to tell me he had a baby with his *sister*?!" I'm thoroughly disgusted. What is *wrong* with every man I meet?

"Listen!" Mama hollers at me in the way you holler at a person who's gone temporarily insane, just before you slap them. Then she calms herself and visibly searches for enough patience to deal with me. Imagine that—*she's* frustrated with *me*.

"Okay," she speaks slower and more clearly, "he is not the daddy. The baby is his family—niece or nephew, I can't tell if it's a girl or a boy, seems like they don't have sense enough to dress a baby in pink or blue anymore— but he don't have no legal rights for that baby."

I sit down on the edge of the bed again. He never told me she was his sister. This is a nightmare. For him, I mean, and for the baby.

Mama rambles on about young girls having babies, about families sticking together, about how she'd been suspicious of the girl from the moment she'd arrived— but my head swims with this flood of information and I can barely hear her.

"...thought he would have at least come over and asked for some help. Don't no man know how to take care of no little baby by himself." Mama carries on, not really talking to me anymore, just musing out loud.

"Ma. How do you know all of this? You never leave the house."

She scoffs at me like I'm a simple-minded child. "I ain't got to go no further than the front porch to find out all I need to know. People talk and I can see and I can hear." She turns up the volume on the TV and that's my signal to leave.

I lace up my sneakers and walk across the street as soon as Mama tells me what she knows. Through the slender windows on the left and right sides of Glen's front door, I can see there are lights on in the rear of the house, even though the front room is dark. It isn't until I stand at the door, trying to decide between ringing the doorbell or knocking, that Doubt and Indecisiveness double-team me.

What am I doing here? What will I say when he opens the door? What if I wake the baby up and he can't get it to settle down? I turn around and go back home. I'm reminded daily that the tentacles of Fear seem to be tied to my very core. I'll get myself unloosed, but clearly, today isn't the day.

At home, I sit on my bedroom floor and meditate for a few minutes, to calm my breathing. *What are you afraid of, Cynthia?* I'm afraid of embarrassment. I'm ashamed of how easily I tossed aside a friend. I'm afraid he might have wanted to ask me for help but didn't trust me. I'm afraid of offering to help and being taken advantage of. I'm afraid I don't know how to give a little of myself without giving all I've got.

Now breathe. You can face your fears when you can call them all by name. Now, they hold less power, and you can take the focus off yourself. Because it's not about you, Cynthia, this one time, it's not all about you.

I pick up my phone, delete the string of inappropriate messages Victor has sent today, and text Glen:

Me: *What can I do to help?*

Bubbles, and more bubbles show he is responding. Then, finally:

Glen: *Ashamed to say I just need a shower. I'll pay you to babysit for 10 minutes.* 😬

I put my sneakers on again and make my way back to his house. As soon as I step inside, I'm assaulted by the burnt odor of a food I can't readily identify.

I mouth the words, *what's that smell?* because I don't want to wake the baby, if it's sleeping.

Glen laughs and says, "You don't have to whisper. She sleeps through anything." He points to an igloo-shaped contraption near the sofa. "But if I try to move her, she wakes up. I have to take a shower, but I can't move her to the bathroom because she cries. And I'm afraid to leave her out here in the living room alone while

I'm in the shower. Basically," he throws his arms up in bewilderment and I can smell his musky body odor; he's not just-left-the-gym-funky, but the shower is definitely overdue, "I'm afraid to let her out of my sight, so I don't know what I'm supposed to do."

He looks exhausted and I don't know what to say, so I try offering a smile. "New babies are a lot of work. It's definitely a learning…"

He cuts in, interrupting me, and I realize he probably hasn't spoken freely to anyone in a while—since his sister and the baby arrived. "And I'm so hungry! I don't want to leave her alone, but I ran in the kitchen to warm up a microwave dinner, and I left it in there too long and… well, you can smell the outcome."

I walk closer to him and push him in the direction of the bathroom. "Go. Go and shower and rest for a little while. I'll sit in here with—" I glance in the baby's direction. "What's her name?"

The stress literally melts from his face. His eyebrows relax and he looks more like himself. "Naomi." And then he grins. "I've been calling her NayNay." He throws one hand up in the air, feebly mimicking the corny dance of the same name.

I shoo him away with one hand and hold my nose with the other. "Shower. Please."

When he disappears around the corner, I tiptoe towards the igloo thing and peek inside. She's sleeping, but fitfully. Snoozing lightly and then jerking herself awake with her own flailing arms. She's scratched her face, I can see, because there are light brown feathery marks on her cheeks and chin. She smells like…she smells a little sour. I guess all babies aren't born smelling like lavender and powder.

Reaching in to take her out of the igloo, Glen's voice almost makes me pee myself. "Don't! I mean— well, you can try taking her out, but everything I've read online says not to pick her up too much. That's why I put this in there with her—" he reaches past me and feels around inside her blanket, pulling out an old iPhone. "I downloaded this White Noise for Babies app and it's supposed to calm the baby. It promotes self-soothing."

His face, so sweet and genuine, breaks my heart. He believes what he has read, I can tell. And he means well. He's trying, bless his heart.

I slap the iPhone right out of his hand. I know, I know. Rude. But…

"Boy, bye. This baby doesn't need an iPhone and an igloo! She needs a bath and some powder and gloves on her hands—she's scratching her face while she sleeps— and she needs human contact."

I hold my breath, preparing to be thrown out of the house because I keep doing the one thing that always infuriated Victor—trying to control everything—but he stands there for a moment, just looking at me. Then he tosses his hands up in surrender and cracks a soft smile. "Hey! I don't know this stuff! Do you know how long it's been since I was a baby? What can I say? Do your thang, Mama. Teach me."

He trots off to the bathroom.

Right away, I scoop Sour Nay-Nay up and take her to the kitchen. She's so tiny, I can lay her entire body in the space between my right breast and the crook of my neck. Holding her, it only takes a moment to clear out one side of the sink and fill it with warm water.

Searching the area near the igloo, I find an open Amazon box, filled with assorted baby-care items. There's a bottle of gentle baby wash, a package of baby wipes, lotion, and diaper cream.

I grab the baby wash and a pack of baby wipes and then head back into the kitchen.

When I ease Naomi into the warm water, she takes a deep breath and throws her tiny fists into the air, startled.

"It's okay, Little One," I whisper. "You stank." I wrinkle my nose and lean in closely while I work the wet baby wipe into the deep crevices under her chin. "You're a little lady. You can't be stank if you're a little lady."

She protests a bit, widening her eyes but probably not seeing anything, and kicking her legs alternately with her pumping fists.

I whisper to her again, all the while washing away the scent of sour milk from her fleshy rolls. "It's okay. I've got you. I won't let you float away, but I can't let you go around smelling like old milk, can I? Your uncle might, but he doesn't know any better, does he? You'll have to teach him, won't you?"

She doesn't answer me with words, but we have a full conversation, and I can tell my voice soothes her. The pumping fists and kicking legs eventually relax.

When she's clean, I lay her on the couch and dry her carefully, moisturizing her skin, rubbing extra Vaseline into the spots that look like eczema patches, and dress her in a fresh diaper and T-shirt. I slip a pair of baby socks onto her feet and another pair over her fists.

Then, I swaddle her tightly in a blanket so she looks like a fat burrito and hold her as she falls asleep.

When she's finally asleep, I don't want to return her to that igloo contraption, and I carry her into the kitchen with me to inventory Glen's refrigerator. I'm afraid to know what he's been feeding her—from what he says, he's barely been feeding himself.

I'm wholly unprepared for what I see when I open the refrigerator door: Rows and rows of baby bottles, each precisely filled to the four-ounce line with formula, each labeled with the date and time. There is also a well-worn sheet of paper, listing the recommended feeding schedule for infants, by months. One month: four ounces, six to seven times per day. Two to three months: four to five ounces, six to seven times per day.

On the next shelf there are packages of rice cereal, jugs of nursery water—I didn't even know there was a such thing as bottled water for babies!—and a few cans of ready-to-feed infant formula.

The bottom shelf holds only a pizza box and a few energy drinks.

I hadn't expected Glen to be this organized and prepared for the baby. When I realize Glen's fifteen-minute shower has turned into an hour, I return to the living room, stopping at the end of the hallway to listen for the water running. I hear nothing.

Again, I consider laying Naomi down in her igloo but decide against it. Instead, I readjust her in my arms and light-step my way down the hallway towards Glen's room.

I barely breathe, not wanting him to find me snooping through his home, not wanting to catch him undressed or on the toilet.

But he's asleep when I finally peek into his room, sitting in his desk chair, in front of the computer, wearing the kind of plaid, matching pajamas that your grandma might send you for Christmas.

He looks peaceful and sweet, and I make the decision to let him sleep for a while longer. But Naomi makes a sound, softly and suddenly, like the low purr of a tiny kitten, and Glen bolts straight out of the chair, looking frightened for a second, as though he's forgotten where he is.

There isn't time for me to react, and I just stand there, hoping my smile looks more reassuring and less stalker-ish. "Hey! I'm sorry! You were back here for a while and I was just checking to make sure you were okay. You know, people can fall in the shower or pass out or something. I didn't mean to scare you."

"Aw man, I guess I fell asleep, huh?" He looks apologetic and reaches for the baby. "I can take her. Your arm will fall asleep if you hold her for too long. Trust me, my whole arm went numb last night."

I smile at him and turn my body slightly, keeping the baby away, and tease him. "So, you've been holding her, huh? I thought you said you were teaching her how to self-soothe."

He grins, slow and wide, not wanting to admit I've busted him. "I mean, I like holding her sometimes. I'm not some kind of caveman." He presses his hand to his heart and tries to look sensitive. "I do have feelings, you know."

Then he straightens his back and stands a little taller. "And just so you know, you didn't scare me when I woke up." He puffs his chest out just a bit. "I am a man." and then he smiles and relaxes his stance. "You might have startled me a little, but you didn't scare me."

We stand there in the dimly lit hallway, whisper-giggling like kids, trying not to disturb Naomi, and I forget, for the moment, I've got responsibilities waiting for me across the street.

Back at home, I rush around as quietly as possible, doing my nightly routine, hoping not to rouse Mama. It's late, already 9:55, and by the time I finish my bath, brush and floss, scrub my face, and apply my monthly glycolic peel, it's well after 11. While I wait for the peel to begin working, I slather shea body butter on my feet, pull on my spa socks, and then rub more shea butter over my stretch marks…and I hear it: "Cent!"

I freeze, hoping she'll think I'm asleep and just go on back to sleep herself.

"Cynthia! Something is burning! Whatchu doing in there?" There isn't even a hint of sleep in her voice.

"Ma! It's a candle. I lit a candle while I was getting ready for bed! Nothing is burning!" My voice has escalated to a holler and I breathe deeply to calm myself before I walk into her room. Standing in the doorway staring at her, I feel exhaustion creeping up my neck, tightening around my head like a vise.

She clicks on her bedside lamp and studies me, "Everything alright?"

I press my forehead against the worn wooden frame of the doorway and answer quietly. "I'm fine, Ma. I'm just tired and wanted to relax before…"

She shushes me, shaking her head before I can finish the sentence. "I'm talking about over there, across the street. Why did she leave that boy with the baby?"

"I didn't ask him. I just went to see if he needed any help and then I left."

She shakes her head again, disappointed, I'm sure, because I don't have any juicy details for her, and then clicks the lamp off.

Feeling dismissed, I turn to walk away, when she flings one last demand in my direction: "I want you to fix him something to eat tomorrow and take it over there after you get home from work."

Her tone of voice tells me this is not debatable. She's always believed in southern hospitality, especially among neighbors during their time of need. I know she would have personally delivered plenty of hot, cooked meals as soon the baby was born if she'd been able. Now that her strength and mobility are declining, she's passed the torch to me.

Chapter Twenty-Three

The next day I walk across the street carrying a covered casserole dish, like a church lady taking food to a widower. It's baked spaghetti with diced sausage, topped with a cheesy pepper jack crust. It's the best I could do on such short notice and it reheats well.

And that's how it begins. Me, bringing food each day, holding and bathing Naomi so Glen can shower and eat and rest. He's managed to arrange a work-from home schedule that allows him to stay with her all day and still earn a living. But, by the time I get home from work, he's ready for a break.

I've switched my workouts back to mornings, and I look forward to seeing Glen and Naomi after work each day. Our evenings are peaceful, smooth, and Glen's mood is always light-hearted and welcoming. Around 9 each night, I make my way back to my house and he watches me from his front porch until I'm safely inside.

Each night, before I fall asleep, Glen sends a simple text:

I appreciate you.
Dinner was on point.
Thank you.

Even in the midst of this unthinkable tragedy, he's remained humble and appreciative—even apologetic for asking so much of me. The thing is, I still don't know much about how things will turn out for him. He barely speaks of the future, and I've been careful not to ask too many questions about his sister, but he's not volunteering any information, either. It's as though he'd simply ordered a new baby on Amazon and now, she's here.

On the weekend, we decide to walk the neighborhood, pushing Naomi in the massive stroller Glen has ordered online. '*It had the highest safety ratings,*' he'd said when it arrived. '*It had great reviews. I guess I overlooked the fact that it's built for multiple babies.*'

He's talking about work, software development and testing, the weather, pointing out the yards with the best grass, noting the differences between fescue and Bermuda.

Naomi has managed to shake one glove off so she can chew her fingers.

"What's going to happen to her?" I just blurt it out because I don't know how else to start the conversation.

He pauses and looks confused. "I don't know. I guess if she doesn't get the lawn mowed, then the HOA will probably give her a citation. Personally, I think it's—"

I stop walking and touch his arm lightly, slowing him to a halt. "Glen. The baby. What's going to happen to the baby?"

He hesitates for a second and then he shrugs. "I've been talking to everyone—the police, detectives, child protective services, my parents, my attorney. What it comes down to is this: my sister abandoned this baby, my only niece, and I think she planned to do this from the start. Before she got pregnant, I hadn't heard from her since we were eighteen. We're twins by birth, but she's always been different. As a kid, I couldn't understand it, I just knew we weren't alike— not in the way I saw other twins connect. My parents pretended not to see it for a long time. And by the time they started taking her to a therapist, she was too defiant to cooperate. She wouldn't take her meds, and after she turned eighteen, they couldn't force her to go to therapy anymore. Eventually she left home."

He steers the stroller onto our street and up his driveway in silence. I don't know what to say, either.

We sit together on the small bench on his front porch and watch Naomi sleeping in her stroller. She's a perfect baby, healthy and beautiful.

"Looking back on it now, I wonder if she would have been diagnosed on the autism spectrum—maybe like Asperger's or something. But, then again, it seems like it's a condition that mostly affects boys, not girls. Anyways, she needed help and she didn't receive it. She left home twenty-one years ago and then pops up, out of the blue on my doorstep—pregnant."

He taps his foot, a nervous tap without any rhythm, and pulls the stroller closer to us.

"I'm still not entirely sure how she found me. She claimed she found me on some job recruiting website, but I'm not registered with any I know of, and I'm not on social media. But she lies a lot, and it's hard to know what's true and what isn't with her."

My phone vibrates in my pocket and I reach in to silence it. The strain of recounting this story has etched unfamiliar lines in Glen's face and I realize I've taken his goofy smile for granted.

"But she was here, telling me she wanted a fresh start for her and the baby, so I let her stay. She's my *sister*. I hooked her up with a part-time job doing data entry from home for a few weeks up until the baby was born. The plan was she could stay here for a while to save her money and get herself established, and then get a place for herself and the baby."

I remember now, seeing him with the pregnant girl, coming and going, walking in the neighborhood, assuming she was his girlfriend.

"So, anyways," he breathes, thick and heavy, trying to tell the story objectively. "She was doing well, working, eating right, walking with me in the evenings—but I could *feel* something was wrong. I could see she hadn't bonded with Naomi, so I stepped in and tried to help. I encouraged her, told her she was a great mom, suggested she speak to someone—a professional. But she didn't. She left one morning and never came back."

He leans back on the bench and crosses his arms. "I knew she was gone. I could just feel it. She wasn't just gone, but *gone*. When I called the police, they said she hadn't been gone long enough to warrant an alert. They told me to call again when she'd been gone longer. Funny thing is, *they* ended up calling *me* the next day, to say she'd been found unconscious in a motel room. They couldn't revive her."

He leans forward and scrapes the toe of his sneaker against the concrete flooring as though he could dig a hole there and I cry for him. I cry for Naomi.

"They determined it was suicide, not foul play. They flew her back home and my parents had her cremated, but they're too old to raise a baby, and the father is unknown, so…" he throws his hands up, "that makes me Uncle Daddy Glen."

I reach into the diaper bag and find a tissue, blot my eyes, the space beneath my chin, and try to catch my running nose. "Are they letting you keep the baby? Legally?"

His voice drops an octave, as though he doesn't want Naomi to hear him. "They have granted me immediate temporary custody and I've petitioned the court for extended temporary custody. So now," he leans back and crosses his arms again, searching his mind for the next steps. "Now they have to verify the parental rights can be terminated, which is just a formality since the only known parent is deceased." The word 'deceased' catches at the edge of his throat, a jagged pill that he's learning to swallow.

"Then, there's a home inspection, hearings, an investigation and they'll determine if I qualify to be her guardian. If not," he pulls and pushes the stroller gently, as though Naomi has been fussing, but she's asleep. "If I'm not found to be an adequate guardian then the state will…" His voice trails off and I do not need him to finish the sentence.

I touch his hand and we sit quietly for a moment, before he continues. "At the end of the day, I love my niece and I can't just let her get sucked into the system when I'm right here. She's my family. I'm going to adopt her, if I can, if the courts will let me."

I release his hand and take a good look at his face. "All of this has been going on, you're dealing with an incredibly traumatic event, and you never said a word until now. You probably wouldn't have ever said anything if I hadn't asked. But why? I've been here every day. You could have talked to me. I thought we were friends."

"I don't know." He's digging his toe into the concrete again and I nudge the bottom of his pants leg until he stops.

"I don't really know. I keep a lot of things inside—I didn't want to burden you with my problems. I just figured I'd handle it myself, you know?" He glances over at me and then looks away. "And we *are* friends. For a while, I was hoping we'd be more than that—more than just friends, you know? Then, everything got so crazy with my sister and I thought—*maybe when she gets herself together and can take care of her child on her own, then I could ask you for another chance*—but she's gone and Naomi is here, so..."

So we sit there, in silence, until the streetlights warm to a bold glow, until Naomi awakens and demands attention, and then we move from the porch to the inside of the house, falling seamlessly into our nightly rhythm, leaving the conversation outside the front door like a pair of wet rain boots.

Chapter Twenty-Three

When I walk through the front door at home that night, I hold my breath, listening for Mama to begin hollering out requests and demands, but she doesn't.

When I peek into her room, I see she's already asleep, the plastic tray of a Lean Cuisine perched on her nightstand. She's even wearing a fresh nightgown.

I soft-walk just close enough to plant a feathery kiss on her cheek, whisper a good night, and she stirs around a bit, mumbling incoherently in her sleep.

I realize, as I make my way back to my room, she hasn't been very needy lately. Given all the hours I spend at Glen's house, helping with the baby, she barely texts me, rarely calls— she's become so much more independent.

Thinking back on the times I wanted to spend time with Victor but couldn't because she was so helpless, so sick—it dawns on me, maybe she'd been trying to keep me away from him for a reason.

On my bed, the thick envelope that must have come in the mail today reminds me of the appointment I've scheduled with the fertility specialist for next month. It's funny, it seems like the age of forty is racing toward me, but the date for my doctor's appointment has taken forever to get here. I push the envelope aside and call Julene.

"Are you excited about your appointment? Do you need me to go with you?" She's full of questions.

"To be honest, I almost forgot about it. I've been so focused on helping Glen with the baby I haven't thought about the fertility thing very much lately."

That's a lie, of course, because, even as I say these words to Julene, I'm bookmarking an article on PCOS and hormonal imbalances on my iPad.

I haven't lost enough weight— Dr. Gandhi wants me to lose sixty to seventy pounds, but I can't seem to shake the last twenty to thirty. I'm continually conscious of the velvety, dark patches of skin on my neck and elbows and inner thigh, the acne along my jawline and the stray chin hairs I pluck from my face as soon as they appear—all side effects of PCOS. These constant reminders won't let me forget how it will take a monumental effort if my body is to ever conceive a child.

I've also bookmarked a website that explains how diabetes medication has helped lots of PCOS sufferers lose weight and become mothers.

I don't tell Julene any of this, though. I don't know why I don't tell her I've been researching my options or that I plan to ask the doctor to prescribe diabetes medication. I usually tell her everything, and the things I don't tell her she figures out anyway. What I do tell her is this:

"I don't even know if I want to go through with any of it. Do I really want to have a baby alone? If I have a child through artificial insemination, then that's one more kid in this world without a dad. I would want my kid to have everything that other kids have—including a mother *and* a father."

Julene mmhmm's softly, thoughtfully. "I get it. Sometimes things happen and a child *has* to grow up with only one parent, and that scenario can work out okay. God always provides a way. But if you have the *opportunity* to give a child two parents, then why not?"

Her words send my mind racing across the street to Glen, the inadvertent single parent. What are his thoughts on this subject, now that he's in the thick of it himself? I make a mental note to ask him how he's feeling about everything when I see him tomorrow.

"Then, are you going to keep the appointment? It kind of sounds like you've changed your mind…" Julene's voice bursts through my thoughts and brings me back to our conversation.

"Yeah, I think I'll still go. It's just a meeting with the specialist and bloodwork. You know, checking my hormone levels again. Part of me still wants to know if I *can* get pregnant, even if I don't do it artificially."

"Well, you…" muffled baby sounds followed by a man's deep voice fill the background and I know my friend has to get back to her real life. I speak into the commotion that comes through the phone line and tell her I'll call her later.

Not sure if she hears me or not, I hang up and know she'll understand.

Instead of sleeping, I stay up a few minutes longer to fill out the new patient forms the specialist has sent. It's the usual—insurance information, contact information, health history, and consent forms—plus an additional questionnaire about family planning, spousal information, long term goals…stuff that applies to a traditionally married couple, of which I am not. I skip this sheet altogether.

In the morning, I am awakened by the water droplet notification sound of a text message. Grabbing the phone from the night stand, I barely have to peel my eyelids apart to see the message:

Victor: *Good morning, beautiful.*

Instantly, my stomach lurches and I close the message.

And then:

Victor: *I've been trying to get in touch with you for a while.*

Victor: *I know you hate me. Just wanted to apologize. It's not what you think.*

Then, a meme of a puppy with a blanket over his head, only the tip of his shiny nose exposed:

Victor: *I miss my friend. I miss you.*

Now, I'm awake, stirred to the point of fury by the inappropriate use of the word friend. It's been so long since I've replied to his messages—at least a few weeks, and, I'd hoped he'd tire of my silent treatment, get the message and find someone else to harass. Better yet, I wished he'd make things work with the mother of his unborn child. But it seems I'm still on his radar and something in me is still pissed.

I text him back:

Me: *We are not friends. We were never friends. Friends don't sleep together. Friends don't forget to mention they are having children with other friends. We crossed the line of friendship a long time ago but you didn't honor it. You used it to your advantage, and you didn't care who got hurt in the process.*

Me: *So now, as a friend, I wish you the best. I'll give you all the space you need to take care of your family and handle your business.*

After a series of bubbles that stop and begin over and over like an animation, he finally replies.

Victor: *You're right. I was wrong to take you for granted and I should have given you more respect. I should have told you everything. I was afraid of losing your friendship when I should have been open with you.*

Victor: *But I'm not with that girl. I never was. I mean, not like in a relationship. It's like she set me up and we don't even know if the baby is mine.*

Victor: *And that doesn't change how I feel about you.*

Victor: *Come on! I miss you. Empress misses you. You've been my best friend. No lie. You still are. The only one.*

I stare at his words for a long time, picking them apart individually and non-sequentially rather than seeing them as complete, orderly thoughts. They are all the words that would have made me follow him to a goat farm in Jamaica a few months ago, just to be with him. *Miss you. Beautiful. Feel. Baby. Relationship. Respect.*

But, when I read the words in the proper order, they make me sick and I can't believe we are here—talking about a baby, another woman, a new baby mama, and paternity testing. It's too much. It's wrong for his children, and it's wrong for me.

I click the phone shut and toss it on the nightstand while I lay for another moment and try to… another water droplet sound and the phone screen illuminates again. I almost ignore it, but I pick it up despite my better judgement.

It's a Sprinkle of Jesus and not Victor at all.

Stop looking for happiness in the same place you lost it.

Just for a second, I clutch the phone close to my chest and thank God for bringing Ruth into my life, even if he'd taken her away too soon. *You're right*, I think to God or to Ruth—perhaps both.

And then I pop out of bed before I change my mind.

Chapter Twenty-Four

It's early and Mama's not up yet, but I put on a pot of coffee for her, make her some toast and bacon, then get myself washed and dressed before heading across the street.

Today, Glen and I have plans. He wants to clean out the room once occupied by his sister and drop the stuff off at the Goodwill. I'm all about purging, cleaning out, and getting rid of clutter, but today's mission feels different

It seems so sad, and I didn't even know her.

When I get there, it's 8:30 A.M. and he's up and dressed in a t-shirt and sweatpants, but Naomi is wearing a complete Easter Sunday outfit: ruffled dress, frilly socks, patent leather Mary Janes, and a soft yellow hair bow strategically positioned in the center-left of her head.

I burst out laughing when I see her, until I see the expression of pride plastered across Glen's face. I think he's serious.

Per protocol, I walk past him and toss up a fist bump and then scoop Naomi into my arms. She smells like... Heaven, all baby powdery and clean. I inhale her scent and look toward Glen who is beaming proudly.

"She said she wanted to get dressed up for you." His smile is adorable, and I can't help but smile back. Suddenly, I look down at my own yoga pants and Disney t-shirt and laugh.

"I wish I had known. I would have dressed up for her, too." I nuzzle her neck and she coos in her gurgling baby voice. I look over at Glen. "I love this girl."

He grins, scanning me from head to toe. "You look perfect in anything. The walking and working out is looking good on you."

I'm flattered and a little uncomfortable accepting the compliment about my body, so I busy myself by straightening Naomi's dress. I want to tell him I can see some changes in his physique, too. If I had an ounce more courage, I'd tell him I can see the muscle definition in his chest and shoulders through his t-shirt. I keep those thoughts inside, though, and chastise myself inwardly for not being brave enough to be more forward with him.

There are sparks between us that have nothing to do with Naomi or convenience, but here I am, freezing up at the thought of returning a simple compliment. I feel hot and embarrassed, so I turn my attention back to NayNay.

Glen looks wistful for a split second and then turns away. "I got most of her stuff together. There wasn't much."

He fans his hands towards the three black plastic trash bags and two small boxes near his feet. "I'll go drop these off at the Goodwill donation center and come right back, if you want to stay here with NayNay."

I'm already bouncing Naomi on my hip playing peekaboo with her, covering my eyes with her hands and pulling them away until her face splits into a gummy grin. "That's fine because I wanted to go through your refrigerator and clean it out, anyway. How long were you going to keep those takeout containers?"

I lift Naomi's dress and blow a raspberry on her belly, and in my peripheral, I notice Glen's uncharacteristically subdued expression. "What's wrong? I could go with you if you want. We can bring the baby."

But he shakes it off, finds a quick smile, and grabs his keys. "Nah. I can do it. Looks like you and Nay would have more fun here anyways. I'll just make a quick run and come right back."

I'm pretending to bite Naomi's chubby fingers with my lips and she's making sounds that are a hybrid between coughing and snickering, but I hold up my fist in Glen's direction, waiting for a goodbye fist bump. When I hear the door close softly behind me, I realize he's left me hanging.

I snap Naomi into her activity walker, run to open the front door, and wave him down before he backs out of the driveway. He stops and jumps out, but I try waving him back into the car. "You didn't have to get out. I was just going to ask you when you last fed her, or is she due for a bottle?"

He leans into the car door jam and looks so disappointed I know he had been expecting me to ask something else. He looks at his watch. "I gave her a bottle a few hours ago, so she's probably ready for another one soon."

He tries to slip into the car, and I touch his shoulder, squeezing softly to stop him. "What's wrong?"

He doesn't answer, but I can read the unhappiness in his eyes.

I try again. "You're not yourself. I mean, you left me hanging on the fist bump in there." I nod towards the house and look back at Glen with a smile I hope is encouraging.

He sighs lightly and rubs the toe of his sneakers across a groove in the driveway. I know him so well now. His habits, mannerisms, and nuances are languages I can read proficiently, and it matters to me. As much as his quirks used to get on my nerves, today, all I care about is making sure they're protected.

This is the difference between a casual acquaintance and a true friend: care, concern, and a positive vibe. I like that I can feel his vibe and it's the thing that connects us and makes us actual friends. Not the friends of convenience Victor always dangled in my face, but real ones. True ones.

He speaks and it snaps me to attention, not because of his words, but because of his tone. It's the driest I've ever heard from him.

"I told you how I felt about you last night."

There. He's dropped the truth right at our feet, right on the line he's been tracing with his shoe, and it feels like he's thrown down a gauntlet.

I take a deep breath and prepare myself for The Relationship Talk.

He steps around the car door and stands in front of me, looking right into my eyes as he speaks. "What are we doing here?" He uses his hands to stir the air in the space between us as though he's trying to feel if something is there or not.

I shrug my shoulders and try to think quickly. I haven't let myself define our…friendship—I hate the word now that Victor has destroyed it, but I don't know what else to say. "Well, I thought we were friends. You told me you hoped we could be more, but you had too much going on in your life right now, with the baby and everything. What was I supposed to say to that?"

The things I really want to say: *I'm having trouble trusting again, I'm not sure if I've healed from my previous relationship, I'm working on myself right now*—all these excuses sound eerily familiar and I'd call BS on myself if they came out of my mouth right now. I feel like a hypocrite.

And then Naomi inserts herself into our incredibly heavy conversation by letting out a cry strong enough to travel from the house to the driveway where we stand.

The thick energy of our conversation is broken, and I gesture toward the house. "I'll check on her. You go ahead and run your errands and we can finish this when you get back." I shoo him into the car and run back to the house, grateful for the interruption.

Inside the house, I walk towards Naomi who isn't crying at all, but screaming in sheer ecstasy at the mess she's made by knocking over everything within arm's reach on the coffee table.

"Hey, Little Lady! Look at you, screaming like that and making a mess!" I put my hands on my hips and stand in front of her, pretending to look stern, but she's an irresistible baby doll and I can't resist lifting her out of the walker. "Come here, Pumpkin." I hold her and softly sing the cleanup song as I get to work, picking up her mess. "Clean up, everybody clean up, clean up, everybody clean up, time to clean up!" When I glance at her, her expression makes me laugh. "Okay, so you don't like my singing?"

When I stand back and survey the room, I'm pleased. Everything is in its place and I'm ready to tackle the kitchen. I scoot Naomi's walker toward the kitchen with my foot and tell her what we're going to do next. "Your Uncle-Daddy doesn't wash his dishes before he goes night-night, does he?" She doesn't respond, but she's studying my lips and reaching for my chin, so I continue. "No, he doesn't. And he doesn't throw away his takeout boxes, either, does he?"

With the walker in the center of the kitchen, away from anything Naomi can grab, I shh-shh her while snapping her into the seat before backing away slowly so she doesn't think I'm leaving her. "We have to help him, don't we? Let's get it all cleaned up and smelling nice, and then we can play!"

I get to work, washing dishes, cleaning out the fridge, and wiping the counters down-- chatting with Naomi the whole time. She listens as I tell her about how I'm thinking of trying a new hair color, how I've made a board on Pinterest dedicated to new zero-point recipes even though I haven't really been counting points lately, about how much I enjoy hanging with her and her Uncle-Daddy, and how I think his smile is so cute. Then I stop and swear her to secrecy, explaining that we are having Girl Talk and we never tell anyone else what we talk about—especially boys.

Her expression is either one of solidarity or disinterest, and I'm satisfied with both. Plus, the kitchen is sparkling clean now, so I take one of her bottles from the refrigerator and place it into the bottle warmer Glen ordered from Amazon.

I chuckle to myself, recalling how we'd argued about the proper way to warm a baby bottle. Everyone I know just pops the bottle into the microwave for a few seconds and shakes a few drops of milk on their inner wrist to check the temperature.

Glen, on the other hand, has become a baby expert, thanks to the internet, and would only warm a bottle by running it under a stream of warm water—a strategy that is maddeningly slow when you have a fussy, hungry baby waiting.

But the internet had told him microwave bottle warming is unsafe, and so he was unwilling to accept the idea that almost everybody in our generation had survived microwave baby bottle warming with no fatalities. The next day—hastened by Glen's equal love for next-day shipping and gadgets—the electric bottle warmer arrived. It was the compromise that settled our bottle-warming debate.

When the bottle is warm, I take it, along with Naomi and move to her nursery. We sit in the rocking chair while she has her bottle, which she gobbles down so quickly I have to take it away a few times, just so she can catch her breath. I make a mental note to talk to Glen about increasing her bottle size or introducing some cereal.

I'm pleased though, by her healthy appetite, her chunky body, her sharp senses, and her sweet disposition. As I burp her and change her diaper, I sing 'Jesus Loves Me to her' and I wonder for the billionth time, how any mother could walk away from such a perfect little girl. Who couldn't see the blessing in this child?

The trifecta of the full belly, clean diaper, and cozy rocking chair turn Naomi into Sleeping Beauty, and I sit with her in the rocking chair for a while, enjoying the serenity.

"Cynthia. Psst." I hear my name, softly, coming to me through darkness, from a distance, and I open my eyes to see Glen standing in the doorway of the nursery, waving my phone at me. He looks…I can't figure out his expression. He motions for me to put Naomi in her crib and then he disappears around the corner.

Feeling as though I've been summoned to the principal's office, I ease myself out of the rocker, slide Naomi, who is sweating as she sleeps in her frilly dress, into the crib and slow-walk behind Glen. I knew we'd have to finish this conversation, but I didn't expect to have it so abruptly. I sit down and massage my arms in the places that had fallen asleep as I help Naomi.

"Hey…what time is it? I don't know what time Naomi and I…"

He stops me, though, by tossing my phone softly into my lap. "It was chiming like crazy. Apparently your boyfriend is fiending for you."

I look at the phone and there are back to back to back texts from Victor. Memes, lip-biting, long messages, and short messages. *Call me. I need a friend. Never thought you would quit on me. Wouldn't do that to you.*

I glance up at Glen and smile. "This is nothing. This is less than nothing, just someone who can't take 'no' for an answer. As you can see, I never even responded."

"He's definitely persistent. I'll give you that. But you did respond to him, and there seems to be a lot of unfinished business between you two." He holds an imaginary phone in his hand and scrolls through an imaginary list of text messages:

"Good morning, beautiful.
Good morning, beautiful.
Good morning, beautiful.
Good morning, beautiful."

He glances over at me. "I'm guessing this is the reason you're keeping me at a distance—because I don't text you '*Good morning, beautiful*' every day."

He's standing in the center of the living room, arms crossed, staring down at me as I sit on the edge of the couch. The fact that he's gone through my phone, the fact that he's standing there thinking he's giving me the business right now—all of it is secondary to the fact that I've been in his shoes before, trying to figure out if you're being lied to, if you're being played, trying not to look as vulnerable as you feel, all heart-on-sleeve and whatnot. I feel a wave of sympathy for him—but not much.

I learned some hard lessons in my dealings with Victor, primarily that I'll never again let a man press me down into a state of weakness. I'll never let one think for a moment he has the upper hand with me. Never again. So, I stand up, and get myself on eye-level with him so he isn't looking down on me. I change our dynamic to let him know he can't take a position of power over me. And then, when I have evened the playing field, I address him.

"Here's the thing: first, I'm not upset with you for going through my phone. I don't have anything to hide. Second, whatever I had with Victor is over. He was horrible to me. He was horrible *for* me, and he hurt me a lot. I never want to speak to him again, and I've told him that. That's why he's blowing up my phone. He hates being ignored, but I've made the decision to eliminate him from my life because that's what's healthiest for me. I'm putting myself first. But sometimes a message from him really strikes a nerve and I feel like I need to get it off my chest, so that's when I text him back."

Glen sits down in the armchair then, and I pause to let him speak. But he doesn't say a word, just extends his hand towards me, motioning for me to continue.

And I do continue. "So, the issue with Victor is a nonfactor. I'll never do that to myself again. However, I *am* slow to get into another relationship because I want to be smarter next time. I'll make sure the man in my life doesn't just make my heart beat fast but is also careful with it. I need to trust him not to hurt me, and he has to put me first in his life instead of hiding me on the sidelines."

I pause and catch my breath. I hadn't planned to say so much, but it's the truth and now it's out in the open. Glen's face looks so calm and so kind, I feel foolish for standing up like this. It seems like he's watching me, really watching me, and letting me get my thoughts out rather than simply waiting to make his own argument. I sit down again and then he speaks.

"If you want to make sure someone doesn't call you, that's easy. You block their number, you change your number, you report it as harassment—whatever's necessary. So that's what gets me. If you really wanted him out of your life, then he'd be out of your life—period. But, whatever, that's your thing. You're damaged. I get it. You've been hurt. I can respect that."

He crosses and uncrosses his legs, and then leans towards me before he continues. "But all the other stuff—

finding someone who makes your heart beat fast and puts you first in their life—that's stuff's going to cause you to miss out on a great relationship. It's what's making it so hard for you right now."

His words have sharp edges, but he delivers them with care, as though he's a big brother trying to teach his younger sister how the game of love is played.

"You need to know the love of your life might not make your heart beat fast every day. A rapid heartbeat is a sign of distress, anxiety, maybe even fear, and sometimes love. But, a heart that's always racing is unhealthy. The love of your life should be putting your heart at ease—the love of your life should feel calming and relaxing and safe. And you can't always be first, I'm sorry to tell you. This is real life. People have parents to care for, kids to raise, and careers to manage. You might have to take a backseat sometimes, but that doesn't mean you're not cared for or loved. It just means life is happening. People in love give each other space to live their lives and they're still able to enjoy one another, unselfishly."

When Naomi's protests become increasingly consistent, its apparent she's done with her nap, and Glen stands up to check on her. When he reaches the doorway, he turns back to me and adds another layer to his lecture:

"Cynthia, you're beautiful, and not because of the physical stuff. You're a cool person, smart and thoughtful. You're cautious when you need to be and you're vulnerable inside. I can see it, and that's what makes you beautiful to me—not just in the morning, as old boy seems to think, but all day, every day."

He takes another step into the baby's room, has a second thought, turns and wags his finger at me with an energy that toes the line between playfulness and a stern warning. "But I'll tell you this: If I was your man, I'd make sure your heart was always calm. I'd make sure you felt secure about your place in my life and I'd date you in real life, not via text. And all this bossy stuff you do," he swirls his finger around in the air to illustrate the range of my bossiness, "That stuff you do because you're a little insecure…I'd make sure you felt safe enough to let down your guard when you're with me. But you know," he flashes the smile I've grown to adore. "Do you, booboo."

And then he leaves me sitting there in silence while he goes into the next room to attend to Naomi.

After a moment, I stand and walk to the doorway of Naomi's room, peek inside and wave at Glen. "Hey! I'll let you get her settled down and I'm going to run over and check on Mama. But," I can't help smiling at him, standing knee-deep in a disgusting diaper change. "Give me a call after you put her down for the night. I'll come back over and hang out with you."

He smiles at me, a glimmer of confusion in his eyes, and, despite what he'd said earlier, my heartbeat picks up the pace just a little.

Chapter Twenty-Five

I. Am. On. The. Phone!" Julene hollers at whomever is being disobedient, a door slams, her voice is overlapped by an echo, and I know she's in the bathroom.

"Okay! Tell me again! From the beginning. He told you he what?" Julene is breathless and, to be honest, I am too. It's been two days since I spent the night at Glen's, and I've replayed the scene in my head a million times since then. Julene is the only person I can talk to about it. Still, I haven't been able to tell her about it until today.

"So, after he told me about the kind of man he'd be in my life, he went to go check on the baby. I told him to call me after he put her down for the night and I'd come back over to hang out for a while.

"Then, I went home, had a few glasses of wine, and waited for him to call me. When he did, I showered, shaved *everywhere*, twisted my hair up into a funky Mohawk, did a full face of makeup, and put on my sexiest bra and panty set. Then I put on my leather trench coat, a pair of heels, and went back to his house. I told Mama Glen needed me to watch the baby overnight."

Julene laughs at that. "She knows better than that!"

I laugh a little too. "She probably did, but she didn't say anything. So, I knock on his door, feeling brave, and when he opens it, I don't say anything. I just push him backwards and play the role of The Stranger. You know, I untie my coat and push him down onto the couch."

"Girl, no you didn't!" Julene is whisper-shouting into the phone and she hasn't even heard the whole story yet.

"Yeah, I did. So, at first he was like, *'You don't have any clothes on,'* like I was accidentally naked. Then he was like, *'What are you doing? I think we should wait…we don't have to do this…'* But I dropped my coat on the floor and stood in front of him. Here I am, messing with him, tickling his ears and doing my best strip-tease."

Julene is screaming, then shushes herself so I can continue.

"…and he tried his hardest to resist. He kept trying to show me something on his phone, and I kept pushing the phone away. Next thing I know, he throws the phone down—I thought he was mad—and it scared me a little bit. And then, girl! He picked me up! Literally lifted me up, carried me into his room and laid me on the bed."

I can hear Julene's gasp, but there's still more to the story.

"Right. He picked up all this." She can't see me as I wave my hand across my body, but I know she gets it. "So, girl, he took control and I wasn't ready! I didn't expect him to be so…I don't know what I was expecting, but O-M-G! When we finished, I cried."

Julene sucks in her breath. "You cried? In front of him? Why?"

I laugh at the sound of it, now, the whole scenario is so crazy. "Yes, honey! I don't know! I just felt so emotional

I cried, and he just laid with me, wiping my face until I stopped. Then he went to the kitchen to get us some juice and we fell asleep."

Julene lets out a long, low whistle. "Wow. I didn't know Glen had it in him! He let you know he ain't nothing to play with."

She's quiet for a moment, and I'm quiet, too, thinking about what's happened, and then Julene asks the million-dollar question: "So what's next? Are you two a thing, or what?"

I answer, almost before she's finished asking the question because I'm already thinking about it, too. "So, the first thing I did was block Victor from all of my social media and block his number on my phone. Glen was right about that part—if you want someone out of your life then you can make it happen."

"True that."

"And I decided to face myself in the mirror every morning and say 'Good morning, beautiful.' Out loud. I've gotta learn how to greet and validate myself instead of waiting for someone else to do it. Glen hasn't changed. He hasn't pressured me or questioned me. It's like, it happened, we're adults, he's told me how he feels, and he's left the ball in my court."

"Okay. He's being a grown man about it. I like that."

"But I don't know what to do with my feelings. It's sad to say, but I'm not used to a man being so nice to me-- consistently. He's not like run-all-over-me nice—he's a strong man, a manly man—he just doesn't throw it in my face all the time. So, this is new for me, but I think I like it. I think I *need* it."

"Okay…"

"The thing is, I was in a good place, you know, with the whole 'Year of Selfie' thing, and I've been on this path with my health and the PCOS. So, now that Glen's come along, do I just drop my plans and jump into a relationship? Seems like I have a bad habit of doing that and it's always turned out terrible. I'm supposed to be finding myself right now and I think I've been doing pretty good so far."

"Alright." Julene exhales and I can tell she's choosing her words carefully. "Okay. You're right. Don't stop what you're doing. You've been working towards the things you want in your life—health, wealth, self-control, confidence—and you shouldn't have to give anything up. But if you like him, if you don't have to set yourself on fire just to keep him warm. If he adds more to your life than he takes away then I think that's worth something."

I'm listening to her, and she makes perfect sense. Truthfully, it's what I've already known. I know how I feel about him, and I think I know what a healthy relationship should look like. I've never had one of my own, but I've seen enough inspirational posts on Pinterest, read enough self-help books to get the idea.

Why, then, did I waste so much time and energy waiting for Victor to provide me with a healthy love? The truth is this: I knew he had issues—everyone does, but I could also see he had the potential to be a great guy if he could only learn to trust someone. And I believe everyone deserves a second chance, so I couldn't hold his past mistakes against him. So, I thought, if I could heal him—rebuild him—then he would appreciate me love and loyalty. I believed he would overlook my issues and repay me with the same.

I'm not the skinniest girl in the room, and my OCD tendencies can be frustrating, but I maintain a good appearance, I'm a good listener, I can cook and clean, I'd protect his child with my life, and I'm no gold-digger. Either I was worried his own brokenness was keeping him from seeing my worth or I was afraid I didn't deserve anyone better.

Once again, it comes down to Fear, an old foe whom I've come to recognize in various forms, no matter how its disguised. From where I'm lying on my bed, I only have to roll my head to the left to see the book with Ruth's bookmark sticking out of the section I've read so many times already. I've read it so often, the book falls open to page 240 as soon as I toss it on the bed.

I skim the page, refreshing my memory on the way fear, if left unchecked, can shift the mind into a state of chronic worrying, which, in turn, paralyzes our ability to make decisions. It keeps our minds unsettled, destroys our self-confidence, and prevents us from making confident decisions we can stand by.

The line in the center of the page, the one that draws my attention as though it is highlighted, basically says, *'We will not worry about the obstacles or challenges, once we have made up our minds to a definite line of action based on our decision.'*

"Make a decision, stick to it, and don't worry about the rest." I blurt the words out loud as if to confirm to myself what I've just read.

"What?" Julene sounds confused, "I was only saying I'm either making spaghetti or letting the kids eat breakfast for dinner again…what were you…?"

Her bewilderment makes me laugh out loud. "I'm sorry. I wasn't talking about your dinner. I didn't even hear what you said! I was reading about Fear, rereading it, actually, and this one part finally clicked for me. I know what I have to do. I just need to make a decision, and move forward. I have to stop worrying about what could go wrong."

Julene laughs, and then the sound is drowned out by the flushing of the toilet. "Okay, good, because I'm making spaghetti again. I know we eat it every week, but I'm running out of stuff to cook! So, you go on and make your decision and stick to it and all that stuff, and I'm going in here to make spaghetti."

I take a deep breath and blow it out. The feeling of decisiveness works for me; it feels nice. So, I tell Julene, "Alright girl! Go make that spaghetti and call me later."

I can already hear cartoons and kids in the background when she says, "Okay, talk to you later."

And just before I press 'end' I hear her yelling, "Cynthia! Hey! Wait a sec!"

I whip the phone back to me ear. "Huh?"

"What is this decision that you made? You didn't tell me."

Her question makes me pause for a second. I can barely remember what I've said to myself and what I've said out loud. "Oh! Right. Well, I've decided to choose me and I'm choosing Glen too. I'm taking care of myself and I'm having him too. I've made a decision and I won't be afraid. If it's meant for me, then it is for me. Period."

The sound of Julene snapping her fingers through the phone is as good as a high-five in real life. She gets it.

"I hear you, honey! Go on out there and live your life and get your man, too!"

We laugh together for a moment, and then, "Okay, girl, I gotta go, for real this time! These kids are demanding spaghetti, like, *right now.*"

When we hang up, I feel good. I peek through the window shades, see that Glen's house is dark, but for the warm glow from the nightlight in Naomi's room, and head toward my bathroom to start my evening routine.

CHAPTER TWENTY-SIX

Don't get me wrong. What happened the other night was…" Glen is the embodiment of Fred Sanford as he clutches his chest like he's having a heart-attack and looks towards the heavens. "You tried to give a brother a heart attack!"

He takes my hand and leads me onto his front porch, stopping before I can open the door. He called me last night, asked if I'd be available this evening, and told me to meet him in front of his house at 7 P.M. Although I'd asked in a million different ways, he had firmly refused to give me any other details about his invitation.

He takes a deep breath and smiles at me for a long second. "You surprised me the other night. Tonight, I have a surprise for you."

"You got the house cleaned, didn't you? I saw the car from the maid service parked here when I was leaving for work this morning." I blurt it out, and then peek at his face to see if I'm right.

He shakes his head at me, but the smile never leaves his adorable face. "I can't slip anything past you, huh? You just think you got my number, don't you?" When he reaches out to push the door open, he taunts me. "What you gotta say now, girlfriend? I bet you weren't expecting this!"

The house is spotless. I can smell the freshness as soon as I step inside, but that isn't the shocker. Ms. Emma Lee's granddaughters, Mecca and Amethyst, are sitting on the living room floor, playing with Naomi. They both look up at me at the same time and burst out laughing.

"Mr. Glen said you'd be surprised!" The girls are speaking in unison, and I must admit, I'm confused. I look to Glen for an explanation, even as I walk towards the girls, hugging each of them and kissing Naomi.

"Alright, that's enough of that. We have to go." Glen's hand is gentle but firm as he guides me towards the front door, stopping to give the girls some instructions. "Help yourselves to anything in the kitchen. There's juice in the fridge and pizza in the oven. I ordered one cheese, one pepperoni, and one veggie, because I didn't know what you might like. Naomi's had her bath already, so you'll just need to feed her around 7:30 and she should fall right asleep. You have my number saved in your phones and there are some emergency numbers written on the whiteboard on the fridge." He pauses for a moment, trying to remember the last-minute instructions.

"Bye, Mr. Glen! We got this. Don't worry." Mecca is walking towards us, shooing us out the door.

Glen takes my hand and walks towards the door with me but stops again. "I left the Netflix account logged in for you and you just hit that button on the left for the surround sound."

"Bye, Mr. Glen! We'll call you if we need anything!" I can hear Amethyst giggling as Mecca closes the door behind us.

Outside, I look at him and shake my head slowly. "Babysitters? Cleaning service? How did you know to hire Mecca and Amethyst?"

He hugs me and then takes a small step backwards to look at me. "I asked your mom for a recommendation. She came to the door when I was pulling her trash bins to the side of the house the other day and she gave me their grandmother's phone number. I got the house cleaned because I know you're a neat freak and I want you to feel comfortable whenever you're here. I'm not the best housekeeper, personally, but I don't want you to feel like you need to clean up every time you come over."

I laugh out loud. "Am I that bad? I know I'm OCD about certain things, but…"

He laughs too. "Yeah, you're that bad, but cleanliness is important, especially with a baby in the house, so I'm stepping up to make sure it's handled. The cleaning crew will be here every other week to do the kitchen, bathroom, and floors."

Leading me to the car, he opens the passenger side door and waits for me to get in.

I hesitate, with one leg in. "Where are we going?"

"Woman, will you just get in the car? I'm handling this." He's still laughing as he closes me inside the car and trots around to the driver's side. He's in such a great mood, the energy is contagious.

Once he's inside, he steers the car out of the driveway and passes me his cellphone. "Find us some music. I have a few playlists saved, just pick whatever you want."

I accept the phone, but I don't play a song right away. "Do you hear that?"

He slows the car to a crawl and all but stops breathing to listen for whatever I'm hearing. "What? I don't hear anything."

I look over at him. "You hear that dinging sound? It usually means *put on your seatbelt!*" I can no longer contain my giggles. "Put your seatbelt on, man! Click it or ticket!"

His expression is priceless as he realizes I'm teasing him, but he clicks his seatbelt on anyway. "Thanks for looking out for me." His voice sounds more serious as he drives us out of the neighborhood. "You're good at that, you know—looking out for everybody else and taking care of things. I appreciate it."

"I feel like I've heard this kind of speech before. What's wrong? Just tell me, I can handle it." I twist myself to the left so I can watch his face for clues.

This makes Glen laugh, but I'm not kidding. Whatever it is he's trying to say, I need him to just spit it out.

"Look Cynthia," he reaches over to squeeze my hand. "Nothing is wrong. I appreciate you and I just need you to know it. Also, I really care about *you*." He jabs my knee with his finger and it tickles. "I care about having you in my life. Not to take care of Naomi, and not for that thing you did the other night—even though I'd love to have a replay—but I want to *date* you. Properly. I know we're grown, we have so many responsibilities, and we can't just take off whenever, like two teenagers, but I've hired Mecca and Amethyst to babysit every other weekend so we can hang out together as adults instead of caretakers. We can do whatever you like, or we can do nothing."

When he stops speaking, I try to make sure I'm hearing what I'm hearing. "You want to date me every other weekend…?"

The smile drops from his face. "I'm sorry if I assumed…was I wrong to plan things in advance? I just want to spend time with you and I don't want you to feel like you have to tend to Naomi all the time. You said you wanted to be a top priority in your next relationship…"

I can't help but smile. "And you told me I was being unrealistic. Also, are we officially calling this a relationship?"

He glances at me for a second before returning his attention to the road. I watch as a brilliant smile spreads across his face. "You just gonna use my own words against me? Yes, I said it, and it's true sometimes, but not always. For something as important as this," he jabs my knee again, "it's my job to make you a top priority."

He said real love shouldn't make my heart feel like it's racing, but I guess that isn't a hard and fast rule, either, because, this evening, I'm full of butterflies. I reach over and trace his freshly-edged hairline with my finger. "You got a haircut, too? You really went all out, huh? Where are we going?"

Turning his face to the side, he kisses my hand and laughs. "Don't worry about that, sweetheart. Just sit back and ride-- and find us some music!"

I give his neck a tickle and pick up his phone to choose a station. I'm grinning as I select 90s R&B radio, while a single, joyous tear frees itself from the corner of my eye.

I wipe it away before Glen can see it, place the phone in his lap, sit back, and ride.

CHAPTER TWENTY-SEVEN

I have a boyfriend now. Sounds silly, doesn't it, for an almost forty-year-old woman to have her first, real, out-in-public boyfriend since high school? Stranger things have happened, maybe, but for me, it's completely foreign. And then again, it feels like it's always been this way. Like the rhythm of my life: Mama, work, working out, girl's nights, recipes, Target, and Pinterest have always included Glen and Naomi. But it hasn't, and now it does.

However, there's one thing my life always included which has all but gone away: the texting. The countless, predictable, lengthy, ambiguous, provocative, inappropriate, misleading, often one-sided text messages that basically comprised my relationship with Victor—that's no longer a thing.

Glen isn't big on texting, and on the rare occasion he does it's purely for sharing pertinent information: *home security alarm code is 0819* or *I'm grilling out tonight*—that kind of thing. But never, *never* does he allow his texts to stand as a substitute for a real conversation.

Now, if I'm honest, this change has been a blessing and a curse. For me, it's so much easier to have certain conversations—the touchy subjects—via text. It's easier for me to hide my feelings or my expressions. Maybe that's why I allowed it with Victor—because I could hide myself behind a text without having to let my guard down. Maybe that's why I decide to text Glen about my doctor's appointment rather than telling him in person.

Me: *I have a doctors appointment this morning but I'll come over after.*

The phone rings in my hand as I'm waiting for him to respond and I'm busted.

"Hey GlenGlen!" I don't know why I say his name twice, and even to me, it sounds unbelievably phony.

"What's wrong? Are you okay?" He skips my introduction and gets to the point.

I laugh it off to downplay the whole topic. "I'm okay. I had scheduled this appointment for a physical a while back and I almost forgot about it. No big deal, though."

His tone is more relaxed now, but still he asks, "Do you want me to go with you?"

"No… Nope. No, it's fine. It won't take long and I'll meet you after. Are we still taking Naomi to the aquarium?" I say all of this quickly. Probably too quickly to sound trustworthy, and a suspicious or insecure man would have picked up on it in an instant. Hell, if the conversation had been the other way around, *my* radar would have gone up.

But Glen? He's a different type of man. Without more questions or scrutiny, he accepts my response, tells me he hopes all is well, and asks if I'd like him to grill chicken or shrimp kabobs for lunch after the aquarium.

On my end of the phone, I do a quick happy dance to thank God for a man who likes to eat nutritionally sound meals, and then I say, "I like both. You can mix chicken and shrimp on the same skewer, with pineapple, sweet red peppers, and onions—or you can put all the chicken on one skewer, the shrimp on another, and grill all the veggies separately. Either way will be good. Just be sure to save me some."

He laughs, thinking I must be kidding. "Save you some? Won't you be there?"

"We're having a book club meeting later this afternoon, but it shouldn't last long. If you keep my kabobs warm for me, I'll see you when the meeting's over."

"You're a busy woman. First, a doctor's appointment and now a book club meeting? I'm starting to think you only want me for my kabobs." He's still chuckling, and the word 'kabobs' suddenly sounds flirtatious.

I play along, assuring him there's more to his charm than just 'kabobs' before I say goodbye and hang up.

What's kept me from talking to Glen about my medical concerns? I can't put my finger on it, but words like 'inadequacy' and 'self-consciousness' come to mind. Why haven't I told him what we really do at our book club meetings? In weakness, I violated our club's code of silence in the past, but I'm stronger now. Now, I hold my cards close to my chest and get ready for my appointment.

"How's Cynthia doing today?" Dr. Stovall breezes into the room as though we've known each other forever. She extends her hand and I reach up to shake it.

"I'm doing well. It's nice to meet you. Dr. Gandhi spoke very highly of you." I take note of her kind face and warm hands. I like her already, but I'm not here to make a new friend, I'm here to figure out if I'll ever be a mom.

She pulls a stool towards me and sits down. "Dr. Gandhi. Yes, yes. I've known her for a long time. I'll have to thank her for the referral." As she speaks, she flips open the cover of her iPad and taps the screen a few times, scrolling for a bit and then stopping to look at me. "So, tell me, have you ever been pregnant or have you been actively trying to conceive?"

I shake my head slowly.

Dr. Stovall raises her eyebrows. "I'm surprised. I typically assist women who have been unable to conceive, but you haven't tried yet. What makes you feel as though you can't?"

I take a deep breath and jump in. "So, as you can probably see in my chart, I'm approaching forty. Actually, I'll be forty in a few months, and I'm just trying to find out if I can still have children. And I know," I want her to know I've done my research, "I know lots of women have children past the age of forty—I mean, look at Janet Jackson!—but I've had PCOS almost all of my life, so…"

She scrolls through the iPad a little more, not speaking right away. "You are correct, the ability to conceive beyond the age of forty is not impossible. There are certainly some risk factors as we age, but these don't mean a mature woman can't become a mother." She flips the iPad closed and positions herself right in front of me. "Now, the PCOS, that's a condition that makes it hard for your body to regulate your hormone levels. Too much of one hormone, or not enough of another hormone, can prevent the follicles in your ovaries from releasing eggs. So," she shrugs her shoulders. "No egg, no baby. But you already knew that, am I right?"

I nod, hardly breathing, hating to hear this information about myself again.

Dr. Stovall continues. "Okay, and you also know PCOS is linked to obesity, right?"

I nod again. "I've been working on the weight loss, though. I've lost some weight since I saw Dr. Gandhi the last time, but it seems like I hit a plateau and..."

"Good. That's alright. That's your first step. Getting healthy. But PCOS doesn't go away overnight, and there are things we can do to help nature to take its course, so to speak." She raises an eyebrow towards me, giving me a chance to respond.

"We're talking about artificial insemination, and in vitro fertilization, right?" I raise my eyebrow back at her.

She smiles. "Yes and no. Those are just a few of the options available, but we have to find the treatment plan that is most appropriate for you and for your family planning goals. For a woman who wants to be a mother right away, there are fertility injections and various insemination techniques. For a woman who has more time, we can be more conservative. There is nutritional counselling, medication, and hormone monitoring. So, the real question is: where do you fall on that spectrum?"

I'm ready for this question, it's the reason I'm here. "I'm not married, but I hope to be one day. There was a time when I would have been open to choosing a *sperm donor*," I don't know why I whisper the words, "but I've decided I don't want to bring a fatherless child into the world if I can avoid it."

I take a deep breath and try to slow down a little. "I want to know more about my chances for becoming a mother in the future. You know, just to make sure I can still have a child in the next two to three years. Dr. Gandhi did some preliminary tests at my last visit and said some of my hormone levels were low, and she explained why my ovaries will release fewer and fewer eggs. But some time has passed, I've lost some weight, and I want to make sure things haven't gotten much worse. Is the PCOS destroying my ovaries?"

Dr. Stovall puts the iPad down and grabs my hands. "I want you to listen to me: this is not impossible. You are still a young woman, but you are wise to recognize the challenges you face…"

"I just like to be prepared and know what I'm dealing with." I nod my head and allow her to continue.

"Right. I get it. Here's what we're going to do. Let's start with a diabetes medication regimen. It will…"

I jump in, finishing her sentence, "…help me lose some weight and boost my ovulation. I've been reading about that."

Dr. Stovall holds up her hand to stop me and I nod, again. "It's technically used to treat diabetes and insulin resistance, but it has been found to help regulate reproductive hormones and stimulate weight loss. So, it's not a weight loss drug or fertility drug—please don't misunderstand—but it's a good place to begin and I think it will keep you moving in the right direction so you'll have a better chance at success when the time comes."

She releases my hand and pats the side of my thigh like I'm a little girl. "What do we think about that?"

She makes me smile, puts me at ease. I shrug my shoulders. "Sounds good to me. So…?"

"So," she picks the iPad up again and taps the screen. "You'll start this. I just sent the prescription to your pharmacy. You'll take it once a day, with a meal if possible. It can cause some nausea, diarrhea, or stomach upset while your body gets used to it. Also, I'll have you go down to the lab for your bloodwork and a urine sample before you leave today. Let's get a baseline reading before you start the medication and let's check it again in three months. I know your menstrual cycle has been irregular, but it should level out with the medication so I want you to start tracking your cycle for me. Sound good?" She stands up.

I smile and stand up to hug her. "Thank you, Dr. Stovall. I'm on board with the plan. It's exactly what I wanted to hear."

She grabs my hands and pats them. "Alright, then. Wait right here. Elise will be in in a moment and she'll walk you over to the lab. Give them about two weeks to send you the report and give me a call if you have any questions or concerns."

Just a few hours after I've peed in a cup and been poked with needles in both arms because the phlebotomist didn't listen when I told her no one has ever been able to get blood out of the veins in my left arm, I'm walking through the aquarium with Glen and Naomi.

While Glen pushes the empty stroller, I hold Naomi up so she can see the colorful creatures inside the massive tanks, but she's more fascinated with my earrings. She's doing her best to grab hold of the hoops and yank them from my earlobes. I dodge her advances and our game makes her laugh.

"See! Y'all aren't even paying attention!" Glen wants to sound stern with us, but I mimic him and he laughs, too.

"You were the one who wanted to bring a ten-month-old *baby* to an *aquarium*! She don't know a jellyfish from a Finding Nemo fish!" I walk close to him and bump his hip with mine.

He bumps me back and lifts Naomi from my arms. "If you *show* her the fish, she'll *look* at them. Besides, there's no such thing as a Finding Nemo Fish. It's called a clownfish and they're very interesting."

He holds Naomi closer to the tank. "Did you know they're all born as boys? What happens is, the biggest male in a group of clownfish will actually *turn himself into a female* and then he/she becomes the boss of the group! Can you believe that? He/she can lay eggs and everything! Like 1000 eggs at a time!"

I can't tell if he's talking to me or to Naomi, but she reaches out her hand and slaps the glass, shrieking and kicking her feet as though she wants to jump down. He immediately grabs her hand and the fish dart away from the glass, disappearing behind glowing rocks and underwater shrubbery.

When Glen turns around to face me, still clutching Naomi's tiny hand, he looks mortified, but I bust out laughing. "First of all, we aren't in a library, so she can scream all she wants. Second, just admit it. Ain't *nobody* want to come to this dark dungeon of an aquarium but *you*." I jab my finger into his chest and let it linger there for a second before opening my hand and squeezing his pecs playfully. "You been working out? Huh? Let me feel the other side!"

We're laughing like we're the only ones in the whole place, but we stop when we hear someone else laughing nearby. It's a middle-aged woman wearing a turquoise polo shirt embroidered with bold lettering that says Volunteers Help Keep Us Afloat and a badge that says Ask Me!

When we stop laughing, she steps towards us and says, "Sounds like you're having a great time here! I have to say, you are the most *adorable family*! Maybe your little one will grow up to be one of our Marine Life Specialists one day. You're getting an early introduction, aren't you, little lady?" She reaches over to tickle Naomi's hand and I instinctively step to the side, out of the way. This lady thinks we're a family, mother, father, baby—which we aren't—and I have a sickening flashback of the time it happened with Victor and Empress. Of how badly I'd wanted the picture from that day to reflect reality.

Glen doesn't seem to notice any of this, or at least it doesn't strike him as odd that a stranger misunderstands our dynamic, because he's grabbing me by the waist and pulling me into himself at the same time he's passing the volunteer lady his phone. "Would you mind taking a picture of us?"

She takes the phone and aims it at us, then lowers it. "Come on, Mom! Let's see that smile!"

Glen's hand leaves my hip, softly tickles my back, and jostles Naomi around a bit in the opposite arm. The tickle makes me laugh and I look over at him, he tosses me a sideways grin, and Naomi reaches across to grab my earring, the lady snaps the picture.

"I think I got a good one!" She hands the phone back to Glen. "I took a few, though, just in case. And hey," she winks at him, "you have a beautiful family. Take care of them."

When she walks away, Glen and I stand together, reviewing the seven pictures she's taken, each one practically the same as the next, except for the slightest differences in our expressions and positions.

"Look how far away you are in this one." Glen zooms in on one picture where I'm a full six inches away from him and Naomi.

"And then, look at this one." He scrolls to the next picture, in which I'm a step closer, and the next, where I'm even closer, and the last, where I'm snuggled next to him smiling and Naomi is reaching for my earring. "This one is my favorite. It's like you finally decided to join us." He laughs and wraps his arm around my shoulder, pulling me into him again. Then he teases in a playfully menacing voice, "You're one of us now."

With his voice lowered, I assume to build suspense, he passes Naomi to me. "Smells like you and Nay-Nay need a trip to the lady's room."

I hate disgusting, germ-infested public restrooms. If it is humanly possible, I always wait until I get home. But, I've had enough outings with Naomi to know waiting isn't always an option when a bad diaper is involved.

I find the cleanest-looking family restroom, balance Naomi on my hip, and spray the changing table down with the small can of Lysol I keep in my purse. Then I grab a wad of paper towels, wipe the surface down—careful not to let the soiled side of the paper touch my hand—and cover the table with a fresh layer of paper towels.

My phone rings as soon as I lay Naomi down on the nest of paper towels and I steady her with one hand while I dig my phone from my purse with the other. I don't recognize the number.

"Hello?"

Dr. Stovall's warm voice comes through. "Cynthia? How are you, dear?"

Her voice is pleasant, but eerily calm, and I ignore her greeting. "What's wrong?"

"I'm calling to let you know I've added another prescription for you. Have you already picked up the other one?"

I relax myself and nestle the phone between my shoulder and my ear so I can finish changing Naomi's diaper. "Not yet. I'll pick it up this afternoon and I was planning to start it tonight. What's the new prescription for?"

In seconds, I've wrangled Naomi into a fresh diaper, and she's balanced on my hip again as I wash my hands at the bathroom sink.

Dr. Stovall speaks too slowly and deliberately for my liking—it's not the most convenient time for me to take a phone call—but I try not to rush her off the phone. Instead, I dry my hands and carry Naomi back to the spot where Glen is waiting for us. I pass the baby to him, I mouth the words *Doctor's office*, and signal with one finger it will be just another moment before we can get back to the exhibits. I cover one ear with my hand and press the phone closer to the other ear, straining to hear, just as Dr. Stovall finishes her explanation, but it sounds like a chopped up foreign language to me. "...preliminary urinalysis confirms you are pregnant...so pleased for you...conceived naturally...called in prenatal supplements...long road ahead."

When I push the phone back into my purse, I move towards Glen as though I'm underwater. He rushes to meet me, concern registering on his face at the sight of mine. "What's wrong?"

I'm in tears, now, and I can tell I'm freaking him out, but I try to smile through it, to reassure him these are *happy* tears as I blubber the words, "We're going to be a mom."

I shake my head and try again to make sense of what I'm saying. "No. *I'm* going to be a mom. We're pregnant."

We stand in the middle of the cold-water exhibit, overlooking the Belugas, silent, but for the sound of my sniffling and Naomi's shrieking. Glen pulls me close enough to give Naomi access to my earring again. "There are no mistakes, you know?" He whispers this into my ear with a steadiness that calms my breathing.

Gently, I untangle Naomi's small fingers from my earring and blow raspberries into her hand until she laughs. Then, I exhale and try to find words for Glen, but he stops me.

"I know, I know...you're strong. You can handle yourself. But listen," he squeezes my hand just a little, "I'm right here, you're not in this alone, and we're not reckless teenagers. I don't believe in accidents or mistakes, but I do believe in blessings, especially this one." He taps my stomach so gently it tickles, and he hugs me when I smile. "We weren't very careful the night you played The Stranger, huh?"

When he leads us outside to the parking lot, he hugs me again and says, "I know you like to have a plan for everything and that's cool. But one thing I've learned in my life is this: just because something doesn't go according to *your* plan doesn't mean it's not part of *THE* plan. Everything will be absolutely alright. This is going to be great—for all of us. Trust me."

I take a deep breath and nod like a child, hoping he'll understand my need to process the impact of the doctor's overwhelming phone call. Then I hug him, plant kisses on his face as well as Naomi's, and promise to meet him at his house after my book club meeting.

"You're still going to the meeting? Are you sure you're okay?" Concern registers in his eyes and I know he means well, but there's been an intermittent tremble in my knees ever since I heard Dr. Stovall say the word 'pregnant,' and I'm desperate to be in a place where the earth feels steady beneath my feet.

"I'm okay, don't worry. Just get those kabobs ready and I'll see you in a little while." I say as I buckle my seatbelt and drive away.

Chapter Twenty-Eight

Pulling into Irene's yard, I can see from the number of cars, I'm the last to arrive. I feel lightheaded with nausea over Dr. Stovall's phone call, and I'm fighting an incredible battle of the what-if's as I walk through Irene's front door.

Everyone stops, mid-prayer, when I drift into the room, and I realize I hadn't even knocked.

Julene's the first to say anything: "Girl, what's wrong? You look like you're sick or something!"

"Don't say that!" Irene rushes to defend me. "You don't tell somebody they look sick!" Then she peers a little closer into my face. "Your eyes do look a little glassy, though. Are you coming down with something?"

I nod my head, forcing myself to pull it together, and smile at everyone. "Sorry I'm late. I had a lot going on today, but I'm here now! What'd I miss?"

"We were just about to start the meeting with a prayer. Come on in." Irene ushers me towards the circle of ladies gathered in her living room, and we join hands.

"Lord, we come to..." Just as Ms. Emma Lee begins to pray, Julene's phone rings.

"Sorry y'all. I meant to turn my ringer off!" Julene laughs as she reaches for her phone and presses a button to silence it.

"Lord God, we..." As Ms. Emma Lee begins again, so does the vibrating sound from Julene's phone.

"I'll turn the whole phone off. Sorry y'all. This number has been calling me all day and I don't answer unknown numbers." She reaches for it again, and I noticed a fleeting change in her expression when she takes note of whatever's on the screen.

"Bill collector?" Someone jokes across our prayer circle, but I notice my friend doesn't laugh.

Ms. Emma Lee begins for a third time: *"God we just want to thank you for your unending Grace and Mercy. We thank you for bringing us together, for keeping us in perfect peace, and for protecting us against all manner of harm. We ask you to keep your hand on us—each one of us and our families too—so that we can continue to do the work you have called us to do. Guide us in our meeting today and bless the hands which have prepared our food.*

Thank you for your son Jesus and thank you for continuing to light the way. Amen."

When we all say amen, fill our plates with meatballs and deviled eggs, and take our seats, Irene begins the meeting.

"I'm glad we could all make it this time. It's been too long since we've gathered together..."

I'm sitting, small plate perched on my lap, trying to listen to the details of the meeting but Irene sounds like she's speaking a foreign language. I try harder to focus, to be present in this moment, until I can... I don't know what my next step is. What's the plan, now that I'm within inches of all I've ever wanted? There's self-love, a healthy relationship, and a new life blossoming inside me. I'm the Queen of Best Laid Plans, yet I've never thought to plan beyond this moment.

While I wrestle with my own thoughts, Ms. Emma Lee stands near the front of the room to make an announcement.

"The Lord put something on my mind the other day and I just want to run it by all y'all. I'm proud of what we've done and I believe God has more for us to do. I believe we can grow a little more. What do you think about our group getting into real estate?"

The room is dead silent for a breath. At nearly eighty years old, Ms. Emma Lee is still searching for ways to move us toward our original vision, and her suggestion makes us all pause to think.

"I used to have my real estate license back in the day—somebody told me it would be easy money—but I'm here to tell you, it wasn't." Ms. Irene isn't fond of the idea, and she enlightens us with her reasons: "First of all, I spent all my weekends driving people around looking at houses they couldn't afford, then I had other agents trying to steal my clients, I had clients trying to short-change me on my commission, and people who wouldn't follow the lender's directions. It was nothing but a headache. You couldn't pay me enough to go down that road again."

There's some head-nodding around the group, to confirm Irene isn't the only one who isn't too keen on the business of real estate, but Julene speaks up to encourage Ms. Emma Lee. "Real estate isn't all about selling houses to your friends. and it can be a smart way to add assets to our trust," her phone buzzes in her pocket and she reaches in to silence it without looking, "but Ms. Irene is right too. It can get complicated and it can be time consuming, so what exactly did you have in mind?"

"There's an apartment house next door to me—y'all know that little brick house on the corner of my street? It was just a house, but the owner rents the upstairs as an apartment, the downstairs as another apartment, and the room over the garage as another one." Ms. Emma Lee glances around the room and, seeing that everyone knows the house to which she refers, she continues. "The people living there ain't doing nothing but running drugs out of it! I've sit there and watched them from my kitchen window—cars coming and going all times of the night, different people in and out of there, and not one of them has a real job, from what I can tell. Just the other day, somebody drove by and tried to shoot the house up. One of the bullets came right through the wall of the shed on the side of my house!"

"Have you called the police?" Tamara, head of security at the hospital, puts her plate down and scoots to the edge of her seat. "If you report drug activity, the police will patrol the area more often. You just have to keep calling."

"Aww… the police ain't gonna do nothing but take a report and lose it in a pile of all the other reports from our community!" Irene leans forward in her own chair and offers her own suggestion. "What you have to do is call Randy Watson. He's the one who owns that house and he just rents the rooms out to anyone with a sob-story. You need to call him and say you're gonna tell his wife about that side-baby he got down there in Riceboro if he doesn't get those drug dealers out of that house!"

Ms. Emma Lee laughs—we all laugh—at the thought of blackmailing Randy Watson, but she has her own answer to the problem: "I've called the police already—they didn't do squat. And I spoke to Randy several times—he's too busy juggling women and loan sharks to care. What I want to do is buy the house from him. I know he'll sell because he's in debt…"

Julene jumps up then, suddenly understanding Ms. Emma Lee's idea. "We can buy the house, evict the tenants, clean the place up, and rent it out! I was reading about this investment group in Minnesota who buys apartment homes and rents them out to generate income for their investors. We could start with this one house—it would make Ms. Emma Lee feel safer and the rental income would increase the value of our trust. Who knows? If this one works out, eventually we could buy another rental property, and we'll have a substantial stream of revenue to…"

"Pass on to our children." The words tumble out of my mouth too quickly and suddenly all eyes are on me, but Ms. Emma Lee speaks again, reclaiming everyone's attention.

"This investment rental stuff—that's up to y'all. I just want those hooligans gone and it seems we have the means to get rid of them for good." She looks towards me. "Cynthia, baby, you're always talking about passing something on to the children. When you gonna have some children of your own to help manage this thing?"

She's chuckling—everyone's laughing, as we always have, about my concern for everyone else's children when I have none of my own—but the hee-hees and haw-haws dissipate into silence when I rub my belly and answer:

"In about seven months."

"So, I'm going to be an Auntie, huh?" Julene's walking me down Irene's front steps, escorting me as though I'm suddenly disabled, but I feel amazing at the moment.

After I shared the news of my pregnancy, everyone laid hands on me, praying for my health, praying for my child, thanking God for our blessings—and then we voted and agreed to acquire the drug-infested property next door to Ms. Emma Lee's house.

"Yeah, you're going to be an Auntie! Finally! It doesn't seem real. Glen and I haven't even talked about it since I got the phone call today." I'm laughing as I link my arm through hers. "He's home right now, grilling kabobs for us."

Standing next to my car, I hug my friend, and I can feel the vibration of her phone buzzing in her pocket. "You gonna answer that or nah? Somebody's been blowing your phone up all day."

I expect her to laugh and tell me something: the kids are calling, her husband is annoying, a telemarketer wants to sell her a timeshare property—but she doesn't. She glances at the phone, presses a button to send the caller to voicemail, and leans in to kiss my cheek.

She says, "Get home to your man and enjoy those kabobs. I'll holler at you later."

When she turns to leave, I have the urge to grab her arm—to pull her back and let her know I saw the word 'Mother' on her phone screen as she was rejecting the call, but I decide to give her some space. I'll be here for her when she's ready to talk about it, just as she's always been here for me.

Inside my car, before I drive away, I send her a simple text:

Me: 😚

And she replies almost instantly:

Julene: 🖤

Satisfied for now, I rub my belly softly, and drive towards home.

THE END

Thanks for reading Good Morning Beautiful. If you'd like to stay in touch with me, join my newsletter and follow me on social media.
https://booksbydaines.com
https://twitter.com/booksbydaines
https://www.facebook.com/BooksbyDaines/
https://www.instagram.com/booksbydaines/
If you enjoyed this story, please kindly leave a review on Amazon.
Also, stay tuned for the next book in the Trust series.

ABOUT THE AUTHOR

Author Daines L. Reed, a wildly optimistic lover of words, resides in a small town just outside of Charlotte, NC with her husband, daughters, and pair of miniature Schnauzers. She is a registered dental hygienist, an avid reader, lifelong learner, and emerging storyteller.

Good Morning Beautiful is the second novel in the Trust Series.